Fict w

TOBACCO
ODOR

262501
5A/WB

BY EVELYN WAUGH

Novels
DECLINE AND FALL
VILE BODIES
BLACK MISCHIEF
A HANDFUL OF DUST
SCOOP
PUT OUT MORE FLAGS
WORK SUSPENDED
BRIDESHEAD REVISITED
SCOTT-KING'S MODERN EUROPE
THE LOVED ONE
HELENA
MEN AT ARMS
LOVE AMONG THE RUINS
OFFICERS AND GENTLEMEN
UNCONDITIONAL SURRENDER
THE ORDEAL OF GILBERT PINFOLD

Biography
ROSSETTI
EDMUND CAMPION
MSGR. RONALD KNOX

Autobiography
A LITTLE LEARNING

Travel
LABELS
REMOTE PEOPLE
NINETY-TWO DAYS
WAUGH IN ABYSSINIA
ROBBERY UNDER LAW
WHEN THE GOING WAS GOOD
A TOURIST IN AFRICA

Short Stories
MR. LOVEDAY'S LITTLE OUTING, AND OTHER SAD STORIES
BASIL SEAL RIDES AGAIN

Put Out More Flags

EVELYN WAUGH

PUT

OUT

MORE

FLAGS

Little, Brown and Company · Boston

LIBRARY OF CONGRESS CATALOG CARD NO. 77–88246

REPUBLISHED OCTOBER 1977

PRINTED IN THE UNITED STATES OF AMERICA

TO
RANDOLPH CHURCHILL

Dedicatory Letter

to

MAJOR RANDOLPH CHURCHILL,
4th Hussars, Member of Parliament

Dear Randolph,

I am afraid that these pages may not be altogether acceptable to your ardent and sanguine nature. They deal, mostly, with a race of ghosts, the survivors of the world we both knew ten years ago, which you have outflown in the empyrean of strenuous politics, but where my imagination still fondly lingers. I find more food for thought in the follies of Basil Seal and Ambrose Silk than in the sagacity of the Higher Command. These characters are no longer contemporary in sympathy; they were forgotten even before the war; but they lived on delightfully in holes and corners and, like everyone else, they have been disturbed in their habits by the rough intrusion of current history. Here they are in that odd, dead period before the Churchillian renaissance which people called at the time "the Great Bore War."

So please accept them with the sincere regards of

Your affectionate friend,

THE AUTHOR

"A man getting drunk at a farewell party should strike a musical tone, in order to strengthen his spirit . . . and a drunk military man should order gallons and put out more flags in order to increase his military splendour.

CHINESE SAGE, *quoted and translated by Lin Yutang in* THE IMPORTANCE OF LIVING.

"A little injustice in the heart can be drowned by wine; but a great injustice in the world can be drowned only by the sword."

EPIGRAMS OF CHANG CH'AO; *quoted and translated by Lin Yutang in* THE IMPORTANCE OF LIVING.

The military operation described in Chapter III is wholly imaginary. No existing unit of His Majesty's Forces is represented there, or anywhere, directly or indirectly. No character is derived from any living man or woman.

Contents

CHAPTER I

Autumn, 3

CHAPTER II

Winter, 89

CHAPTER III

Spring, 172

EPILOGUE

Summer, 273

Put Out More Flags

Autumn

1. IN THE WEEK which preceded the outbreak of the Second World War — days of surmise and apprehension which cannot, without irony, be called the last days of "peace" — and on the Sunday morning when all doubts were finally resolved and misconceptions corrected, three rich women thought first and mainly of Basil Seal. They were his sister, his mother and his mistress.

Barbara Sothill was at Malfrey; in recent years she had thought of her brother as seldom as circumstances allowed her, but on that historic September morning, as she walked to the village, he predominated over a multitude of worries.

She and Freddy had just heard the Prime Minister's speech, broadcast by wireless. "It is an evil thing we are fighting," he had said and as Barbara turned her back on the house where, for the most part, the eight years of her marriage had been spent, she felt personally challenged and threatened, as though, already, the mild, autumnal sky were dark with circling enemies and their shadows were trespassing on the sunlit lawns.

There was something female and voluptuous in the

beauty of Malfrey; other lovely houses maintained a virginal modesty or a manly defiance, but Malfrey had no secret from the heavens; it had been built more than two hundred years ago in days of victory and ostentation and lay, spread out, sumptuously at ease, splendid, defenceless and provocative — a Cleopatra among houses; across the sea, Barbara felt, a small and envious mind, a meanly ascetic mind, a creature of the conifers, was plotting the destruction of her home. It was for Malfrey that she loved her prosaic and slightly absurd husband; for Malfrey, too, that she had abandoned Basil and with him the part of herself which, in the atrophy endemic to all fruitful marriages, she had let waste and die.

It was half a mile to the village down the lime avenue. Barbara walked because, just as she was getting into the car, Freddy had stopped her saying, "No petrol now for gadding about."

Freddy was in uniform, acutely uncomfortable in ten-year-old trousers. He had been to report at the yeomanry headquarters the day before, and was home for two nights collecting his kit, which, in the two years since he was last at camp, had been misused in charades and picnics and dispersed about the house in a dozen improbable places. His pistol, in particular, had been a trouble. He had had the whole household hunting it, saying fretfully, "It's all very well but I can get court-martialled for this," until, at length, the nursery-maid found it at the back of the toy cupboard. Barbara was now on her way to look for his binoculars which she remembered vaguely having lent to the scoutmaster.

The road under the limes led straight to the village; the park gates of elaborately wrought iron swung on rusticated stone piers, and the two lodges, formed one side of the village green; opposite them stood the church; on the other sides, two inns, the vicarage, the shop and a row of grey cottages; three massive chestnuts grew from the roughly rectangular grass plot in the centre. It was a "beauty spot," justly but reluctantly famous, too much frequented of late by walkers but still, through Freddy's local influence, free of charabancs; a bus stopped three times a day on weekdays, four times on Tuesdays when the market was held in the neighbouring town, and to accommodate passengers Freddy had that year placed an oak seat under the chestnuts.

It was here that Barbara's thoughts were brought up sharply by an unfamiliar spectacle: six dejected women sat in a row staring fixedly at the closed doors of the Sothill Arms. For a moment Barbara was puzzled; then she remembered. These were Birmingham women. Fifty families had arrived at Malfrey late on Friday evening, thirsty, hot, bewildered and resentful after a day in train and bus. Barbara had chosen the five saddest families for herself and dispersed the rest in the village and farms.

Punctually next day the head housemaid, a veteran of old Mrs. Sothill's regime, had given notice of leaving. "I don't know how we shall do without you," said Barbara.

"It's my legs, madam. I'm not strong enough for the work. I could just manage as things were, but now with children all over the place . . ."

"You know we can't expect things to be easy in wartime. We must expect to make sacrifices. This is our war work."

But the woman was obdurate. "There's my married sister at Bristol," she said. "Her husband was on the Reserve. I ought to go and help her now he's called up."

An hour later the remaining three housemaids had appeared with prim expressions of face.

"Edith and Olive and me have talked it over and we want to go and make aeroplanes. They say they are taking on girls at Brakemore's."

"You'll find it terribly hard work, you know."

"Oh, it's not the work, madam. It's the Birmingham women. The way they leave their rooms."

"It's all very strange for them at first. We must do all we can to help. As soon as they settle down and get used to our ways . . ." But she saw it was hopeless while she spoke.

"They say they want girls at Brakemore's," said the maids.

In the kitchen Mrs. Elphinstone was loyal. "But I can't answer for the girls," she said. "They seem to think war is an excuse for a lark."

It was the kitchen-maids, anyway, and not Mrs. Elphinstone, thought Barbara, who had to cope with the extra meals . . .

Benson was sound. The Birmingham women caused *him* no trouble. But James would be leaving for the Army within a few weeks. It's going to be a difficult winter, thought Barbara.

These women, huddled on the green, were not Barbara's guests, but she saw on their faces the same look of frustration and defiance. Dutifully, rather than prudently, she approached the group and asked if they were comfortable. She spoke to them in general and each felt shy of answering; they looked away from her sullenly towards a locked inn. Oh dear, thought Barbara, I suppose they wonder what business it is of mine.

"I live up there," she said, indicating the gates. "I've been arranging your billets."

"Oh have you?" said one of the mothers. "Then perhaps you can tell us how long we've got to stop."

"That's right," said another.

"D'you know," said Barbara, "I don't believe anyone has troubled to think about that. They've all been too busy getting you away."

"They got no right to do it," said the first mother. "You can't keep us here compulsory."

"But surely you don't *want* to have your children bombed, do you?"

"We won't stay where we're not wanted."

"That's right," said the yes-woman.

"But of *course* you're wanted."

"Yes, like the stomach-ache."

"That's right."

For some minutes Barbara reasoned with the fugitives until she felt that her only achievement had been to transfer to herself all the odium which more properly belonged to Hitler. Then she went on her way to the scoutmaster's, where, before she could retrieve the binoculars, she had to listen to the story of the Birmingham schoolmistress, billeted on him, who refused to help wash up.

As she crossed the green on her homeward journey, the mothers looked away from her.

"I hope the children are enjoying themselves a little," she said, determined not to be cut in her own village.

"They're down at the school. Teacher's making them play games."

"The park's always open you know, if any of you care to go inside."

"We had a park where we came from. With a band Sundays."

"Well I'm afraid I can't offer a band. But it's thought rather pretty, particularly down by the lake. Do take the children in if you feel like it."

When she had left the chief mother said: "What's she? Some kind of inspector, I suppose, with her airs and graces. The idea of inviting us into the park. You'd think the place belonged to her the way she goes on."

Presently the two inns opened their doors and the scandalized village watched a procession of mothers assemble from cottage, farm and mansion and make for the bar parlours.

Luncheon decided him; Freddy went upstairs immediately he left the dining-room and changed into civilian clothes. "Think I'll get my maid to put me into something loose," he had said in the voice he used for making jokes. It was this kind of joke Barbara had learned to recognize during her happy eight years in his company.

Freddy was large, masculine, prematurely bald and superficially cheerful; at heart he was misanthropic and gifted with that sly, sharp instinct for self-preservation that passes for wisdom among the rich; his indolence was qualified with enough basic bad temper to ensure the respect of those about him. He took in most people, but not his wife or his wife's family.

Not only did he have a special expression of face for making jokes; he had one for use when discussing his brother-in-law Basil. It should have conveyed lofty disapproval tempered by respect for Barbara's loyalty; in fact it suggested sulkiness and guilt.

The Seal children, for no reason that was apparent to the rest of the world, had always held the rest of the world in scorn. Freddy did not like Tony; he found him supercilious and effeminate, but he was prepared to concede to him certain superiorities; no one doubted that there was a brilliant career ahead of him in diplomacy. The time would come when they would all be very proud of Tony. But Basil from his earliest days had been a source of embarrassment and reproach. On his own terms Freddy might have been willing to welcome a black sheep in the Seal family, someone who was "never mentioned," to whom he might, every now and then, magnanimously unknown to anyone except Barbara, extend a helping hand; someone, even, in whom he might profess to see more good than the rest of the world. Such a kinsman might very considerably have redressed the balance of Freddy's self-esteem. But, as Freddy found as soon as he came to know the Seals intimately, Basil, so far from being never mentioned, formed the subject of nearly half their conversation. At that time they were ever ready to discuss with relish his latest outrage, ever hopeful of some splendid success for him in the immediate future, ever contemptuous of the disapproval of the rest of the world. And Basil himself regarded Freddy pitilessly, with eyes which, during his courtship and the first years of marriage, he had recognized in Barbara herself.

For there was a disconcerting resemblance between Basil and Barbara; she, too, was *farouche* in a softer and deadlier manner, and the charm which held him breathless flashed in gross and acquisitive shape in Basil. Maternity and the tranquil splendour of Malfrey had wrought changes in her; it was very rarely, now, that the wild little animal in her came above ground; but it was there, in its earth, and from time to time he was aware of it, peeping out, after long absences; a pair of glowing eyes at the twist in the tunnel watching him as an enemy.

Barbara herself pretended to no illusions about Basil. Years of disappointment and betrayal had convinced her, in the reasoning part of her, that he was no good. They had played pirates together in the nursery and the game was over. Basil played pirates alone. She apostatized from her faith in him almost with formality, and yet, as a cult will survive centuries after its myths have been exposed and its sources of faith tainted, there was still deep in her that early piety, scarcely discernible now in a little residue of superstition, so that this morning when her world seemed rocking about her, she turned back to Basil. Thus, when earthquake strikes a modern city and the pavements gape, the sewers buckle up and the great buildings tremble and topple, men in bowler hats and natty, ready-made suitings, born of generations of literates and rationalists, will suddenly revert to the magic of the forest and cross their fingers to avert the avalanche of concrete.

Three times during luncheon Barbara had spoken of Basil and now, as she and Freddy walked arm-in-arm on the terrace, she said: "I believe it's what he's been waiting for all these years."

"Who, waiting for what?"

"Basil, for the war."

"Oh . . . Well, I suppose in a way we all have really . . . the gardens are going to be a problem. I suppose we could get some of the men exemption on the grounds that they're engaged in agriculture, but it hardly seems playing the game."

It was Freddy's last day at Malfrey and he did not want to spoil it by talking of Basil. It was true that the yeomanry were not ten miles away; it was true, also, that they were unlikely to move for a very long time; they had recently been mechanized, in the sense that they had had their horses removed; few of them had ever seen a tank; he would be back and forwards con‑ tinually during the coming months; he meant to shoot the pheasants; but although this was no final leave‑ taking he felt entitled to more sentiment than Barbara was showing.

"Freddy, don't be bloody." She kicked him sharply on the ankle for she had found, early in married life, that Freddy liked her to swear and kick in private. "You know exactly what I mean. Basil's *needed* a war. He's not meant for peace."

"That's true enough. The wonder is he's kept out of prison. If he'd been born in a different class he wouldn't have."

Barbara suddenly chuckled. "D'you remember how he took Mother's emeralds, the time he went to Azania? But then you see that would never have happened if there'd been a war of our own for him to go to. He's always been mixed up in fighting."

"If you call living in a gin palace in La Paz and seeing generals shoot one another . . ."

"And Spain."

"Journalist and gun runner."

"He's always been a soldier *manqué*."

"Well, he hasn't done much about it. While he's been gadding about the rest of us have been training as territorials and yeomanry."

"Darling, a fat lot of training you've done."

"If there'd been more like us and fewer like Basil there'd never have been a war. You can't blame Ribbentrop for thinking us decadent when he saw people like Basil about. I don't suppose they'll have much use for him in the Army. He's thirty-six. He might get some sort of job connected with censorship. He seems to know a lot of languages."

"You'll see," said Barbara. "Basil will be covered with medals while your silly old yeomanry are still messing in a Trust House and waiting for your tanks."

There were duck on the lake and she let Freddy talk about them. She led him down his favourite paths. There was a Gothic pavilion where by long habit Freddy often became amorous; he did become amorous. And all the time she thought of Basil. She thought of him in terms of the war books she had read. She saw him as Siegfried Sassoon, an infantry subaltern in a mud-bogged trench, standing-to at dawn, his eyes on his wrist watch, waiting for zero hour; she saw him as Compton Mackenzie, spider in a web of Balkan intrigue, undermining a monarchy among olive trees and sculptured marble; she saw him as T. E. Lawrence and Rupert Brooke.

Freddy, assuaged, reverted to sport. "I won't ask any

of the regiment over for the early shoots," he said. "But I don't see why we shouldn't let some of them have a bang at the cocks round about Christmas."

2. LADY SEAL was at her home in London. She had taken fewer precautions against air raids than most of her friends. Her most valuable possession, her small Carpaccio, had been sent to safe-keeping at Malfrey; the miniatures and Limoges enamels were at the bank; the Sèvres was packed in crates and put below-stairs. Otherwise there was no change in her drawing-room. The ponderous old curtains needed no unsightly strips of black paper to help them keep in the light.

The windows were open now on the balcony. Lady Seal sat in an elegant rosewood chair gazing out across the square. She had just heard the Prime Minister's speech. Her butler approached from the end of the room.

"Shall I remove the radio, my lady?"

"Yes, by all means. He spoke very well, very well indeed."

"It's all very sad, my lady."

"Very sad for the Germans, Anderson."

It was quite true, thought Lady Seal; Neville Chamberlain had spoken surprisingly well. She had never liked him very much, neither him nor his brother — if anything she had preferred the brother — but they were uncomfortable, drab fellows both of them. However, he had spoken very creditably that morning, as though at last he were fully alive to his responsibilities. She would ask him to luncheon. But perhaps he would be busy; the most improbable people were busy in wartime, she remembered.

Her mind went back to the other war, which until that morning had been The War. No one very near to her had fought. Christopher had been too old, Tony just too young; her brother Edward had begun by commanding a brigade — they thought the world of him at the Staff College — but, inexplicably, his career had come to very little; he was still brigadier in 1918, at Dar-as-Salaam. But the war had been a sad time; so many friends in mourning and Christopher fretful about the coalition. It had been a bitter thing for them all: accepting Lloyd George; but Christopher had patriotically made the sacrifice with the rest of them; probably only she knew how much he had felt it. The worst time had been after the armistice, when peerages were sold like groceries and the peace terms were bungled. Christopher had always said they would have to pay for it in the long run.

The hideous, then unfamiliar shriek of the air raid sirens sang out over London.

"That was the warning, my lady."

"Yes, Anderson, I heard it."

"Will you be coming downstairs?"

"No, not yet at any rate. Get all the servants down and see they are quiet."

"Will you require your respirator, my lady?"

"I don't suppose so. From what Sir Joseph tells me the danger of gas is very slight. In any case I daresay this is only a practice. Leave it on the table."

"Will that be all, my lady?"

"That's all. See that the maids don't get nervous."

Lady Seal stepped onto the balcony and looked up into the clear sky. They'll get more than they bargain for if they try and attack *us*, she thought. High time that man was taught a lesson. He's made nothing but trouble for years. She returned to her chair thinking, Anyway *I* never made a fuss of that vulgar man von Ribbentrop. I wouldn't have him inside the house, even when that goose Emma Granchester was plaguing us all to be friendly to him. I hope she feels foolish this morning.

Lady Seal waited with composure for the bombardment to begin. She had told Anderson it was probably only a practice. That was what one told servants; otherwise they might panic — not Anderson but the maids. But in her heart Lady Seal was sure that the attack was coming; it would be just like the Germans, always blustering and showing off and pretending to be efficient. The history Lady Seal had learned in the schoolroom had been a simple tale of the maintenance of right against the superior forces of evil, and the battle honours of her country rang musically in her ears — Crecy, Agincourt, Cádiz, Blenheim, Gibraltar, Inkerman, Ypres. England had fought many and various enemies with many and various allies, often on quite recondite pretexts, but always justly, chivalrously, and with ultimate success. Often, in Paris, Lady Seal had been proud that her people had never fallen to the habit of naming streets after their feats of arms; that was suitable enough for the short-lived and purely professional triumphs of the French, but to put those great manifestations of divine rectitude which were the victories of England to the use, for their postal addresses, of milliners and chiropodists, would have been a baseness to which even the radicals had not stooped. The steel engravings of her schoolroom lived before her eyes, like tableaux at a charity fête — Sidney at Zutphen, Wolfe at Quebec, Nelson at Trafalgar (Wellington, only, at Waterloo was excluded from the pageant by reason of the proximity of Blücher, pushing himself forward with typical Prussian effrontery to share the glory which the other had won); and to this tremendous assembly (not unlike, in Lady Seal's mind, those massed groups of wealth and respectability portrayed on the Squadron Lawn at Cowes and hung with their key plans in lobbies and billiard rooms) was added that morning a single new and rather improbable figure, Basil Seal.

The last war had cost her little; nothing, indeed, except a considerable holding of foreign investments and her brother Edward's reputation as a strategist. Now she had a son to offer her country. Tony had weak eyes and a career, Freddy was no blood of hers and was not cast in a heroic mould, but Basil — her wayward and graceless and grossly disappointing Basil, whose unaccountable taste for low company had led him into so many vexatious scrapes in the last ten years, whose wild oats refused to correspond with those of his Uncle Edward — Basil, who had stolen her emeralds and made Mrs. Lyne distressingly conspicuous — Basil, his peculiarities merged in the manhood of England, at last was entering on his inheritance. She must ask Jo about getting him a commission in a decent regiment.

At last, while she was still musing, the sirens sounded the All Clear.

Sir Joseph Mainwaring was lunching with Lady Seal that day. It was an arrangement made early in the preceding week before either of them knew that the day they were choosing was one which would be marked in the world's calendars until the end of history. He arrived punctually, as he always did; as he had done, times out of number, in the long years of their friendship.

Sir Joseph was not a church-going man except when he was staying at one of the very rare, very august houses where it was still the practice; on this Sunday morning, however, it would not have been fantastic to describe his spirit as inflamed by something nearly akin to religious awe. It *would* be fantastic to describe

him as purged, and yet there had been something delicately purgative in the experiences of the morning and
there was an unfamiliar buoyancy in his bearing as
though he had been at somebody's Eno's. He felt ten
years younger.

Lady Seal devoted to this old booby a deep, personal
fondness which was rare among his numerous friends
and a reliance which was incomprehensible but quite
common.

"There's only ourselves, Jo," she said as she greeted
him. "The Granchesters were coming but he had to go
and see the King."

"Nothing could be more delightful. Yes, I think we
shall all be busy again now. I don't know exactly what
I shall be doing yet. I shall know better after I've been
to Downing Street to-morrow morning. I imagine it
will be some advisory capacity to the War Cabinet. It's
nice to feel in the centre of things again, takes one back
ten years. Stirring times, Cynthia, stirring times."

"It's one of the things I wanted to see Emma Granchester about. There must be so many committees we
ought to start. Last war it was Belgian refugees. I suppose it will be Poles this time. It's a great pity it isn't
people who talk a language one knows."

"No; no Belgians this time. It will be a different war
in many ways. An economic war of attrition, that is
how I see it. Of course we had to have all this A.R.P.
and shelters and so on. The radicals were making copy
out of it. But I think we can take it there won't be any

air raids, not on London at any rate. Perhaps there may be an attempt on the seaports, but I was having a most interesting talk yesterday to Eddie Beste-Bingham at the Beefsteak; we've got a most valuable invention called R.D.F. That'll keep 'em off."

"Dear Jo, you always know the most encouraging things. What is R.D.F.?"

"I'm not absolutely clear about that. It's very secret."

"Poor Barbara has evacués at Malfrey."

"What a shocking business! Dear, dreaming Malfrey. Think of a Birmingham board school in that exquisite Grinling Gibbons salon! It's all a lot of nonsense, Cynthia. You know I'm the last man to prophesy rashly, but I think we can take one thing as axiomatic. There will be no air attack on London. The Germans will never attempt the Maginot Line. The French will hold on for ever, if needs be, and the German air bases are too far away for them to be able to attack us. If they do, we'll R.D.F. them out of the skies."

"Jo," said Lady Seal, when they were alone with the coffee. "I want to talk to you about Basil."

How often in the last twenty years had Sir Joseph heard those heavy words, uttered with so many intonations in so wide a variety of moods, but always, without fail, the prelude, not, perhaps, to boredom, but to a lowering of the interest and warmth of their converse! It was only in these material conferences that Cynthia Seal became less than the perfect companion, only then that, instead of giving, she demanded, as it were, a small sumptuary duty upon the riches of her friendship.

Had he been so minded Sir Joseph could have drawn a graph of the frequency and intensity of these discussions. There had been the steady rise from nursery through school to the university, when he had been called on to applaud each new phase of Basil's precocious development. In those days he had accepted Basil at his face value as an exceptionally brilliant and beautiful youth in danger of being spoiled. Then, towards the end of Basil's second year at Balliol, had come a series of small seismic disturbances, when Cynthia Seal was alternately mutely puzzled or eloquently distressed; then the first disaster, rapidly followed by Christopher's death. From then onwards for fifteen years the line had dipped and soared dizzily as Basil's iniquities rose on the crest or fell into the trough of notoriety, but with the passing years there had been a welcome decline in the mean level; it was at least six months since he had heard the boy's name.

"Ah," he said, "Basil, eh?" trying to divine from his hostess's manner whether he was required to be judicial, compassionate or congratulatory.

"You've so often been helpful in the past."

"I've tried," said Sir Joseph, recalling momentarily his long record of failures on Basil's behalf. "Plenty of good in the boy."

"I feel so much happier about him since this morning, Jo. Sometimes, lately, I've begun to doubt whether we shall ever find the proper place for Basil. He's been a square peg in so many round holes. But this war seems to take the responsibility off our hands. There's room for everyone in war-time, every *man*. It's always been Basil's *individuality* that's been wrong. You've said that often, Jo. In war-time individuality doesn't matter any more. There are just *men*, aren't there?"

"Yes," said Sir Joseph doubtfully. "Yes, Basil's individuality has always been rather strong, you know. He must be thirty-five or thirty-six now. That's rather old for starting as a soldier."

"Nonsense, Jo. Men of forty-five and fifty enlisted in the ranks in the last war and died as gallantly as anyone else. Now I want you to see the Lieutenant-Colonels of the foot guard regiments and see where he will fit in best . . ."

In her time Cynthia Seal had made many formidable demands on Basil's behalf. This, which she was now asking with such an assumption of ease, seemed to Sir Joseph one of the most vexatious. But he was an old and loyal friend and a man of affairs, moreover, well-practised, by a lifetime of public service, in the evasion of duty. "Of course, my dear Cynthia, I can't promise any results . . ."

3. ANGELA LYNE was returning by train from the South of France. It was the time when, normally, she went to Venice, but this

year, with international politics tediously on every
tongue, she had lingered at Cannes until and beyond
the last moment. The French and Italians whom she
met had said war was impossible; they said it with assurance before the Russian pact, with double assurance
after it. The English said there would be war, but not
immediately. Only the Americans knew what was coming, and exactly when. Now she was travelling in un-
wonted discomfort through a nation moving to action
under the dour precepts *"Il faut en finir"* and *"Nous
gagnerons parce que nous sommes les plus forts."*

It was a weary journey; the train was already eight
hours late; the restaurant car had disappeared during
the night at Avignon. Angela was obliged to share a
two-berth sleeper with her maid and counted herself
lucky to have got one at all; several of her acquaintances
had stayed behind, waiting for things to get better; at
the moment no reservations were guaranteed and the
French seemed to have put off their politeness and
packed it in moth-balls for the duration of hostilities.

Angela had a glass of Vichy water on the table before her. She sipped, gazing out at the passing land-
scape, every mile of which gave some evidence of the
changing life of the country; hunger and the bad night
she had spent raised her a hair's breadth above reality,
and her mind, usually so swift and orderly, fell into
pace with the train — now rocking in haste, now, barely
moving, seeming to grope its way from point to point.

A stranger passing the open door of her compartment

might well have speculated on her nationality and place in the world and supposed her to be American, the buyer perhaps for some important New York dress shop — whose present abstraction was due to the worries of war-time transport for her "collection." She wore the livery of the highest fashion, but as one who dressed to inform rather than to attract; nothing which she wore, nothing it might be supposed in the pigskin jewel-case above her head, had been chosen by or for a man. Her smartness was individual; she was plainly not one of those who scrambled to buy the latest gadget in the few breathless weeks between its first appearance and the inundation of the cheap markets of the world with its imitations; her person was a record and criticism of succeeding fashions, written, as it were, year after year, in one clear and characteristic fist. Had the curious fellow passenger stared longer — as he was free to do without offence, so absorbed was Angela in her own thoughts — he would have been checked in his hunt when he came to study his subject's face. All her properties — the luggage heaped above and around her, the set of her hair, her shoes, her finger-nails, the barely perceptible aura of scent that surrounded her, the Vichy water and the paper-bound volume of Balzac on the table before her — all these things spoke of what (had she been, as she seemed, American) she would have called her "personality." But the face was mute. It might have been carved in jade, it was so smooth and cool and conventionally removed from the human. A stranger might have watched her for mile after mile, as a spy or a lover or a newspaper reporter will loiter in the street before a closed house, and see no chink of light, hear no whisper of movement behind the shuttered façade, and in direct proportion to his discernment, he would have gone on his way down the corridor baffled and disturbed. Had he been told the bare facts about this seemingly cosmopolitan, passionless, barren, civilized woman, he might have despaired of ever again forming his judgment of a fellow being; for Angela Lyne was Scottish, the only child of a Glasgow millionaire — a jovial, rascally millionaire who had started life in a street gang — she was the wife of a dilettante architect, the mother of a single robust and unattractive son (the dead spit, it was said, of his grandfather), and her life had so foundered on passion that this golden daughter of fortune was rarely spoken of by her friends without the qualifying epithet of "poor" Angela Lyne.

Only in one respect would the casual observer have hit upon the truth. Angela's appearance was not designed for man. It is sometimes disputed — and opinions canvassed in popular papers to decide the question — whether woman, alone on a desert island, would concern herself with clothes; Angela, as far as she herself was concerned, disposed of the question finally. For seven years she had been on a desert island; her appearance had become a hobby and distraction, a pursuit entirely self-regarding and self-rewarding; she

watched herself moving in the mirrors of the civilized
world as a prisoner will watch the antics of a rat which
he has domesticated to the dungeon. (In the case of
her husband grottoes took the place of fashion. He
had six of them now, bought in various parts of Europe — some from Naples, some from Southern Germany — and painfully transported, stone by stone, to
Hampshire.)

For seven years, ever since she was twenty-five and
two years married to her dandy-aesthete, "poor" Angela Lyne had been in love with Basil Seal. It was one
of those affairs which, beginning light-heartedly as an
adventure and accepted light-heartedly by their friends
as an amusing scandal, seemed somehow petrified by
a Gorgon glance and endowed with an intolerable
permanence; as though in a world of capricious and
fleeting alliances, the ironic Fates had decided to set
up a standing, frightful example of the natural qualities of man and woman, of their basic aptitude to fuse
together; a label on the packing case "These chem-
icals are dangerous" — an admonitory notice, like the
shattered motor-cars erected sometimes at dangerous
turns in the road; so that the least censorious were
chilled by the spectacle and recoiled saying, "Really,
you know, there's something rather squalid about
those two."

It was a relationship which their friends usually described as "morbid," by which they meant that sensuality played a small part in it, for Basil was only at-

tracted to very silly girls and it was by quite other bonds that he and Angela were fettered together.

Cedric Lyne, pottering disconsolately in his baroque solitudes and watching with dismay the progress of his blustering son, used to tell himself, with the minimum of discernment, that a *béguin* like that could not possibly last. For Angela there seemed no hope of release. Nothing, she felt in despair, would ever part them but death. Even the flavour of the Vichy water brought thoughts of Basil as she remembered the countless nights in the last seven years when she had sat late with him, while he got drunk and talked more and more wildly, and she sipping her water waited her turn to strike, hard and fierce, at his conceit, until as he got more drunk he became superior to her attacks and talked her down and eventually came stupidly away.

She turned to the window as the train slackened to walking pace, passing truck after truck of soldiers. *Il faut en finir, Nous gagnerons parce que nous sommes les plus forts.* A hard-boiled people, the French. Two nights ago at Cannes, an American had been talking about the mutinous regiments decimated in the last war. "It's a pity they haven't got anyone like old Pétain to command them this time," he had said.

The villa at Cannes was shut now and the key was with the gardener. Perhaps she would never go back. This year she remembered it only as the place where she had waited in vain for Basil. He had telegraphed

"International situation forbids joy-riding." She had sent him the money for his journey but there had been no answer. The gardener would make a good thing out of the vegetables. A hard-boiled people, the French; Angela wondered why that was thought to be a good thing; she had always had a revulsion from hard-boiled eggs, even at picnics in the nursery — hard-boiled; over-cooked; over-praised for their cooking. When people professed a love of France, they meant a love of eating; the ancients located the deeper emotions in the bowels. She had heard a commercial traveller in the Channel packet welcome Dover and English food: "I can't stomach that French messed-up stuff." A commonplace criticism, thought Angela, that applied to French culture for the last two generations — "messed-up stuff," stale ingredients from Spain and America and Russia and Germany, disguised in a sauce of white wine from Algeria. France died with her monarchy. You could not even eat well, now, except in the provinces. It all came back to eating. "What's eating you?" . . . Basil claimed to have eaten a girl once in Africa; he had been eating Angela now for seven years. Like the Spartan boy and the fox . . . Spartans at Thermopylae, combing their hair before the battle; Angela had never understood that, because Alcibiades had cut off his hair in order to make himself acceptable. What did the Spartans think about hair really? Basil would have to cut his hair when he went into the Army. Basil the Athenian would have to sit at the public tables of Sparta, clipped blue at the neck where before his dark hair had hung untidily to his collar. Basil in the pass at Thermopylae . . .

Angela's maid returned from gossiping with the conductor. "He says he doesn't think the sleeping cars will go any further than Dijon. We shall have to change into day coaches. Isn't it wicked, madam, when we've paid?"

"Well, we're at war now. I expect there'll be a lot to put up with."

"Will Mr. Seal be in the Army?"

"I shouldn't be surprised."

"He will look different, won't he, madam?"

"Very different."

They were both silent, and in the silence Angela knew, by an intuition which defied any possible doubt, exactly what her maid was thinking. She was thinking, "Supposing Mr. Seal gets himself killed. Best thing really for all concerned."

. . . Flaxman Greeks reclining in death among the rocks of Thermopylae; riddled scarecrows sprawling across the wire of no man's land . . . Till death us do part . . . Through the haphazard trail of phrase and association, a single, unifying thought recurred, like the sentry posts at the side of the line, monotonously in Angela's mind. Death. "Death the Friend" of the sixteenth-century woodcuts, who released the captive and bathed the wounds of the fallen; Death in frock coat and whiskers, the discreet undertaker,

spreading his sable pall over all that was rotten and
unsightly; Death the macabre paramour in whose em-
brace all earthly loves were forgotten; Death for Basil,
that Angela might live again . . . that was what she
was thinking as she sipped her Vichy water, but no
one, seeing the calm and pensive mask of her face,
could ever possibly have guessed.

4. RUPERT BROOKE, Old

Bill, the Unknown Soldier — thus three fond women
saw him, but Basil breakfasting late in Poppet Green's
studio fell short and wide of all these ideals. He was
not at his best that morning, both by reason of his
heavy drinking with Poppet's friends the night before
and the loss of face he was now suffering with Poppet
in his attempts to explain his assertion that there would
be no war. He had told them this the night before,
not as a speculation, but as a fact known only to himself and half a dozen leading Germans; the Prussian
military clique, he had told them, were allowing the
Nazis to gamble just as long as their bluff was not
called; he had had this, he said, direct from von
Fritsch. The Army had broken the Nazi Party in the
July purge of 1936; they had let Hitler and Goering
and Goebbels and Ribbentrop remain as puppets just

as long as they proved valuable. The Army, like all Armies, was intensely pacifist; as soon as it became clear that Hitler was heading for war, he would be shot. Basil had expounded this theme not once but many times, over the table of the Charlotte Street restaurant, and because Poppet's friends did not know Basil, and were unused to people who claimed acquaintance with the great, Poppet had basked in vicarious esteem. Basil was little used to being heard with respect and was correspondingly resentful at being reproached with his own words.

"Well," Poppet was saying crossly, from the gas stove. "When does the Army step in and shoot Hitler?"

She was a remarkably silly girl, and, as such, had commanded Basil's immediate attention when they met, three weeks earlier, with Ambrose Silk. With her Basil had spent the time he had promised to Angela at Cannes; on her he had spent the twenty pounds Angela had sent him for the journey. Even now, when her fatuous face pouted in derision, she found a soft place in Basil's heart.

Evidence of her silliness abounded in the canvases, finished and unfinished, which crowded the studio. Eighty years ago her subjects would have been knights in armour, ladies in wimples and distress; fifty years ago "nocturnes"; twenty years ago Pierrots and willow trees; now, in 1939, they were bodiless heads, green horses and violet grass, seaweed, shells and funguses, neatly executed, conventionally arranged in the manner of Dali. Her work in progress on the easel was an overlarge, accurate but buttercup-coloured head of the Aphrodite of Melos, poised against a background of bull's-eyes and barley-sugar.

"My dear," Ambrose had said, "you can positively hear her imagination *creaking* as she does them, like a pair of old, old *corsets*, my dear, on a *harridan*."

"They'll destroy London. What shall I do?" asked Poppet plaintively. "Where can I go? It's the end of my painting. I've a good mind to follow Parsnip and Pimpernell" (two great poets of her acquaintance who had recently gone to New York).

"You'll be in more danger crossing the Atlantic than staying in London," said Basil. "There won't be any air raids on London."

"For God's sake don't say that." Even as she spoke the sirens wailed. Poppet stood paralyzed with horror. "Oh God," she said. "You've done it. They've come."

"Faultless timing," said Basil cheerfully. "That's always been Hitler's strong point."

Poppet began to dress in an ineffectual fever of reproach. "You *said* there wouldn't be a war. You *said* the bombers would never come. Now we shall all be killed and you just sit there talking and talking."

"You know I should have thought an air raid was just the thing for a *surréaliste*; it ought to give you plenty of compositions — limbs and things lying about in odd places you know."

"I wish I'd never met you. I wish I'd been to church. I was brought up in a convent. I wanted to be a nun once. I wish I was a nun. I'm going to be killed. Oh, I wish I was a nun. Where's my gas-mask? I shall go mad if I don't find my gas-mask."

Basil lay back on the divan and watched her with fascination. This was how he liked to see women behave in moments of alarm. He rejoiced, always, in the spectacle of women at a disadvantage: thus he would watch, in the asparagus season, a dribble of melted butter on a woman's chin, marring her beauty and making her ridiculous, while she would still talk and smile and turn her head, not knowing how she appeared to him.

"Now do make up your mind what you're frightened of," he urged. "If you're going to be bombed with high explosive run down to the shelter; if you're going to be gassed, shut the skylight and stay up here. In any case I shouldn't bother about that respirator. If they use anything it'll be arsenical smoke and it's no use against that. You'll find arsenical smoke quite painless at first. You won't know you've been gassed for a couple of days; then it'll be too late. In fact for all we know we're being gassed at this moment. If they fly high enough and let the wind carry the stuff they may be twenty miles away. The symptoms when they do appear are rather revolting . . ."

But Poppet was gone, helter-skelter, downstairs, making little moaning noises as she went.

Basil dressed and, only pausing to paint in a ginger moustache across Poppet's head of Aphrodite, strolled out into the streets.

The normal emptiness of Sunday in South Kensington was made complete that morning by the air raid scare. A man in a tin helmet shouted at Basil from the opposite pavement, "Take cover, there. Yes, it's you I'm talking to."

Basil crossed over to him and said in a low tone, "M.I.9."

"Eh?"

"M.I.9."

"I don't quite twig."

"But you *ought* to twig," said Basil severely. "Surely you realize that members of M.I.9 are free to go everywhere at all times?"

"Sorry, I'm sure," said the warden. "I was only took on yesterday. What a lark getting a raid second time on!" As he spoke the sirens sounded the All Clear. "What a sell!" said the warden.

It seemed to Basil that this fellow was altogether too cheerful for a public servant in the first hours of war; the gas scare had been wasted on Poppet; in her panic she had barely listened; it was worthy of a more receptive audience. "Cheer up," he said. "You may be breathing arsenical smoke at this moment. Watch your urine in a couple of days' time."

"Coo. I say, what did you say you was?"

"M.I.9."

"Is that to do with gas?"

"It's to do with almost everything. Good morning."

He turned to walk on but the warden followed. "Wouldn't we smell it or nothing?"

"No."

"Or cough or anything?"

"No."

"And you think they've dropped it, just in that minute, and gone away leaving us all for dead?"

"My dear fellow, I don't think so. It's your job as a warden to find out."

"Coo."

That'll teach him to shout at me in the street, thought Basil.

After the All Clear various friends of Poppet's came together in her studio.

"I wasn't *the least* frightened. I was so surprised at my own courage I felt quite giddy."

"I wasn't *frightened*, I just felt glum."

"I felt positively glad. After all we've all said for years that the present order of things was doomed, haven't we? I mean it's always been the choice for *us* between concentration camp and being blown up, hasn't it? I just sat thinking how much I preferred being blown up to being beaten with rubber truncheons."

"I was frightened," said Poppet.

"Dear Poppet, you always have the *healthiest* reactions. Erchman really did wonders for you."

"Well I'm not sure they *were* so healthy this time. D'you know, I found myself actually *praying*."

"I say, did you? That's bad."

"Better see Erchman again."

"Unless he's in a concentration camp."

"We shall all be in concentration camps."

"If anyone so much as mentions concentration camps again," said Ambrose Silk, "I shall go frankly haywire." ("He had an unhappy love affair in Munich," one of Poppet's friends explained to another, "then they found he was half-Jewish and the Brown Shirt was shut away.") "Let's look at Poppet's pictures and forget the war. Now *that*," he said, pausing before the Aphrodite, "*that* I consider *good*. I consider it *good*, Poppet. The moustache . . . it shows you have crossed one of the artistic rubicons and feel strong enough to be facetious. Like those wonderfully dramatic old *chestnuts* in Parsnip's *Guernica Revisited*. You're growing up, Poppet, my dear."

"I wonder if it's the effect of that old adventurer of hers."

"Poor Basil, it's sad enough for him to be an *enfant terrible* at the age of thirty-six; but to be regarded by the younger generation as a kind of dilapidated Bulldog Drummond . . ."

Ambrose Silk was older than Poppet and her friends; he was, in fact, a contemporary of Basil's, with whom he had maintained a shadowy, mutually derisive acquaintance since they were undergraduates. In those

days, the mid-twenties at Oxford, when the last of the
ex-service men had gone down and the first of the puri-
tanical, politically minded had either not come up or,
at any rate, had not made himself noticed, in those
days of broad trousers and high-necked jumpers and
cars parked nightly outside the Spread Eagle at
Thame, there had been few subdivisions; a certain
spiritual extravagance in the quest for pleasure had
been the sole common bond between friends, who in
subsequent years had drifted far apart, beyond hailing
distance, on the wider seas. Ambrose, in those days,
had ridden ridiculously and ignominiously in the
Christ Church Grind, and Peter Pastmaster had gone
to a *palais de danse* in Reading dressed as a woman.
Alastair Digby-Vane-Trumpington, absorbed in immature experiments into the question of how far various lewd debutantes would go with him, still had time
when tippling his port at Mickleham to hear, without
disapproval, Ambrose's recitals of unrequited love for
a rowing blue. Nowadays Ambrose saw few of his old
friends except Basil. He fancied that he had been
dropped and sometimes in moments of vainglory, to
the right audience, represented himself as a martyr to
Art; as one who made no concessions to Mammon.
"I can't come all the way with you," he said once to
Parsnip and Pimpernell when they explained that
only by becoming proletarian (an expression to which
they attached no pedantic suggestion of childbearing;
they meant that he should employ himself in some ill-

paid, unskilled labour of a mechanical kind) could he hope to be a valuable writer, "I can't come all the way with you, dear Parsnip and Pimpernell. But at least you know I have never sold myself to the upper class." In this mood he saw himself as a figure in a dream, walking down an endless fashionable street; every door stood open and the waiting footmen cried, "Come in and join us; flatter our masters and we will feed you," but Ambrose always marched straight ahead unheeding. "I belong, hopelessly, to the age of the ivory tower," he said.

It was his misfortune to be respected as a writer by almost everyone except those with whom he most consorted. Poppet and her friends looked on him as a survival from the *Yellow Book*. The more conscientiously he strove to put himself in the movement and to ally himself with the dour young proletarians of the new decade, the more antiquated did he seem to them. His very appearance, with the swagger and flash of the young Disraeli, made him a conspicuous figure among them. Basil with his natural shabbiness was less incongruous.

Ambrose knew this, and repeated the phrase "old adventurer" with relish.

5. ALASTAIR and Sonia Trumpington changed house, on an average, once a year, ostensibly for motives of economy, and were now

in Chester Street. Wherever they went they carried
with them their own inalienable, inimitable disorder.
Ten years ago, without any effort or desire on their
part, merely by pleasing themselves in their own way,
they had lived in the full blaze of fashionable notoriety; to-day without regret, without in fact being aware
of the change, they formed a forgotten cove, where
the wreckage of the "roaring twenties," long tossed
on the high seas, lay beached, dry and battered, barely
worth the attention of the most assiduous beach-
comber. Sonia would sometimes remark how odd it
was that the papers nowadays never seemed to mention anyone one had ever heard of; they had been such
a bore once, never leaving one alone.

Basil, when he was in England, was a constant visi-
tor. It was really, Alastair said, in order to keep him
from coming to stay that they had to live in such painfully cramped quarters.

Wherever they lived Basil developed a homing instinct towards them; an aptitude which, in their swift
moves from house to house, often caused consterna-
tion to subsequent tenants, who, before he had had
time to form new patterns of behaviour, would quite
often wake in the night to hear Basil swarming up the
drainpipes and looming tipsily in the bedroom window, or, in the morning, to find him recumbent and
insensible in the area. Now, on this catastrophic morning, Basil found himself orientated to them as surely
as though he were in wine, and he arrived on their new
doorstep without conscious thought of direction. He

went upstairs immediately, for, wherever they lived, it was always in Sonia's bedroom, as though it were the scene of an unending convalescence, that the heart of the household beat.

Basil had attended Sonia's levees (and there were three or four levees daily for, whenever she was at home, she was in bed) off and on for nearly ten years, since the days of her first, dazzling loveliness, when, almost alone among the chaste and daring brides of London, she had admitted mixed company to her bathroom. It was an innovation, or rather the revival of a more golden age, which, like everything Sonia did, was conceived without any desire for notoriety; she enjoyed company, she enjoyed her bath. There were usually three or four breathless and giddy young men, in those days, gulping Black Velvet in the steam, pretending to take their reception as a matter of common occurrence.

Basil saw little change in her beauty now and none in the rich confusion of letters, newspapers, half-opened parcels and half-empty bottles, puppies, flowers and fruit which surrounded the bed where she sat sewing (for it was one of the vagaries of her character to cover acres of silk, yearly, with exquisite embroidery).

"Darling Basil, have you come to be blown up with us? Where's your horrible girl friend?"

"She took fright."

"She was a beast, darling, one of your very worst.

Look at Peter. Isn't it all crazy?" Peter Pastmaster sat
at the foot of her bed in uniform. Once, for reasons
he had now forgotten, he had served, briefly, in the
cavalry; the harvest of that early sowing had ripened,
suddenly, overnight. "Won't it be too ridiculous, starting all over again, lunching with young men on guard?"

"Not young, Sonia. You should see us. The average
age of the subalterns is about forty, the Colonel finished the last war as a brigadier, and our troopers are
all either weatherbeaten old commissionaires or fifteen-
stone valets."

Alastair came in from the bathroom. "How's the
art-tart?" He opened bottles and began mixing stout
and champagne in a deep jug. "Blackers?" They had
always drunk this sour and invigorating draught.

"Tell us all about the war," said Sonia.

"Well — " Basil began.

"No, darling, I didn't mean that. Not *all*. Not about
who's going to win or why we are fighting. Tell us what
everyone is going to do about it. From what Margot
tells me the last war was absolute heaven. Alastair
wants to go for a soldier."

"Conscription has rather taken the gilt off that particular gingerbread," said Basil. "Besides, this isn't going to be a soldier's war."

"Poor Peter," said Sonia, as though she were talking
to one of the puppies. "It isn't going to be your war,
sweetheart."

"Suits me," said Peter.

"I expect Basil will have the most tremendous adventures. He always did in peace-time. Goodness knows what he'll do in war."

"There are too many people in on the racket," said Basil.

"Poor sweet, I don't believe any of you are nearly as excited about it as I am."

The name of the poet Parsnip, casually mentioned, reopened the great Parsnip-Pimpernell controversy which was torturing Poppet Green and her friends. It was a problem which, not unlike the Schleswig-Holstein question of the preceding century, seemed to admit of no logical solution, for, in simple terms, the postulates were self-contradictory. Parsnip and Pimpernell, as friends and collaborators, were inseparable; on that all agreed. But Parsnip's art flourished best in England, even an embattled England, while Pimpernell's needed the peaceful and fecund soil of the United States. The complementary qualities which, many believed, made them together equal to one poet, now threatened the dissolution of partnership.

"I don't say that Pimpernell is the *better* poet," said Ambrose. "All I say is that I *personally* find him the more nutritious; so I *personally* think they are right to go."

"But I've always felt that Parsnip is so much more dependent on environment."

"I know what you mean, Poppet, but I don't agree

. . . Aren't you thinking only of *Guernica Revisited* and forgetting the Christopher Sequence . . ."

Thus the aesthetic wrangle might have run its familiar course, but there was in the studio that morning a cross, red-headed girl in spectacles from the London School of Economics; she believed in a People's Total War; an uncompromising girl whom none of them liked; a suspect of Trotskyism.

"What I don't see," she said (and what this girl did not see was usually a very conspicuous embarrassment to Poppet's friends), "what I don't see is how these two can claim to be *contemporary* if they run away from the biggest event in contemporary history. They were contemporary enough about Spain when no one threatened to come and bomb *them*."

It was an awkward question; one that in military parlance was called "a swift one." At any moment, it was felt in the studio, this indecent girl would use the word "escapism"; and, in the silence which followed her outburst, while everyone in turn meditated and rejected a possible retort, she did, in fact, produce the unforgivable charge. "It's just sheer escapism," she said.

The word startled the studio, like the cry of "Cheat" in a card-room.

"That's a foul thing to say, Julia."

"Well, what's the answer?" . . .

The answer, thought Ambrose; he knew an answer or two. There was plenty that he had learned from his new friends, that he could quote to them. He could say that the war in Spain was "contemporary" because it was a class war; the present conflict, since Russia had declared herself neutral, was merely a phase in capitalist disintegration; that would have satisfied, or at least silenced, the red-headed girl. But that was not really the answer. He sought for comforting historical analogies but every example which occurred to him was on the side of the red-head. She knew them too, he thought, and would quote them with all her postgraduate glibness — Socrates marching to the sea with Xenophon, Virgil sanctifying Roman military rule, Horace singing the sweetness of dying for one's country, the troubadours riding to war, Cervantes in the galleys at Lepanto, Milton working himself blind in the public service, even George IV, for whom Ambrose had a reverence which others devoted to Charles I, believed he had fought at Waterloo. All these, and a host of other courageous contemporary figures, rose in Ambrose's mind. Cézanne had deserted in 1870, but Cézanne in the practical affairs of life was a singularly unattractive figure; moreover, he was a painter whom Ambrose found insufferably boring. There was no answer to be found on those lines.

"You're just sentimental," said Poppet, "like a spinster getting tearful at the sound of a military band."

"Well, they have military bands in Russia, don't they? I expect plenty of spinsters get tearful in the

Red Square when they march past Lenin's tomb."

You can always stump them with Russia, thought Ambrose; they can always stump each other. It's the dead end of all discussion.

"The question is: Would they write any better for being in danger?" said one.

"Would they help the People's Cause?" said another.

It was the old argument, gathering speed again after the rude girl's interruption. Ambrose gazed sadly at the jaundiced, mustachioed Aphrodite. What was he doing, he asked himself, in this galley?

Sonia was trying to telephone to Margot, to invite themselves all to luncheon.

"An odious man says that only official calls are being taken this morning."

"Say you're M.I.9," said Basil.

"I'm M.I.9. . . . What can that mean? Darling, I believe it's going to work . . . It *has* worked . . . Margot, this is Sonia . . . I'm dying to see you, too. . . ."

Aphrodite gazed back at him, blind, as though sculptured in butter; Parsnip and Pimpernell, Red Square and Brown House, thus the discussion raged. What had all this to do with him?

Art and Love had led him to this inhospitable room.

Love for a long succession of louts — rugger blues,

all-in wrestlers, naval ratings; tender, hopeless love that had been rewarded at the best by an occasional episode of rough sensuality, followed, in sober light, with contempt, abuse and rapacity.

A pansy. An old queen. A habit of dress, a tone of voice, an elegant, humorous deportment that had been admired and imitated, a swift, epicene felicity of wit, the art of dazzling and confusing those he despised — these had been his; and now they were the current exchange of comedians; there were only a few restaurants, now, which he could frequent without fear of ridicule, and there he was surrounded, as though by distorting mirrors, with gross reflections and caricatures of himself. Was it thus that the rich passions of Greece and Arabia and the Renaissance had worn themselves out? Did they simper when Leonardo passed and imitate with mincing grace the warriors of Sparta? Was there a snigger across the sand outside the tents of Saladin? They burned the Knights Templars at the stake; their loves, at least, were monstrous and formidable, a thing to call down destruction from heaven if man neglected his duty of cruelty and repression. Beddoes had died in solitude, by his own hand; Wilde had been driven into the shadows, tipsy and garrulous, but, to the end, a figure of tragedy looming big in his own twilight. But Ambrose, thought Ambrose, what of him? Born after his time, in an age which made a type of him, a figure of farce; like mothers-in-law and kippers, the century's

contribution to the national store of comic objects;
akin with the chorus boys who tittered under the lamps
of Shaftesbury Avenue . . . And Hans, who at last,
after so long a pilgrimage, had seemed to promise rest,
Hans so simple and affectionate, like a sturdy young
terrier, Hans lay in the unknown horrors of a Nazi concentration camp.

The huge, yellow face with scrawled moustaches
offered Ambrose no comfort.

There was a young man of military age in the studio;
he was due to be called up in the near future. "I don't
know what to do about it," he said. "Of course I could
always plead conscientious objections, but I haven't
got a conscience. It would be a denial of everything
we've stood for if I said I had a conscience."

"No, Tom," they said to comfort him. "We know
you haven't a conscience."

"But then," said the perplexed young man, "if I
haven't got a conscience, why in God's name should I
mind so much saying that I have?"

". . . Peter's here and Basil. We're all feeling very
gay and warlike. May we come to luncheon? Basil says
there's bound to be an enormous air raid to-night so it
may be the last time we shall ever see each other . . .
What's that? Yes, I told you I'm (What am I, Basil?)
— I'm M.I.9. (There's a ridiculous woman on the line
saying, 'Is this a private call?') . . . Well, Margot,

then we'll all come round to you. That'll be heaven
. . . Hello, *hello* . . . I do believe that damned
woman has cut us off."

Nature I loved, and next to Nature, Art. Nature in
the raw is seldom mild: red in tooth and claw; matelots
in Toulon smelling of wine and garlic, with tough
brown necks, cigarettes stuck to the lower lip, lapsing
into unintelligible contemptuous argot.

Art: this was where Art had brought him, to this
studio, to these coarse and tedious youngsters, to that
preposterous yellow face among the boiled sweets.

It had been a primrose path in the days of Diaghilev;
at Eton he had collected Lovat-Fraser Rhyme-sheets;
at Oxford he had recited "In Memoriam" through a
megaphone to an accompaniment hummed on combs
and tissue paper; in Paris he had frequented Jean Coc-
teau and Gertrude Stein; he had written and pub-
lished his first book there, a study of Montparnasse
Negroes that had been banned in England by Sir William Joynson-Hicks. That way the primrose path led
gently downhill to the world of fashionable photographers, stage sets for Cochrane, Cedric Lyne and his
Neapolitan grottoes.

He had made his decision then, turned aside from
the primrose path; had deliberately chosen the austere
and the heroic; it was the year of the American slump,
a season of heroic decisions, when Paul had tried to
enter a monastery and David had succeeded in throw-

ing himself under a train. Ambrose had gone to Germany, lived in a workmen's quarter, found Hans, begun a book — a grim, abstruse, interminable book, a penance for past frivolity; the unfinished manuscript lay somewhere in an old suitcase in Central Europe; and Hans was behind barbed wire; or worse, perhaps, had given in — as, with his simple easy-going acceptance of things, was all too likely; was back among the Brown Shirts, a man with a mark against his name, never again to be trusted, but good enough for the firing line, good enough to be jostled into battle.

The red-headed girl was asking inconvenient questions again. "But Tom," she was saying. "Surely if it was a good thing to share the life of the worker in a canned fruit factory, why isn't it a good thing to serve with him in the Army?"

"Julia's just the type who used to go about distributing white feathers."

"If it comes to that, why the hell not?" said Julia.

Ars longa, thought Ambrose, a short life but a grey one.

Alastair plugged his electric razor into the lamp on Sonia's writing table and shaved in the bedroom, so as not to miss what was going on. He had once in the past seen Peter in full dress uniform at a Court Ball and had felt sorry for him because it meant that he could not come on afterwards to a night club; this was the first time he had seen him in khaki and he was jealous as a schoolboy. There was still a great deal of the schoolboy about Alastair; he enjoyed winter sports and sailing and squash racquets and the chaff round the bar at Bratt's; he observed certain immature taboos of dress, such as wearing a bowler hat in London until after Goodwood Week; he had a firm, personal sense of schoolboy honour. He felt these prejudices to be peculiar to himself; none of them made him at all censorious of anyone else; he accepted Basil's outrageous disregard for them without question. He kept his sense of honour as he might have kept an expensive and unusual pet; as, indeed, once, for a disastrous month, Sonia had kept a small kangaroo named Molly. He knew himself to be as eccentric, in his own way, as Ambrose Silk. For a year, at the age of twenty-one, he had been Margot Metroland's lover; it was an apprenticeship many of his friends had served; they had forgotten about it now, but at the time all their acquaintances knew about it; but never, even to Sonia, had Alastair alluded to the fact. Since marriage he had been unfaithful to Sonia for a week every year, during Bratt's Club golf tournament at Le Touquet, usually with the wife of a fellow member. He did this without any scruple because he believed Bratt's Week to be in some way excluded from the normal life of loyalties and obligations; a Saturnalia when the laws did not run. At all other times he was a devoted husband.

Alastair had never come nearer to military service than in being senior private in the Corps at Eton; during the General Strike he had driven about the poorer quarters of London in a closed van to break up seditious meetings and had clubbed several unoffending citizens; that was his sole contribution to domestic politics, for he had lived, in spite of his many moves, in uncontested constituencies. But he had always held it as axiomatic that, should anything as preposterous and antiquated as a large-scale war occur, he would take a modest but vigorous part. He had no illusions about his abilities, but believed, justly, that he would make as good a target as anyone else for the King's enemies to shoot at. It came as a shock to him now, to find his country at war and himself in pyjamas, spending his normal Sunday noon with a jug of Black Velvet and some chance visitors. Peter's uniform added to his uneasiness. It was as though he had been taken in adultery at Christmas or found in mid-June on the steps of Bratt's in a soft hat.

He studied Peter, with the rapt attention of a small boy, taking in every detail of his uniform, the riding boots, Sam Browne belt, the enamelled stars of rank, and felt disappointed but, in a way, relieved, that there was no sword; he could not have borne it if Peter had had a sword.

"I know I look awful," Peter said. "The Adjutant left me in no doubt on that subject."

"You look sweet," said Sonia.

"I heard they had stopped wearing cross straps on the Sam Browne," said Alastair.

"Yes, but technically *we* still carry swords."

Technically. Peter *had* a sword, technically.

"Darling, do you think that if we went past Buckingham Palace the sentries would salute?"

"It's quite possible. I don't think Belisha has quite succeeded in putting it down yet."

"We'll go there at once. I'll dress. Can't wait to see them."

So they walked from Chester Street to Buckingham Palace; Sonia and Peter in front, Alastair and Basil a pace or two behind. The sentries saluted and Sonia pinched Peter as he acknowledged it. Alastair said to Basil:

"I suppose we'll be doing that soon."

"They don't want volunteers in this war, Alastair. They'll call people up when they want them without any recruiting marches or popular songs. They haven't the equipment for the men in training now."

"Who do you mean by 'they'?"

"Hore-Belisha."

"Who cares what *he* wants?" said Alastair. For him there was no "they." England was at war; he, Alastair Trumpington, was at war. It was not the business of any politician to tell him when or how he should fight. But he could not put this into words; not into words, anyway, which Basil would not make ridiculous, so he walked on in silence behind Peter's martial figure until Sonia decided to take a cab.

"I know what I want," said Basil. "I want to be one

of those people one heard about in 1919: the hard-
faced men who did well out of the war."

6. ALTHOUGH it was com-
mon for Freddy Sothill and Sir Joseph Mainwaring,
and various others who from time to time were enlisted
to help solve the recurrent problem of Basil's future, to
speak of him in terms they normally reserved for the
mining community of South Wales, as feckless and
unemployable, the getting of jobs, of one kind and another, had, in fact, played a large part in his life; for it
was the explanation and excuse of most of Basil's vagaries that he had never had any money of his own.
Tony and Barbara by their father's will each enjoyed
a reasonable fortune, but Sir Christopher Seal had
died shortly after the first of Basil's major disgraces.
If it were conceivable that one who held the office of
Chief Whip for a quarter of a century could be shocked
at any spectacle of human depravity, it might have
been thought that shame hastened his end, so fast did
one event follow upon the other. Be that as it may, it
was on his death-bed that Sir Christopher, in true mel-
odramatic style, disinherited his younger son, leaving
his future entirely in his mother's hands.

Lady Seal's most devoted friend — and she had

many — would not have credited her with more than human discretion, and some quite preternatural power would have been needed to deal with Basil's first steps in adult life. The system she decided on was, at the best, unimaginative and, like many such schemes, was suggested to her by Sir Joseph Mainwaring; it consisted, in his words, of "giving the boy his bread and butter and letting him find the jam." Removed from the realm of metaphor to plain English, this meant allowing Basil £400 a year, conditional on his good behaviour, and expecting him to supplement it by his own exertions if he wished for a more ample way of life.

The arrangement proved disastrous from the first. Four times in the last ten years Lady Seal had paid Basil's debts; once on condition of his living at home with her; once on condition of his living somewhere, anywhere, abroad; once on condition of his marrying; once on condition of his refraining from marriage. Twice he had been cut off with a penny; twice taken back to favour; once he had been set up in chambers in the Temple with an allowance of a thousand a year; several times, a large lump sum of capital had been dangled before his eyes as the reward of his giving himself seriously to commerce; once he had been on the verge of becoming the recipient of a sisal farm in Kenya. Throughout all these changes of fortune Sir Joseph Mainwaring had acted the part of political

agent to a recalcitrant stipendiary sultan, in a way
which embittered every benevolence and minimized
the value of every gift he brought. In the intervals of
neglect and independence, Basil had fended for himself and had successively held all the jobs which were
open to young men of his qualifications. He had never
had much difficulty in getting jobs; the trouble had always been in keeping them, for he regarded a poten-
tial employer as his opponent in a game of skill. All
Basil's resource and energy went into hoodwinking him
into surrender; once he had received his confidence he
lost interest. Thus English girls will put themselves to
endless exertion to secure a husband and, once married, will think their labour at an end.

Basil had been leader writer on the *Daily Beast*, he
had served in the personal entourage of Lord Mono-
mark, he had sold champagne on commission, composed dialogue for the cinema and given the first of
what was intended to be a series of talks for the B.B.C.
Sinking lower in the social scale he had been press
agent for a female contortionist and had once con-
ducted a party of tourists to the Italian lakes. (He
dined out for some time on the story of that tour,
which had, after a crescendo of minor vexations, cul-
minated in Basil's making a bundle of all the tickets
and all the passports and sinking them in Lake Garda.
He had then travelled home alone by an early train,
leaving fifty penniless Britons, none of whom spoke a

word of any foreign language, to the care of whatever deity takes charge of forsaken strangers; for all Basil knew, they were still there.)

From time to time he disappeared from the civilized area and returned with tales to which no one attached much credence — of having worked for the secret police in Bolivia and advised the Emperor of Azania on the modernization of his country. Basil was in the habit, as it were, of conducting his own campaigns, issuing his own ultimatums, disseminating his own propaganda, erecting about himself his own blackout; he was an obstreperous minority of one in a world of otiose civilians. He was used, in his own life, to a system of push, appeasement, agitation and blackmail, which, except that it had no more distinct aim than his own immediate amusement, ran parallel to Nazi diplomacy.

Like Nazi diplomacy it postulated for success a peace-loving, orderly and honourable world in which to operate. In the new, busy, secretive, chaotic world which developed during the first days of the war, Basil, for the first time in his life, felt himself at a disadvantage. It was like being in Latin America at a time of upheaval and, instead of being an Englishman, being oneself a Latin-American.

The end of September found Basil in a somewhat fretful mood. The air raid scare seemed to be over for the time, and those who had voluntarily fled from London were beginning to return, pretending that they

had only been to the country to see that everything
was all right there. The women and children of the
poor, too, were flocking home to their evacuated
streets. The newspapers said that the Poles were holding out; that their cavalry was penetrating deep into
Germany; that the enemy was already short of motor
oil; that Saarbrücken would fall to the French within
a day or two; air raid wardens roamed the remote ham-
lets of the kingdom, persecuting yokels who walked
home from the inn with glowing pipes. Londoners,
who were slow to acquire the habit of the domestic
hearth, groped their way in darkness from one place of
amusement to another, learning their destination by
feeling the buttons on the commissionaires' uniforms;
revolving black-glass doors gave access to a fairyland;
it was as though, when children, they had been led
blindfold into the room with the lighted Christmas
tree. The casualty list of street accidents became formidable, and there were terrifying tales of footpads
who leaped on the shoulders of old gentlemen on the
very steps of their clubs, or beat them to jelly on Hay
Hill.

Everyone whom Basil met was busy getting a job.
Some consciously or unconsciously had taken out an
insurance policy against unemployment by joining some
military unit in the past; there were those like Peter,
who in early youth had gratified a parental whim by
spending a few expensive years in the regular Army,
and those like Freddy who had gone into the yeomanry

as they sat on the Bench and the county council as part of the normal obligations of rural life. These were now in uniform with their problems solved. In later months, as they sat idle in the Middle East, they were to think enviously of those who had made a more deliberate and judicious choice of service, but at the moment their minds were enviably at rest. The remainder were possessed with a passion to enroll in some form of public service, however uncongenial. Some formed ambulance parties and sat long hours at their posts waiting for air raid victims; some became firemen, some minor civil servants. None of these honourable occupations made much appeal to Basil.

He was exactly the type of man who, if English life had run as it did in books of adventure, should at this turn in world affairs have been sent for. He should have been led to an obscure address in Maida Vale and there presented to a lean, scarred man with hard grey eyes — one of the men behind the scenes; one of the men whose names were unknown to the public and the newspapers, who passed unnoticed in the street, a name known only to the inner circle of the Cabinet and to the heads of the secret police of the world. . . . "Sit down, Seal. We've followed your movements with interest ever since that affair in La Paz in '32. You're a rascal, but I'm inclined to think you're the kind of rascal the country needs at this moment. I take it you're game for anything?"

"I'm game."

"That's what I expected you to say. These are your orders. You will go to Uxbridge aerodrome at 4:30 this afternoon, where a man will meet you and give you your passport. You will travel under the name of Blenkinsop. You are a tobacco grower from Latakia. A civil aeroplane will take you by various stages to Smyrna, where you will register at the Miramar Hotel and await orders. Is that clear? . . ."

It was clear, and Basil, whose life up to the present had been more like an adventure story than most people's, did half expect some such summons. None came. Instead he was invited to luncheon by Sir Joseph Mainwaring at the Travellers' Club.

Basil's luncheons at the Travellers' with Sir Joseph Mainwaring had for years formed a series of monuments in his downward path. There had been the luncheons of his four major debt settlements, the luncheon of his political candidature, the luncheons of his two respectable professions, the luncheon of the threatened divorce of Angela Lyne, the Luncheon of the Stolen Emeralds, the Luncheon of the Knuckledusters, the Luncheon of Freddy's Last Cheque — each would provide both theme and title for a work of popular fiction.

Hitherto these feasts had taken place *à deux* in a secluded corner. The Luncheon of the Commission in the Guards was altogether a more honourable affair and its purpose was to introduce Basil to the Lieutenant-Colonel of the Bombardiers — an officer whom Sir

Joseph wrongly believed to have a liking for him.

The Lieutenant-Colonel did not know Sir Joseph well and was surprised and slightly alarmed by the invitation, for his distrust was based not, as might have been expected, on any just estimate of his capabilities, but, paradoxically, on the fear of him as a politician and man of affairs. All politicians were, to the Lieutenant-Colonel, not so much boobies as bogies. He saw them all, even Sir Joseph, as figures of Renaissance subtlety and intrigue. It was by being in with them that the great professional advances were achieved; but it was by falling foul of them that one fell into ignominy. For a simple soldier — and if ever anyone did, the Lieutenant-Colonel qualified for that honourable title — the only safe course was to avoid men like Sir Joseph. When met with, they should be treated with bluff and uncompromising reserve. Sir Joseph thus found himself, through his loyal friendship with Cynthia Seal, in the equivocal position of introducing, with a view to his advancement, a man for whom he had a deep-seated horror to a man who had something of the same emotion towards himself. It was not a concurrence which, on the face of it, seemed hopeful of good results.

Basil, like "Lord Monmouth," "never condescended to the artifice of the toilet," and the Lieutenant-Colonel studied him with distaste. Together the ill-assorted trio went to their table.

Soldier and statesman spread their napkins on their

knees and in the interest of ordering their luncheon allowed a silence to fall between them into which Basil cheerfully plunged.

"We ought to do something about Liberia, Colonel," he said.

The Colonel turned on him the outraged gaze with which a good regimental soldier always regards the discussion of war in its larger aspects.

"I expect those whose business it is have the question in hand," he said.

"Don't you believe it," said Basil. "I don't expect they've given it a thought," and for some twenty minutes he explained why and how Liberia should be immediately annexed.

The two older men ate in silence. At length a chance reference to Russia gave Sir Joseph the chance to interpose an opinion.

"I always distrust prophecy in any form," he said. "But there is one thing of which I am certain. Russia will come in against us before the end of the year. That will put Italy and Japan on our side. Then it is simply a question of time before our blockade makes itself felt. All kinds of things that you and I have never heard of, like manganese and bauxite, will win the war for us."

"And infantry."

"*And* infantry."

"Teach a man to march and shoot. Give him the right type of officer. Leave the rest to him."

This seemed to Basil a suitable moment to introduce his own problems. "What do you think is the right type of officer?"

"The officer-type."

"It's an odd thing," Basil began, "that people always expect the upper class to be good leaders of men. That was all right in the old days when most of them were brought up with tenantry to look after. But now three-quarters of your officer-type live in towns. *I* haven't any tenantry."

The Lieutenant-Colonel looked at Basil with detestation. "No, no. I suppose not."

"Well, have *you* any tenantry?"

"*I?* No. My brother sold the old place years ago."

"Well, there you are."

It was crystal-clear to Sir Joseph, and faintly perceptible to Basil, that the Lieutenant-Colonel did not take this well.

"Seal was for a time Conservative candidate down in the West," said Sir Joseph, anxious to remove one possible source of prejudice.

"Some pretty funny people have been calling themselves Conservatives in the last year or two. Cause of half the trouble if you ask me." Then, feeling he might have been impolite, he added graciously: "No offence to you. Daresay you were all right. Don't know anything about you."

Basil's political candidature was not an episode to be enlarged upon. Sir Joseph turned the conversation. "Of course the French will have to make some concessions to bring Italy in. Give up Djibouti or something like that."

"Why the devil should they?" asked the Lieutenant-Colonel petulantly. "Who wants Italy in?"

"To counterbalance Russia."

"How? Why? Where? I don't see it at all."

"Nor do I," said Basil.

Threatened with support from so unwelcome a quarter, the Lieutenant-Colonel immediately abandoned his position. "Oh, don't you?" he said. "Well, I've no doubt Mainwaring knows best. His job is to know these things."

Warmed by these words Sir Joseph proceeded for the rest of luncheon to suggest some of the concessions which he thought France might reasonably make to Italy — Tunisia, French Somaliland, the Suez Canal. "Corsica, Nice, Savoy?" asked Basil. Sir Joseph thought not.

Rather than ally himself with Basil the Lieutenant-Colonel listened to these proposals to dismember an ally in silence and fury. He had not wanted to come out to luncheon. It would be absurd to say that he was busy, but he was busier than he had ever been in his life before and he looked on the two hours or so which he allowed himself in the middle of the day as a time for general recuperation. He liked to spend them among people to whom he could relate all that he had done in the morning; to people who would appreciate the importance and rarity of such work; either that, or with a handsome woman. He left the Travellers' as early as he decently could and returned to his mess. His mind was painfully agitated by all he had heard and particularly by the presence of that seedy-looking young radical whose name he had not caught. That at least, he thought, he might have hoped to be spared at Sir Joseph's table.

"Well, Jo, is everything arranged?"

"Nothing is exactly *arranged* yet, Cynthia, but I've set the ball rolling."

"I hope Basil made a good impression."

"I hope he did, too. I'm afraid he said some rather unfortunate things."

"Oh dear. Well, what is the next step?"

Sir Joseph would have liked to say that there was no next step in that direction; that the best Basil could hope for was oblivion; perhaps in a month or so, when the luncheon was forgotten . . . "It's up to Basil now, Cynthia. I have introduced him. He must follow it up himself if he really wants to get into that regiment. But I have been wondering, since you first mentioned the matter, do you really think it is quite suitable . . ."

"I'm told he could not do better," said Lady Seal proudly.

"No, that is so. In one way he could not do better."

"Then he shall follow up the introduction," said that unimaginative mother.

The Lieutenant-Colonel was simmering quietly in his office; an officer — not a young officer but a mature reservist — had just been to see him without gloves, wearing suède shoes; the consequent outburst had been a great relief; the simmering was an expression of content, a kind of mental purr; it was a mood which his subordinates recognized as a good mood. He was feeling that as long as there was someone like himself at the head of the regiment, nothing much could go wrong with it (a feeling which, oddly enough, was shared by the delinquent officer). To the Lieutenant-Colonel, in this mood, it was announced that a civilian gentleman, Mr. Seal, wanted to see him. The name was unfamiliar; so, for the moment, was Basil's appearance, for Angela had been at pains and expense to fit him up suitably for the interview. His hair was newly cut, he wore a stiff white collar, a bowler hat, a thin gold watch-chain and other marks of respectability, and he carried a new umbrella. Angela had also schooled him in the first words of his interview. "I know you are very busy, Colonel, but I hoped you would spare me a few minutes to ask your advice . . ."

All this went fairly well. "Want to go into the Army?" said the Lieutenant-Colonel. "Well I suppose we must expect a lot of people coming in from outside nowadays. Lot of new battalions being formed, even in the Brigade. I presume you'll join the infantry. No point in going into the cavalry nowadays. All these machines. Might just as well be an engine driver and have done with it. There's a lot of damn fool talk about this being a mechanized war and an air war and a commercial war. All wars are infantry wars. Always have been."

"Yes, it was infantry I was thinking of."

"Quite right. I hear some of the line regiments are very short of officers. I don't imagine you want to go through the ranks, ha! ha! There's been a lot of nonsense about that lately. Not that it would do any harm to some of the young gentlemen I've seen about the place. But for a fellow of your age the thing to do is to join the Supplementary Reserve, put down the regiment you want to join — there are a number of line regiments who do very useful work in their way — and get the commanding officer to apply for you."

"Exactly, sir, that's what I came to see you about. I was hoping that *you* — "

"That *I* . . . ?" Slowly to that slow mind there came the realization that Basil, this dissolute-looking young man who had so grossly upset his lunch interval the day before, this radical who had impugned the efficiency of the officer-type, was actually proposing to join the Bombardier Guards.

"I've always felt," said Basil, "that if I had to join the foot guards, I'd soonest join yours. You aren't as stuffy as the Grenadiers and you haven't got any of those bogus regional connections like the Scots and Irish and Welsh."

Had there been no other cause of offence; had Basil come to him with the most prepossessing appearance, the most glittering sporting record, a manner in which deference to age was most perfectly allied with social equality, had he been lord of a thousand loyal tenants, had he been the nephew of the Colonel-in-chief, the use by a civilian of such words as "stuffy" and "bogus" about the Brigade of Guards would have damned him utterly.

"So what I suggest," Basil continued, "is that I sign up for this Supplementary Reserve and put you down as my choice of regiment. Will that be O.K.?"

The Lieutenant-Colonel found his voice; it was not a voice of which he had full control; it might have been the voice of a man who had been suspended for a few seconds from a gibbet and then cut down. He fingered his collar as though, indeed, expecting to find the hangman's noose there. He said: "That would *not* be O.K. We do not take our officers from the Supplementary Reserve."

"Well how *do* I join you?"

"I'm afraid I must have misled you in some way. I have no vacancy for you in the regiment. I'm looking for platoon commanders. As it is I've got six or seven ensigns of over thirty. Can you imagine yourself leading a platoon in action?"

"Well, as a matter of fact I can, but that's the last thing I want. In fact that's why I want to keep away from the line regiments. After all there is always a number of interesting staff jobs going for anyone in the Guards, isn't there? What I thought of doing was to sign up with you and then look round for something more interesting. I should be frightfully bored with regimental life you know, but everyone tells me it's a great help to start in a decent regiment."

The noose tightened about the Lieutenant-Colonel's throat. He could not speak. It was with a scarcely human croak and an eloquent gesture of the hand that he indicated that the interview was over.

In the office it quickly became known that he was in one of his bad moods again.

Basil went back to Angela.

"How did it go, darling?"

"Not well. Not well at all."

"Oh dear, and you looked so particularly presentable."

"Yes; it can't have been that. And I was tremendously polite. Said all the right things. I expect that old snake Jo Mainwaring has been making mischief again."

7. "WHEN WE SAY that Parsnip can't write in war-time Europe, surely we mean that he can't write as he has written up till now. Mightn't it be better for him to stay here, even if it meant holding up production for a year or so, so that he can *develop*?"

"Oh, I don't think Parsnip and Pimpernell *can* develop. I mean an organ doesn't *develop*; it just goes on playing different pieces of music but remains the same. I feel Parsnip and Pimpernell have perfected themselves as an instrument."

"Then suppose Parsnip were to develop and Pimpernell didn't. Or suppose they developed in different directions. What would happen then?"

"Yes, what would happen then?"

"Why does it take two to write a poem?" asked the red-headed girl.

"Now Julia, don't short-circuit the argument."

"I should have thought poetry was a one-man job. Part-time work at that."

"But Julia, you'll admit you don't know very much about poetry, dear."

"That's exactly why I'm asking."

"Don't pay any attention, Tom. She doesn't really want to know. She's only being tiresome."

They were lunching at a restaurant in Charlotte Street; there were too many of them for the table; when you put out your hand for your glass and your neighbour at the same time put out his knife for the butter, he gave you a greasy cuff; too many for the menu, a single sheet of purple handwriting that was passed from hand to hand with indifference and indecision; too many for the waiter, who forgot their various orders; there were only six of them but it was too many for Ambrose. The talk was a series of assertions and interjections. Ambrose lived in and for conversation; he rejoiced in the whole intricate art of it — the timing and striking, the proper juxtaposition of narrative and comment, the bursts of spontaneous parody, the allusion one would recognize and one would not, the changes of alliance, the betrayals, the diplomatic revolutions, the waxing and waning of dictatorships that could happen in an hour's session about a table. But could it happen? Was that, too, most exquisite and exacting of the arts, part of the buried world of Diaghilev?

For months, now, he had seen no one except Poppet Green and her friends, and now, since Angela Lyne's return, Basil had dropped out of the group as abruptly as he had entered it, leaving Ambrose strangely forlorn.

Why, he wondered, do real intellectuals always prefer the company of rakes to that of their fellows? Basil is a Philistine and a crook; on occasions he can be a monumental bore; on occasions a grave embarrassment; he is a man for whom there will be no place in the coming Workers' State; and yet, thought Ambrose, I hunger for his company. It is a curious thing, he thought, that every creed promises a paradise which will be absolutely uninhabitable for anyone of civilized taste. Nanny told me of a Heaven that was full of angels playing harps; the Communists tell me of an earth full of leisured and contented factory hands. I don't see Basil getting past the gate of either. Religion is acceptable in its destructive phase: the desert monks carving up that humbug Hypatia, the anarchist gangs roasting the monks in Spain. Hellfire sermons in the chapels; soap-box orators screaming their envy of the rich. Hell is all right. The human mind is inspired enough when it comes to inventing horrors; it is when it tries to invent a heaven that it shows itself cloddish. But Limbo is the place. In Limbo one has natural happiness without the beatific vision; no harps; no communal order; but wine and conversation and imperfect, various humanity. Limbo for the unbaptized, for the pious heathen, the sincere sceptic. Am I baptized into this modern world? At least I haven't taken a new name. All the rest of the Left Wing writers have adopted plebeian monosyllables. . . . Ambrose was irredeemably bourgeois. Parsnip often said so. Damn Parsnip, damn Pimpernell. Do these atrocious young people never discuss anything else?

They were disputing the bill now, and forgetting what he or she had eaten; passing the menu from hand to hand to verify the prices.

"When you've decided what it is, tell me."

"Ambrose's bill is always the largest," said the red-headed girl.

"Dear Julia, please don't tell me that I could have fed a worker's family for a week. I still feel definitely *peckish*, my dear. I am sure workers eat ever so much more."

"D'you *know* the index figure for a family of four?"

"No," said Ambrose wistfully, "no, I don't know the

index figure. Please don't tell me. It wouldn't surprise me in the least. I like to think of it as dramatically small." (Why do I talk like this? — nodding and fluttering my eyelids, as though with a repressed giggle; why can I not speak like a man? Mine is the brazen voice of Apuleius' ass, turning its own words to ridicule.)

The party left the restaurant and its members stood in an untidy group on the pavement, unable to make up their minds who was going with whom, in what direction, for what purpose. Ambrose bade them good-bye and hurried away, with his absurd, light step and his heavy heart. Two soldiers outside a public-house made rude noises as he passed. "I'll tell your sergeant-major on you," he said gaily, almost gallantly, and flounced down the street. I should like to be one of them, he thought. I should like to go with them and drink beer and make rude noises at passing aesthetes. What does world revolution hold in store for *me?* Will it make me any nearer them? Shall I walk differently, speak differently, be less bored with Poppet Green and her friends? Here is the war, offering a new deal for everyone; I alone bear the weight of my singularity.

He crossed Tottenham Court Road and Gower Street, walking without any particular object except to take the air. It was not until he was under its shadow and saw the vast bulk of London University insulting the autumnal sky that he remembered that here was the Ministry of Information and that his publisher, Mr. Geoffrey Bentley, was working there at the head

of some newly formed department. Ambrose decided
to pay him a call.

It was far from easy to gain admission; only once in
his life, when he had had an appointment in a cinema
studio in the outer suburbs, had Ambrose met such
formidable obstruction. All the secrets of all the services might have been hidden in that gross mass of
masonry. Not until Mr. Bentley had been summoned
to the gate to identify him was Ambrose allowed to
pass.

"We have to be very careful," said Mr. Bentley.

"Why?"

"Far too many people get in as it is. You've no con-
ception how many. It adds terribly to our work."

"What is your work, Geoffrey?"

"Well mostly it consists of sending people who want
to see me on to someone they don't want to see. I've
never liked authors — except of course," he added,
"my personal friends. I'd no idea there were so many
of them. I suppose, now I come to think of it, that ex-
plains why there are so many books. And I've never
liked books — except of course books by personal
friends."

They rose in a lift and walked down a wide corridor,
passing on the way Basil, who was talking a foreign
language which sounded like a series of expectorations
to a sallow man in a tarboosh.

"That's *not* one of my personal friends," said Mr.
Bentley bitterly.

"Does he work here?"

"I don't suppose so. No one works in the Near East Department. They just lounge about talking."

"The tradition of the bazaar."

"The tradition of the Civil Service. This is my little room."

They came to the door of what had once been a chemical laboratory, and entered. There was a white porcelain sink in the corner into which a tap dripped monotonously. In the centre of the oilcloth floor stood a card table and two folding chairs. In his own office Mr. Bentley sat under a ceiling painted by Angelica Kauffmann, amid carefully chosen pieces of Empire furniture. "We have to rough it, you see," he said. "I brought those to make it look more human."

"Those" were a pair of marble busts by Nollekens; they failed, in Ambrose's opinion, to add humanity to Mr. Bentley's room.

"You don't like them? You remember them in Bedford Square."

"I like them very much. I remember them well, but don't you think, dear Geoffrey, that here they are just a weeny bit *macabre*?"

"Yes," said Mr. Bentley sadly. "Yes. I know what you mean. They're really here to annoy the civil servants."

"Do they?"

"To a frenzy. Look at this." He showed Ambrose a long typewritten memorandum which was headed *Furniture, Supplementary to Official Requirements, Un-*

desirability. of. "I sent back this." He showed a still longer message headed *Art, Objets d', Conducive to Spiritual Repose, Absence of in the quarters of advisory staff.* "To-day I got this. *Flowers, Framed Photographs and Other Minor Ornaments. Massive Marble and Mahogany, Decorative features of, Distinction between.* Quite alliterative with rage, you see. There for the moment the matter rests, but as you see, it's uphill work to get anything done."

"I suppose it would make no difference if you explained that Nolleykins had inspired the greatest biography in the English language."

"None, I should think."

"What terrible people to work with! You are *brave*, Geoffrey. I couldn't do it."

"But, bless my soul, Ambrose, isn't that what you came about?"

"No. I came to see you."

"Yes, everyone comes to see me, but they all come hoping to be taken on in the Ministry. You'd better join now you're here."

"No. No."

"You might do worse you know. We all abuse the old M. of I., but there are a number of quite human people here already, and we are gradually pushing more in every day. You might do much worse."

"I don't want to do *anything*. I think this whole war's crazy."

"You might write a book for us then. I'm getting out

a very nice little series on 'What We Are Fighting For.'
I've signed up a retired admiral, a Church of England
curate, an unemployed docker, a Negro solicitor from
the Gold Coast, and a nose-and-throat specialist from
Harley Street. The original idea was to have a sym-
posium in one volume, but I've had to enlarge the idea
a little. All our authors had such very different ideas
it might have been a little confusing. We could fit
you in very nicely. 'I used to think war crazy.' It's a new
line."

"But I *do* think war crazy *still*."

"Yes," said Mr. Bentley, his momentary enthusiasm
waning. "I know what you mean."

The door opened and a drab precise little man entered. "I beg your pardon," he said coldly. "I didn't
expect to find *you* working."

"This is Ambrose Silk. I expect you know his work."

"No."

"No? He is considering doing a book in our 'Why
We Are at War' Series. This is Sir Philip Hesketh-
Smithers, our departmental Assistant Director."

"If you'll excuse me a minute, I came about memorandum RQ/1082/B4. The Director is very worried."

"Was that *Documents, Confidential, Destruction by
fire of?*"

"No. No. *Marble, Decorative features.*"

"*Massive Marble and Mahogany?*"

"Yes. Mahogany has no application to your sub-
department. That has reference to a prie-dieu in the

Religious Department. The Church of England advisor has been hearing confessions there and the Director is very concerned. No, it's these effigies."

"You refer to my Nolleykinses?"

"These great statues. They won't do, Bentley, you know, they really won't do."

"Won't do for what?" said Mr. Bentley bellicosely.

"They won't do for the departmental Director. He says, very properly, that portraits of sentimental association . . ."

"These are full of the tenderest association for me."

"Of relatives . . ."

"These are family portraits."

"Really, Bentley. Surely that is George III?"

"A distant kinsman," said Mr. Bentley blandly, "on my mother's side."

"And Mrs. Siddons?"

"A slightly closer kinswoman, on my father's side."

"Oh," said Sir Philip Hesketh-Smithers. "Ah. I didn't realize . . . I'll explain that to the Director. But I'm sure," he said suspiciously, "that such a contingency was definitely excluded from the Director's mind."

"Flummoxed," said Mr. Bentley, as the door closed behind Sir Philip. "Completely flummoxed. I'm glad you were there to see my little encounter. But you see what we have to contend with. And now to your affairs. I wonder where we can fit you into our little household."

"I don't want to be fitted in."

"You would be a great asset. Perhaps the Religious Department. I don't think atheism is properly represented there."

The head of Sir Philip Hesketh-Smithers appeared round the door. "Could you tell me, please, *how* you are related to George III? Forgive my asking, but the Director is bound to want to know."

"The Duke of Clarence's natural daughter Henrietta married Gervase Wilbraham of Acton — at that time, I need not remind you, a rural district. His daughter Gertrude married my maternal grandfather who was, not that it matters, three times Mayor of Chippenham. A man of substantial fortune — all, alas, now dissipated. . . . Flummoxed again, I think," he added as the door closed.

"Was that true?"

"That my grandfather was Mayor of Chippenham? Profoundly true."

"About Henrietta?"

"It has always been believed in the family," said Mr. Bentley.

In another cell of that great hive, Basil was explaining a plan for the annexation of Liberia. "The German planters there outnumber the British by about fourteen to one. They're organized as a Nazi unit; they've been importing arms through Japan and they are simply waiting for the signal from Berlin to take over the

government of the state. With Monrovia in enemy
hands, with submarines based there, our West Coast
trade route is cut. Then all the Germans have to do is
to shut the Suez Canal, which they can do from Mas-
sawa whenever they like, and the Mediterranean is lost.
Liberia is our one weak spot in West Africa. We've
got to get in first. Don't you see?"

"Yes, yes, but I don't know why you come to me
about it."

"You'll have to handle all the preliminary propaganda there and the explanations in America afterwards."

"But why *me?* This is the Near East Department.
You ought to see Mr. Pauling."

"Mr. Pauling sent me to you."

"Did he? I wonder why. I'll ask him." The unhappy
official took up the telephone and after being successively connected with Films, the shadow cabinet of
the Czecho-Slovaks and the A.R.P. section, said: "Pauling. I have a man called Seal here. He says you sent
him."

"Yes."

"Why?"

"Well you sent me that frightful Turk this morning."

"He was child's play to this."

"Well, let it be a lesson to you not to send me any
more Turks."

"You wait and see what I send you . . . Yes," turning to Basil, "Pauling made a mistake. Your business is really his. It's a most interesting scheme. Wish I could do more for you. I'll tell you who, I think, would like to hear about it — Digby-Smith; he handles propaganda and subversive activities in enemy territory, and, as you say, Liberia is to all intents and purposes enemy territory."

The door opened and there entered a beaming, bearded, hair-bunned figure in a long black robe; a gold cross swung from his neck; a brimless top-hat crowned his venerable head.

"I am the Archimandrite Antonios," he said. "I am coming in please?"

"Come in, Your Beatitude; please sit down."

"I have been telling how I was expulsed from Sofia. They said I must be telling you."

"You have been to our Religious Department?"

"I have been telling your office clergymen about my expulsing. The Bulgar peoples say it was for fornications, but it was for politics. They are not expulsing from Sofia for fornications unless there is politics too. So now I am the ally of the British peoples since the Bulgar people say it was for fornications."

"Yes, yes, I quite understand, but that is not really the business of this department."

"You are not dealing with the business of the Bulgar peoples?"

"Well, yes, but I think your case opens up a wider issue altogether. You must go and see Mr. Pauling. I'll give you someone to show the way. He deals especially with cases like yours."

"So? You have here a Department of Fornications?"

"Yes, you might call it that."

"I find that good. In Sofia is not having any such department."

His Beatitude was sent on his way. "Now you want to see Digby-Smith, don't you?"

"Do I?"

"Yes, he'll be *most* interested in Liberia."

Another messenger came; Basil was led away. In the corridor they were stopped by a small, scrubby man carrying a suitcase.

"Pardon me, can you put me right for the Near East?"

"There," said Basil, "in there. But you won't get much sense out of him."

"Oh, he's bound to be interested in what I've got here. Everyone is. They're bombs. You could blow the roof off the whole of this building with what I got here," said this lunatic. "I've been carting 'em from room to room ever since the blinking war began and often I think it wouldn't be a bad plan if they did go off sudden."

"Who sent you to the Near East?"

"Chap called Smith, Digby-Smith. Very interested in my bombs he was."

"Have you been to Pauling, yet?"

"Pauling? Yes, I was with him yesterday. Very interested he was in my bombs. I tell you everyone is. It was him said I ought to show them to Digby-Smith."

Mr. Bentley talked at length about the difficulties and impossibilities of bureaucratic life. "If it was not for the journalists and the civil servants," he said, "everything would be perfectly easy. They seem to think the whole Ministry exists for their convenience. Strictly, of course, I shouldn't have anything to do with the journalists — I deal with books here — but they always seem to shove them onto me when they get impatient. Not only journalists; there was a man here this morning with a suitcase full of bombs."

"Geoffrey," said Ambrose at length. "Tell me, would you say I was pretty well known as a Left Wing writer?"

"Of course my dear fellow, very well known."

"As a *Left* Wing writer?"

"Of course *very* Left Wing."

"Well known, I mean, outside the Left Wing itself."

"Yes, certainly. Why?"

"I was only wondering."

They were now interrupted for some minutes by an American war correspondent who wanted Mr. Bentley to verify the story of a Polish submarine which was said to have arrived at Scapa; to give him a pass to go there and see for himself; to provide him with a Polish interpreter; to explain why in hell that little runt Pappenhacker of the Hearst press had been told of this submarine and not himself.

"Oh dear," said Mr. Bentley. "Why have they sent you to me?"

"It seems I'm registered with you and not with the Press Bureau."

This proved to be true. As the author of *Nazi Destiny,* a work of popular history that had sold prodigiously on both sides of the Atlantic, this man had been entered as a "man of letters" instead of as a journalist.

"You mustn't mind," said Mr. Bentley. "In this country we think much more of men of letters than we do of journalists."

"Does being a man of letters get me to Scapa?"

"Well, no."

"Does it get me a Polish interpreter?"

"No."

"To hell with being a man of letters."

"I'll get you transferred," said Mr. Bentley. "The Press Bureau is the place for you."

"There's a snooty young man at that bureau looks at me as if I was something the cat brought in," complained the author of *Nazi Destiny.*

"He won't once you're registered with him. I wonder, since you're here, if you'd like to write a book for us."

"No."

"No? Well I hope you get to Scapa all right . . . He won't, you know," added Mr. Bentley as the door closed. "You may be absolutely confident that he'll never get there. Did you ever read his book? It was exceedingly silly. He said Hitler was secretly married to a Jewess. I don't know what he'd say if we let him go to Scapa."

"What do you think he'll say if you don't?"

"Something very offensive I've no doubt. But we shan't be responsible. At least, I wonder, shall we?"

"Geoffrey, when you say well known as a Left Wing writer, do you suppose that if the fascists got into power here, I should be on their black list?"

"Yes, certainly, my dear fellow."

"They did frightful things to the Left Wing intellectuals in Spain."

"Yes."

"And in Poland, now."

"So the Press Department tells me."

"I see."

The Archimandrite dropped in for a few moments. He expressed great willingness to write a book about Axis intrigues in Sofia.

"You think you can help bring Bulgaria in on our side?" asked Mr. Bentley.

"I am spitting the face of the Bulgar peoples," said His Beatitude.

"I believe he'd write a very good autobiography," said Mr. Bentley, when the prelate left them. "In the days of peace I should have signed him up for one."

"Geoffrey, you were serious when you said that I should be on the black list of Left Wing intellectuals?"

"Quite serious. You're right at the top. You and Parsnip and Pimpernell."

Ambrose winced at the mention of those two familiar names. "*They're* all right," he said. "*They're* in the United States."

Basil and Ambrose met as they left the Ministry. Together they loitered for a minute to watch a brisk little scene between the author of *Nazi Destiny* and the policeman on the gate; it appeared that in a fit of nervous irritation the American had torn up the slip of paper which had admitted him to the building; now they would not let him leave.

"I'm sorry for him in a way," said Ambrose. "It's not a place I'd care to spend the rest of the war in."

"They wanted me to take a job there," said Basil, lying.

"They wanted *me* to," said Ambrose.

They walked together through the sombre streets of Bloomsbury. "How's Poppet?" said Basil at length.

"She's cheered up wonderfully since you left. Painting away like a mowing machine."

"I must look her up again sometime. I've been busy lately. Angela's back. Where are we going to?"

"I don't know, I've nowhere to go."

"*I've* nowhere to go."

An evening chill was beginning to breathe down the street.

"I nearly joined the Bombardier Guards a week or two ago," said Basil.

"I once had a *great* friend who was a corporal in the Bombardiers."

"We'd better go and see Sonia and Alastair."

"I haven't been near them for years."

"Come on." Basil wanted someone to pay for the cab.

But when they reached the little house in Chester Street they found Sonia alone and packing. "Alastair's gone off," she said. "He's joined the Army — in the ranks. They said he was too old for a commission."

"My dear, how very 1914."

"I'm just off to join him. He's near Brookwood."

"You'll be beautifully near the Necropolis," said Ambrose. "It's the most enjoyable place. Three public houses, my dear, inside the cemetery, right among the graves. I asked the barmaid if the funeral parties got very tipsy and she said, 'No. It's when they come back to visit the graves. They seem to need something then.' And did you know the Corps of Commissionaires have a special burial place? Perhaps if Alastair is a very good soldier they might make him an honorary member . . ." Ambrose chattered on. Sonia packed. Basil looked about for bottles. "Nothing to drink."

"All packed, darling. I'm sorry. We might go out somewhere."

They went out, later, when the packing was done, into the blackout to a bar. Other friends came to join them.

"No one seems interested in my scheme to annex Liberia."

"Beasts."

"No imagination. They won't take suggestions from outsiders. You know, Sonia, this war is developing into a kind of club enclosure on a race-course. If you aren't wearing the right badge they won't let you in."

"I think that's rather what Alastair felt."

"It's going to be a long war. There's plenty of time. I shall wait until there's something amusing to do."

"I don't believe it's going to be that kind of war."

This is all that anyone talks about, thought Ambrose; jobs and the kind of war it is going to be. War in the air, war of attrition, tank war, war of nerves, war of propaganda, war of defence in depth, war of movement, peoples' war, total war, indivisible war, war infinite, war incomprehensible, war of essence without accidents or attributes, metaphysical war, war in time-space, war eternal . . . all war is nonsense, thought Ambrose. I don't care about their war. It's got nothing to do with me. But if, thought Ambrose, I were one of these people, if I were not a cosmopolitan, Jewish pansy, if I were not all that the Nazis mean when they talk about "degenerates," if I were not a single, sane individual, if I were part of a herd, one of these people, normal and responsible for the welfare of my herd, Gawd strike me pink, thought Ambrose, I wouldn't sit around discussing what kind of war it was going to be. I'd make it *my* kind of war. I'd set about killing and stampeding the other herd as fast and as hard as I could. Lord love a duck, thought Ambrose, there wouldn't be any animals nosing about for suitable jobs in *my* herd.

"Bertie's hoping to help control petrol in the Shetland Isles."

"Algernon's off to Syria on the most secret kind of mission."

"Poor John hasn't got anything yet."

Cor chase my Aunt Fanny round a mulberry bush, thought Ambrose; what a herd.

So the leaves fell and the blackout grew earlier and earlier, and autumn became winter.

CHAPTER II

Winter

1. *W*INTER set in hard. Poland was defeated; east and west the prisoners rolled away to slavery. English infantry cut trees and dug trenches along the Belgian frontier. Parties of distinguished visitors went to the Maginot Line and returned, as though from a shrine, with souvenir-medals. Belisha was turned out; the radical papers began a clamour for his return and then suddenly shut up. Russia invaded Finland and the papers were full of tales of white-robed armies scouting through the forests. English soldiers on leave brought back reports of the skill and daring of Nazi patrols and of how much better the blackout was managed in Paris. A number of people were saying quietly and firmly that Chamberlain must go. The French said the English were not taking the war seriously, and the Ministry of Information said the French were taking it very seriously indeed. Sergeant instructors complained of the shortage of training stores. How could one teach the three rules of aiming without aiming discs?

The leaves fell in the avenue at Malfrey, and this year, where once there had been a dozen men to sweep them, there were now four, and two boys. Freddy was

engaged in what he called "drawing in his horns a bit."
The Grinling Gibbons saloon and the drawing-rooms
and galleries round it were shut up and shut off, carpets
rolled, furniture sheeted, chandeliers bagged, windows
shuttered and barred; hall and staircase stood empty
and dark. Barbara lived in the little octagonal parlour
which opened on the parterre; she moved the nursery
over to the bedrooms next to hers; what had once been
known as "the bachelors' wing" in the Victorian days,
when bachelors were hardy fellows who could put up
with collegiate and barrack simplicity, was given over
to the evacués. Freddy came over for the four good
shoots which the estate provided; he made his guests
stay out this year, one at the farm, three at the bailiff's
house, two at the Sothill Arms. Now, at the end of the
season, he had some of the regiment over to shoot off
the cocks; bags were small and consisted mostly of hens.

When Freddy came on leave, the central heating was
lit; at other times an intense cold settled into the house;
it was a system which had to be all or nothing; it would
not warm Barbara's corner alone but had to circulate,
ticking and guggling, through furlongs of piping, con-
suming cartloads of coke daily. "Lucky we've got plenty
of wood," said Freddy; damp green logs were brought
in from the park to smoke tepidly on the hearths. Barbara used to creep into the orangery to warm herself.
"Must keep the heat up there," said Freddy. "Got some
very rare stuff in it. Man from Kew said some of the
best in the country." So Barbara had her writing table

put there, and sat, absurdly, among tropical vegetation while outside, beyond the colonnade, the ground froze hard and the trees stood out white against the leaden sky.

Then, two days before Christmas, Freddy's regiment was moved to another part of the country. He had friends with a commodious house in the immediate neighbourhood, where he spent his week-ends, so the pipes were never heated and the chill in the house, instead of being a mere negation of warmth, became something positive and overwhelming. Soon after Christmas there was a great fall of snow and with the snow came Basil.

He came, as usual, unannounced. Barbara, embowered in palm and fern, looked up from her letter-writing to see him standing in the glass door. She ran to kiss him with a cry of delight. "Darling, how very nice. Have you come to stay?"

"Yes, Mother said you were alone."

"I don't know where we'll put you. Things are very odd here. You haven't brought anyone else, have you?" It was one of Freddy's chief complaints that Basil usually came not only uninvited but attended by undesirable friends.

"No, no one. There isn't anyone nowadays. I've come to write a book."

"Oh, Basil. I am sorry. Is it as bad as that?" There was much that needed no saying between brother and sister. For years now, whenever things were very bad

with Basil, he had begun writing a book. It was as near
surrender as he ever came and the fact that these books
— two novels, a book of travel, a biography, a work of
contemporary history — never got beyond the first ten
thousand words was testimony to the resilience of his
character.

"A book on strategy," said Basil. "I'm sick of trying
to get ideas into the heads of the people in power. The
only thing is to appeal over their heads to the thinking
public. Chiefly, it is the case for the annexation of
Liberia, but I shall touch on several other vital places
as well. The difficulty will be to get it out in time to
have any influence."

"Mother said you were joining the Bombardier
Guards."

"Yes. Nothing came of it. They say they want
younger men. It's a typical Army paradox. They say
we are too old now and that they will call us up in two
years' time. I shall bring that out in my book. The only
logical policy is to kill off the old first, while there's still
some kick in them. I shan't deal only with strategy. I
shall outline a general policy for the nation."

"Well it's very nice to see you, anyway. I've been
lonely."

"*I've* been lonely."

"What's happened to everyone?"

"You mean Angela. She's gone home."

"Home?"

"That house we used to call Cedric's Folly. It's hers

really of course. Cedric's gone back to the Army. It's
scarcely credible but apparently he was a dashing young
subaltern once. So there was the house and the Lyne
hooligan and the Government moving in to make it a
hospital, so Angela had to go back to see to things. It's
full of beds and nurses and doctors waiting for air raid
victims and a woman in the village got appendicitis and
she had to be taken forty miles to be operated on because she wasn't an air raid victim and she died on the
way. So Angela is carrying on a campaign about it and I
shouldn't be surprised if she doesn't get something
done. She seems to have made up her mind I ought to
be killed. Mother's the same. It's funny. In the old days
when from time to time there really were people gun-
ning for me, no one cared a hoot. Now that I'm living
in enforced safety and idleness, they seem to think it
rather disgraceful."

"No new girls?"

"There was one called Poppet Green. You wouldn't
have liked her. I've been having a very dull time.
Alastair is a private at Brookwood. I went down to see
them. He and Sonia have got a terrible villa on a golf
course where he goes whenever he's off duty. He says
the worst thing about his training is the entertain-
ments. They get detailed to go twice a week and the
sergeant always picks on Alastair. He makes the same
joke each time: 'We'll send the playboy.' Otherwise
it's all very matey and soft, Alastair says . . . Peter
has joined a very secret corps to go and fight in the

Arctic. They had a long holiday doing winter sports in the Alps. I don't suppose you'd remember Ambrose Silk. He's starting a new magazine to keep culture alive."

"Poor Basil. Well I hope you don't have to write the book for long." There was so much between brother and sister that did not need saying.

That evening Basil began his book; that is to say he lay on the rug before the column of smoke which rose from the grate of the octagonal parlour, and typed out a list of possible titles.

A Word to the Unwise.

Prolegomenon to Destruction.

Berlin or Cheltenham; the Choice for the General Staff.

Policy or Generalship; Some Questions Put by a Civilian to Vex the Professional Soldiers.

Policy or Professionalism.

The Gentle Art of Victory.

The Lost Art of Victory.

How to Win the War in Six Months; a Simple Lesson Book for Ambitious Soldiers.

They all looked pretty good to him and looking at the list Basil was struck anew, as he had been constantly struck during the preceding four months, with surprise that anyone of his ability should be unemployed at a time like the present. It makes one despair of winning, he thought.

Barbara sat beside him reading. She heard him sigh and put out a sisterly hand to touch his hair. "It's terribly cold," she said. "I wonder if it would be any good trying to blackout the orangery. Then we could sit there in the evenings."

Suddenly there was a knock on the door and there entered a muffled, middle-aged woman; she wore fur gloves and carried an electric torch, dutifully dimmed with tissue paper; her nose was very red, her eyes were watering and she stamped snow off high rubber boots. It was Mrs. Fremlin of the Hollies. Nothing but bad news would have brought her out on a night like this. "I came straight in," she said superfluously. "Didn't want to stand waiting outside. Got some bad news. The Connollies are back."

It was indeed bad news. In the few hours that he had been at Malfrey, Basil had heard a great deal about the Connollies.

"Oh God," said Barbara. "Where are they?"

"Here, outside in the lobby."

Evacuation to Malfrey had followed much the same course as it had in other parts of the country and had not only kept Barbara, as billeting officer, constantly busy, but had transformed her, in four months, from one of the most popular women in the countryside into a figure of terror. When her car was seen approaching, people fled through covered lines of retreat, through side doors and stable yards, into the snow, anywhere to avoid her persuasive, "But surely you could manage *one* more. He's a boy this time and a very well-behaved little fellow" — for the urban authorities maintained a steady flow of refugees well in excess of the stream of returning malcontents. Few survived of the original party who had sat glumly on the village green on the first morning of war. Some had gone back immediately; others more reluctantly in response to ugly rumours of their husbands' goings on; one had turned out to be a fraud, who, herself childless, had kidnapped a baby from a waiting perambulator in order to secure her passage to safety, so impressed had she been by the propaganda of the local officials. It was mostly children now who assembled, less glumly, on the village green, and showed the agricultural community how another part of the world lived. They were tolerated now as one of the troubles of the time. Some had even endeared themselves to their hosts. But everyone, when evacués were spoken of, implicitly excluded for all generalities the family of Connolly.

These had appeared as an act of God apparently without human agency; their names did not appear on any list; they carried no credentials; no one was responsible for them. They were found lurking under the seats of a carriage when the train was emptied on the evening of the first influx. They had been dragged out and stood on the platform where everyone denied knowledge of them, and since they could not be left there, they were included in the party that was being sent by bus to Malfrey village. From that moment they were on a list; they had been given official existence and their destiny was inextricably involved with that of Malfrey.

Nothing was ever discovered about the Connollies' parentage. When they could be threatened or cajoled into speaking of their antecedents they spoke, with distaste, of an "Auntie." To this woman, it seemed, the war had come as a God-sent release. She had taken her dependents to the railway station, propelled them into the crowd of milling adolescence, and hastily covered her tracks by decamping from home. Enquiry by the police in the street where the Connollies professed to have lived produced no other information than that the woman had been there and was not there any longer. She owed a little for milk; otherwise she had left no memorial on that rather unimpressionable district.

There was Doris, ripely pubescent, aged by her own varied accounts anything from ten years to eighteen. An early and ingenious attempt to have her certified as an adult was frustrated by an inspecting doctor who put her at about fifteen. Doris had dark, black bobbed hair, a large mouth and dark pig's eyes. There was something of the Eskimo about her head but her colouring was ruddy and her manner more vivacious than is common among that respectable race. Her figure was stocky, her bust prodigious, and her gait, derived from the cinematograph, was designed to be alluring.

Micky, her junior by the length of a rather stiff sentence for housebreaking, was of lighter build; a scrawny, scowling little boy; a child of few words and those, for the most part, foul.

Marlene was presumed to be a year younger. But for Micky's violent denials she might have been taken for his twin. She was the offspring of unusually prolonged coincident periods of liberty in the lives of her parents, which the sociologist must deplore, for Marlene was simple. An appeal to have her certified imbecile was disallowed by the same inspecting doctor, who expressed an opinion that country life might work wonders with the child.

There the three had stood, on the eve of the war, in Malfrey Parish Hall, one leering, one lowering, and one drooling, as unprepossessing a family as could be found in the kingdom. Barbara took one look at them, looked again to see that her weary eyes were not playing tricks with her, and consigned them to the Mudges of Upper Lamstock, a tough farming family on a remote homestead.

Within a week Mr. Mudge was at the park, with the three children in the back of his milk truck. "It's not for myself, Mrs. Sothill; I'm out and about all day and in the evenings I'm sleepy, and being with animals so much I don't take on so. But it's my old woman. She *do* take on and she won't stand for it. She've locked herself in upstairs and she won't come down till they've gone and when she do say that she means of it, Mrs. Sothill. We're willing to do anything in reason to help the war, but these brats aren't to be borne and that's flat."

"Oh dear, Mr. Mudge, which of them is giving trouble?"

"Why it's all of 'em, ma'am. There's the boy was the best of 'em at first though you can't understand what he do say, speaking as they do where he come from. Nasty, unfriendly ways he had but he didn't do much that you could call harm not till he'd seen me kill the goose. I took him out to watch to cheer him up like, and uncommon interested he was and I thought I'll make a country lad of you yet. I gave him the head to play with and he seemed quite pleased. Then no sooner was I off down to the root field, than blessed if he didn't get hold of a knife and when I came back supper-time there was six of my ducks dead and the old cat. Yes, mum, blessed if he hadn't had the head off of our old yellow cat. Then the little un, she's a dirty girl begging your pardon, mum. It's not only her wetting the bed; she've wetted everywhere, chairs, floor and not only wetting, mum. Never seem to have been taught to be in a house where she comes from."

"But doesn't the elder girl do anything to help?"

"If you ask me, mum, she's the worst of the lot. My old woman would stick it but for her, but it's that Doris makes her take on like she do. Soft about the men, she is, mum. Why she even comes making up to me and I'm getting on to be her grandf'er. She won't leave our Willie alone not for a minute, and he's a bashful boy our Willie and he can't get on with the work, her always coming after him. So there it is, mum. I'm sorry not to oblige but I've promised my old woman I won't come back with 'em and I dusn't go back on what I've said."

Mr. Mudge was the first of a succession of hosts. The longest that the Connollies stayed in any place was ten days; the shortest was an hour and a quarter. In six weeks they had become a legend far beyond the parish. When influential old men at the Turf in London put their heads together and said, "The whole scheme has been a mistake. I was hearing last night some examples of the way some of the evacués are behaving . . . ," the chances were that the scandal originated with the Connollies. They were cited in the House of Commons; there were paragraphs about them in official reports.

Barbara tried separating them, but in their first night apart Doris climbed out of her window and was lost for two days, to be found in a barn eight miles away, stupefied with cider; she gave no coherent account of her adventure. On the same evening Micky bit the wife of the roadman on whom he was quartered, so that the district nurse had to be called in; while Marlene had a species of seizure which aroused unfulfilled hopes that she might be dead. Everyone agreed that the only place for the Connollies was "an institution"; and at last, just before Christmas, after formalities complicated by the obscurity of their origins, to an in-

stitution they were sent; and Malfrey settled back to
entertain its guests with a Christmas tree and a con-
juror, with an air of relief which could be sensed for
miles around. It was as though the All Clear had
sounded after a night of terror. And now the Connollies were back.

"What's happened, Mrs. Fremlin? Surely the Home
can't send them away."

"It's being evacuated. All the children are being
sent back to the places they came from. Malfrey was
the only address they had for the Connollies, so here
they are. The Welfare Woman brought them to the
Parish Hall. I was there with the Guides so I said I'd
bring them up to you."

"They might have warned us."

"I expect they thought that if we had time we should
try and stop them coming."

"How right they were. Have the Connollies been
fed?"

"I think so. At any rate Marlene was terribly sick
in the car."

"I'm dying to see these Connollies," said Basil.

"You shall," said his sister grimly.

But they were not in the lobby where they had been
left. Barbara rang the bell. "Benson, you remember
the Connolly children?"

"Vividly, madam."

"They're back."

"Here, madam?"

"Here. Somewhere in the house. You'd better institute a search."

"Very good, madam. And when they are found, they will be going away immediately?"

"Not immediately. They'll have to stay here tonight. We'll find somewhere for them in the village to-morrow."

Benson hesitated. "It won't be easy, madam."

"It won't be, Benson."

He hesitated again; thought better of whatever he meant to say, and merely added: "I will start the search, madam."

"I know what that means," said Barbara as the man left them. "Benson is yellow."

The Connollies were found at last and assembled. Doris had been in Barbara's bedroom trying out her make-up, Micky in the library tearing up a folio, Marlene grovelling under the pantry sink eating the remains of the dogs' dinners. When they were together again, in the lobby, Basil inspected them. Their appearance exceeded anything he had been led to expect. They were led away to the bachelors' wing and put together into a large bedroom.

"Shall we lock the door?"

"It would be no good. If they want to get out, they will."

"Could I speak to you for a moment, madam?" said Benson.

When Barbara returned she said, "Benson *is* yellow. He can't take it."

"Wants to leave?"

"It's him or the Connollies, he says. I can't blame him. Freddy will never forgive me if I let him go."

"Babs, you're blubbing."

"Who wouldn't?" said Barbara, pulling out a handkerchief and weeping in earnest. "I ask you, who wouldn't?"

"Don't be a chump," said Basil, relapsing, as he often did with Barbara, into the language of the schoolroom. "I'll fix it for you."

"Swank. Chump yourself. Double chump."

"Double chump with knobs on."

"Darling Basil, it is nice to have you back. I do believe if anyone could fix it, you could."

"Freddy couldn't, could he?"

"Freddy isn't here."

"I'm cleverer than Freddy. Babs, say I'm cleverer than Freddy."

"I'm cleverer than Freddy. Sucks to you."

"Babs, say you love me more than Freddy."

"You love me more than Freddy. Double sucks."

"Say I, Barbara, love you, Basil, more than him, Freddy."

"I won't. I don't . . . Beast, you're hurting."

"Say it."

"Basil stop at once or I shall call Miss Penfold."

They were back twenty years, in the schoolroom again. "Miss Penfold, Miss Penfold, Basil's pulling my hair."

They scuffled on the sofa. Suddenly a voice said, " 'Ere, Missus." It was Doris. "Missus!"

Barbara stood up, panting and dishevelled. "Well, Doris, what is it?"

"Marlene's queer again."

"Oh dear. I'll come up. Run along."

Doris looked languishingly at Basil. " 'Aving a lark, eh?" she said. "I like a lark."

"Run along, Doris. You'll get cold."

"I ain't cold. Pull my hair if you like, mister."

"I wouldn't dream of it," said Basil.

"Dessay I shall. I dream a lot of funny things. Go on, mister, pull it. Hard. I don't mind." She offered her bobbed head to Basil and then with a giggle ran out of the room.

"You see," said Barbara. "A problem child."

When Marlene had been treated for her queerness, Barbara came back to say good night.

"I'll stay up a bit and work on this book."

"All right, darling. Good night." She bent over the back of the sofa and kissed the top of his head.

"Not blubbing any more?"

"No, not blubbing."

He looked up at her and smiled. She smiled back; it was the same smile. They saw themselves, each in the other's eyes. There's no one like Basil, thought

Barbara, seeing herself — no one like him, when he's nice.

2. NEXT MORNING Basil was called by Benson, who was the only manservant indoors since Freddy had drawn in his horns. (He had taken his valet with him to the yeomanry and supported him now, in a very much lower standard of comfort, at the King's expense.) Lying in bed and watching the man put out his clothes, Basil reflected that he still owed him a small sum of money from his last visit.

"Benson, what's this about your leaving?"

"I was cross last night, Mr. Basil. I couldn't ever leave Malfrey, and Mrs. Sothill ought to know that. Not with the Captain away, too."

"Mrs. Sothill was very upset."

"So was I, Mr. Basil. You don't know what those Connollies are. They're not human."

"We'll find a billet for them."

"No one will take the Connollies in these parts. Not if they were given a hundred pounds."

"I have an idea I owe you some money."

"You do, Mr. Basil. Twelve pound ten."

"As much as that? Time I paid it back."

"It is."

"I will, Benson."

"I hope so, sir, I'm sure."

Basil went to his bath pondering. No one will take the Connollies in these parts. Not for a hundred pounds. Not for a hundred pounds.

Since the war began Barbara had taken to breakfasting downstairs in the mistaken belief that it caused less trouble. Instead of the wicker bed-table tray, a table had to be laid in the small dining-room, the fire had to be lit there two hours earlier, silver dishes had to be cleaned and the wicks trimmed under them. It was an innovation deplored by all.

Basil found her crouched over the fire with her cup of coffee; she turned her curly black head and smiled; both of them had the same devastating combination of dark hair and clear blue eyes. Narcissus greeted Narcissus from the watery depths as Basil kissed her.

"Spoony," she said.

"I've squared Benson for you."

"Darling, how clever of you."

"I had to give the old boy a fiver."

"Liar."

"All right, don't believe me then."

"I don't, knowing Benson and knowing you. I remember last time you stayed here I had to pay him over ten pounds that you'd borrowed."

"You paid him?"

"Yes. I was afraid he'd ask Freddy."

"The old double-crosser. Anyway he's staying."

"Yes; thinking it over I knew he would. I don't know why I took it so hard last night. I think it was the shock of seeing the Connollies."

"We must get them settled to-day."

"It's hopeless. No one will take them."

"You've got powers of coercion."

"Yes, but I can't possibly use them."

"*I* can," said Basil. "I shall enjoy it."

After breakfast they moved from the little dining-room to the little parlour. The corridor, though it was one of the by-ways of the house, had a sumptuous cornice and a high, coved ceiling; the door cases were enriched with classic pediments in whose broken entablatures stood busts of philosophers and composers. Other busts stood at regular intervals on marble pedestals. Everything in Malfrey was splendid and harmonious; everything except Doris, who, that morning, lurked in their path rubbing herself on a pilaster like a cow on a stump.

"Hullo," she said.

"Hullo, Doris. Where are Micky and Marlene?"

"Outside. They're all right. They've found the snow-man the others made and they're mucking him up."

"Run along and join them."

"I want to stay here with you — and *him*."

"I bet you do," said Basil. "No such luck. I'm going to find you a nice billet miles and miles away."

"I want to stay with you."

"You go and help muck up the snow-man."

"That's a kid's game. I'm not a kid. Mister, why wouldn't you pull my hair last night? Was it because you thought I had nits? I haven't any more. The nurse combed them all out at the institution and put oil on. That's why it's a bit greasy."

"I don't pull girls' hair."

"You do. I saw you. You pulled *hers*. He's your boy, isn't he?" she said, turning to Barbara.

"He's my brother, Doris."

"Ah," she said, her pig eyes dark with the wisdom of the slums, "but you fancy him, don't you? I saw."

"She really is an atrocious child," said Barbara.

3. BASIL set about the problem of finding a home for the Connollies with zeal and method. He settled himself at a table with an ordnance map, the local newspaper and the little red-leather–covered address book which had been one of old Mrs. Sothill's legacies to Barbara; in this book were registered all her more well-to-do neighbours for a radius of twenty miles, the majority of whom were

marked with the initials G.P.O. — which stood for Garden Party Only. Barbara had done her best to keep this invaluable work of reference up to date and had from time to time crossed out those who had died or left the district, and added the names of newcomers.

Presently Basil said, "What about the Harknesses of Old Mill House, North Grappling?"

"Middle-aged people. He retired from some sort of a job abroad. I think she's musical. Why?"

"They're advertising for boarders." He pushed the paper across to her, where she read, in the *Accommodation* column: —

Paying Guests accepted in lovely modernized fifteenth century mill. Ideal surroundings for elderly or artistic people wishing to avoid war worries. All home produce. Secluded old world gardens. 6 gns weekly. Highest references given and expected. Harkness, Old Mill House, North Grappling.

"How about that for the Connollies?"

"Basil, you can't."

"Can't I just. I'll get to work on them at once. Do they allow you extra petrol for your billeting work?"

"Yes, but . . ."

"That's grand. I'll take the Connollies over there this morning. D'you know, this is the first piece of serious war work I've done so far?"

Normally, whenever the car left the garage there

was a stampede of evacués to the running boards crying "Give us a ride." This morning, however, seeing the three forbidding Connollies in the back seat, the other children fell back silently. They were not allowed by their mothers to play with the Connollies.

"Mister, why can't I sit in front with you?"

"You've got to keep the other two in order."

"They'll be good."

"That's what you think."

"They'll be good if I tell them, mister."

"Then why aren't they?"

"Cos I tell 'em to be bad. In fun you know. Where are we going?"

"I'm finding a new home for you, Doris."

"Away from you?"

"Far away from me."

"Mister, listen. Micky ain't bad really nor Marlene isn't silly. Are you, Marlene?"

"Not very silly," said Marlene.

"She can be clean if she wants to be, if I tell her. See here, mister, play fair. You let us stay with you and I'll see the kids behave themselves."

"And what about you, Doris?"

"I don't have to behave. I'm not a kid. Is it on?"

"It is not."

"You going to take us away?"

"You bet I am."

"Then just you wait and see what we give them where we're going."

"I shan't wait and see," said Basil, "but I've no doubt I shall hear about it in good time."

North Grappling was ten miles distant, a stone-built village of uneven stone-tile roofs none of which was less than a century old. It lay off the main road in a fold of the hills; a stream ran through it following the line of its single street and crossing it under two old stone bridges. At the upper end of the street stood the church, which declared by its size and rich decoration that in the centuries since it was built, while the rest of the world was growing, North Grappling had shrunk; at the lower end, below the second bridge, stood Old Mill House. It was just such a home of ancient peace as a man might dream of who was forced to earn his living under a fiercer sky. Mr. Harkness had in fact dreamed of it, year in, year out, as he toiled in his office at Singapore, or reclined after work on the club verandah, surrounded by gross vegetation and rude colours. He bought it from his father's legacy while on leave, when he was still a young man, meaning to retire there when the time came, and his years of waiting had been haunted by only one fear: that he would return to find the place "developed," new red roofs among the grey and a tarmac road down the uneven street. But modernity spared North Grappling; he returned to find the place just as he had first come upon it, on a walking tour, late in the evening with the stones still warm from the afternoon sun and the scent of the gillyflowers sweet and fresh on the breeze.

This morning, half lost in snow, the stones, which in summer seemed grey, were a golden brown; and the pleached limes, which in their leaf hid the low front of the Old Mill, now revealed the mullions and drip-stones, the sundial above the long, centre window, and the stone hood of the door carved in the shape of a scallop-shell. Basil stopped the car by the bridge.

"Jesus," said Doris. "You aren't going to leave us here?"

"Sit tight," said Basil. "You'll know soon enough."

He threw a rug over the radiator of the car, opened the little iron gate and walked up the flagged path grimly, a figure of doom. The low winter sun cast his shadow before him, ominously, against the door which Mr. Harkness had had painted apple green. The gnarled trunk of a wistaria rose from beside the door-jamb and twisted its naked length between the lines of the windows. Basil glanced once over his shoulder to see that his young passengers were invisible and then put his hand to the iron bell. He heard it ring melodiously, not far away, and presently the door was opened by a maid dressed in apple green, with an apron of sprigged muslin and a starched white cap that was in effect part Dutch, part conventual, and wholly ludicrous. This figure of fancy led Basil up a step, down a step and into a living-room where he was left long enough to observe the decorations. The floor

was covered in coarse rush matting and in places by
bright Balkan rugs. On the walls were Thornton's
flower prints (with the exception of his masterpiece,
"The Night-Flowering Cereus"), samplers and old
maps. The most prominent objects of furniture were
a grand piano and a harp. There were also some tables
and chairs of raw-looking beech. From an open hearth
peat smoke billowed periodically into the room, caus-
ing Basil's eyes to water. It was just such a room as
Basil had imagined from the advertisement and Mr.
and Mrs. Harkness were just such a couple. Mrs.
Harkness wore a hand-woven woollen garment, her
eyes were large and poetic, her nose long and red with
the frost, her hair nondescript in colour and haphazard
in arrangement. Her husband had done all that a man
can to disguise the effects of twenty years of club and
bungalow life in the Far East. He had grown a little
pointed beard; he wore a homespun suit of knicker-
bockers in the style of the pioneers of bicycling; he
wore a cameo ring round his loose silk tie, yet there
was something in his bearing which still suggested the
dapper figure in white ducks who had stood his round
of pink gins, evening after evening, to other dapper
white figures, and had dined twice a year at Government House.

They entered from the garden door. Basil half expected Mr. Harkness to say "take a pew" and clap his
hands for the gin. Instead they stood looking at him
with enquiry and some slight distaste.

"My name is Seal. I came about your advertisement in the *Courier*."

"Our advertisement. Ah yes," said Mr. Harkness vaguely. "It was just an idea we had. We felt a little ashamed here, with so much space and beauty; the place is a little large for our requirements these days. We did think that perhaps if we heard of a few people like ourselves — the same simple tastes — we might, er, join forces as it were during the present difficult times. As a matter of fact we have one newcomer with us already. I don't think we *really* want to take anyone else, do we, Agnes?"

"It was just an idle thought," said Mrs. Harkness. "A green thought in a green place."

"This is not a Guest House, you know. We take in paying guests. Quite a different thing."

Basil understood their difficulties with a keenness of perception that was rare to him. "It's not for myself that I was enquiring," he said.

"Ah, that's different. I daresay we might take in one or two more if they were, if they were *really* . . ."

Mrs. Harkness helped him out. "If we were sure they were the kind of people who would be happy here."

"Exactly. It is essentially a *happy* house."

(It was like his housemaster at school. "We are essentially a keen House, Seal. We may not win many cups but at least we try.")

"I can see it is," he said gallantly.

"I expect you'd like to look round. It looks quite a little place from the road but is surprisingly large, really, when you come to count up the rooms."

A hundred years ago the pastures round North Grappling had all been corn-growing land and the mill had served a wide area. Long before the Harknesses' time it had fallen into disuse and, in the eighties, had been turned into a dwelling house by a disciple of William Morris. The stream had been diverted, the old mill pool drained and levelled and made into a sunken garden. The rooms that had held the grindstones and machinery, and the long lofts where the grain had been stored, had been tactfully floored and plastered and partitioned. Mrs. Harkness pointed out all the features with maternal pride.

"Are your friends who were thinking of coming here artistic people?"

"No, I don't think you could call them that."

"They don't write?"

"No, I don't think so."

"I've always thought this would be an ideal place for someone who wanted to write. May I ask, what *are* your friends?"

"Well, I suppose you might call them evacués."

Mr. and Mrs. Harkness laughed pleasantly at the little joke. "Townsfolk in search of sanctuary, eh?"

"Exactly."

"Well, they will find it here, eh, Agnes?"

They were back in the living-room. Mrs. Harkness

laid her hand on the gilded neck of the harp and looked out across the sunken garden with a dreamy look in her large grey eyes. Thus she had looked out across the Malaya golf course, dreaming of home.

"I like to think of this beautiful old house still being of use in the world. After all it was built for *use*. Hundreds of years ago it gave bread to the people. Then with the change of the times it was left forlorn and derelict. Then it became a home, but it was still out of the world, shut off from the life of the people. And now at last it comes into its own again. Fulfilling a *need*. You may think me fanciful," she said, remote and whimsical, "but in the last few weeks I feel sometimes I can see the old house smiling to itself and hear the old timbers whispering, 'They thought we were no use. They thought we were old stick-in-the-muds. But they can't get on without us, all these busy go-ahead people. They come back to us when they're in trouble.'"

"Agnes was always a poet," said Mr. Harkness. "I have had to be the practical housewife. You saw our terms in the advertisement?"

"Yes."

"They may have seemed to you a little heavy, but you must understand that our guests live exactly as we do ourselves. We live simply but we like our comfort. Fires," he said, backing slightly from the belch of aromatic smoke which issued into the room as he spoke. "The garden," he said, indicating the frozen and buried enclosure outside the windows. "In the summer we take our meals under the old mulberry tree. Music. Every week we have chamber music. There are certain *imponderabilia* at the Old Mill which, to be crude, have their market value. I *don't* think," he said coyly, "I *don't* think that in the circumstances" — and the circumstances, Basil felt, surely were meant to include a good fat slice of Mrs. Harkness' poetic imagination — "six guineas is too much to ask."

The moment for which Basil had been waiting was come. This was the time for the grenade he had been nursing ever since he opened the little, wrought-iron gate and put his hand to the wrought-iron bell-pull. "We pay eight shillings and sixpence a week," he said. That was the safety pin; the lever flew up, the spring struck home; within the serrated metal shell the primer spat and, invisibly, flame crept up the finger's-length of fuse. Count seven slowly, then throw. One, two, three, four . . .

"Eight shillings?" said Mr. Harkness. "I'm afraid there's been some misunderstanding."

Five, six, *seven*. Here it comes. *Bang!* "Perhaps I should have told you at once. I am the billeting officer. I've three children for you in the car outside."

It was magnificent. It was war. Basil was something of a specialist in shocks. He could not recall a better.

After the first tremendous silence there were three stages of Harkness reaction: the indignant appeal to reason and justice, then the humble appeal to mercy, then the frigid and dignified acceptance of the inevitable.

First: —

"I shall telephone to Mrs. Sothill . . . I shall go and see the County authorities . . . I shall write to the Board of Education and the Lord Lieutenant. This is perfectly ridiculous; there must be a hundred cottagers who would be *glad* to take these children in."

"Not *these* children," said Basil. "Besides, you know, this is a war for democracy. It looks awfully bad if the rich seem to be shirking their responsibilities."

"*Rich*. It's only because we find it so hard to make both ends meet that we take paying guests at all."

"Besides this is a *most* unsuitable place for children. They might fall into the stream and be drowned. There's no school within four miles . . ."

Second: —

"We're not as young as we were. After living so long in the East the English winter is very difficult. Any additional burden . . ."

"Mr. Seal, you've seen for yourself this lovely old house and the kind of life we live here. Don't you *feel* that there is something *different* here, something precious that could so easily be killed?"

"It's just this kind of influence these children need," said Basil cheerfully. "They're rather short on culture at the moment."

Third: —

A hostility as cold as the winter hillside above the

village. Basil led the Connollies up the flagged path, through the apple-green door, into the passage which smelled of peat smoke and pot-pourri. "I'm afraid they haven't any luggage," he said. "This is Doris, this is Micky, and that — that is little Marlene. I expect after a day or two you'll wonder how you ever got on without them. We meet that over and over again in our work; people who are a little shy of children to begin with, and soon want to adopt them permanently. Good-bye, kids, have a good time. Good-bye, Mrs. Harkness. We shall drop in from time to time just to see that everything is all right."

And Basil drove back through the naked lanes with a deep interior warmth which defied the gathering blizzard.

That night there was an enormous fall of snow, telephone wires were down, the lane to North Grappling became impassable, and for eight days the Old Mill was cut off physically, as for so long it had been cut in spirit, from all contact with the modern world.

4. BARBARA and Basil sat in the orangery after luncheon. The smoke from Basil's cigar hung on the humid air, a blue line of cloud, motionless, breast-high between the paved floor and the

exotic foliage overhead. He was reading aloud to his sister.

"So much for the supply services," he said, laying down the last sheet of manuscript. The book had prospered during the past week.

Barbara awoke, so gently that she might never have been asleep. "Very good," she said. "First-class."

"It ought to wake them up," said Basil.

"It ought," said Barbara, on whom the work had so different an effect. Then she added irrelevantly, "I hear they've dug the way through to North Grappling this morning."

"There was providence in that fall of snow. It's let the Connollies and the Harknesses get properly to grips. Otherwise, I feel, one or other side might have despaired."

"I daresay we shall hear something of the Harknesses shortly."

And immediately, as though they were on the stage, Benson came to the door and announced that Mr. Harkness was in the little parlour.

"I *must* see him," said Barbara.

"Certainly not," said Basil — "This is my war effort," and followed Benson into the house.

He had expected some change in Mr. Harkness but not so marked a change as he now saw. The man was barely recognizable. It was as though the crust of tropical respectability that had survived below the home-

spun and tie-ring surface had been crushed to pow-
der; the man was abject. The clothes were the same.
It must be imagination which gave that trim beard a
raffish look, imagination fired by the haunted look in
the man's eyes.

Basil on his travels had once visited a prison in Trans-
Jordan where an ingenious system of punishment had
been devised. The institution served the double purpose of penitentiary and lunatic asylum. One of the
madmen was a tough old Arab of peculiar ferocity
who could be subdued by one thing only — the steady
gaze of the human eye. Bat an eyelid, and he was at
you. Refractory convicts were taken to this man's cell
and shut in with him for periods of anything up to
forty-eight hours according to the gravity of their offences. Day and night the madman lurked in his corner with his eyes fixed, fascinated, on those of the
delinquent. The heat of midday was his best opportunity; then even the wariest convict sometimes allowed his weary eyelids to droop and in that moment
he was across the floor, tooth and nail, in a savage attack. Basil had seen a gigantic felon led out after a
two days' session. There was something in Mr. Harkness' eyes that brought the scene back vividly to him.

"I am afraid my sister's away," said Basil.

Whatever hope had ever been in Mr. Harkness'
breast died when he saw his old enemy. "You are Mrs.
Sothill's brother?"

"Yes; we are thought rather alike. I'm helping her here now that my brother-in-law's away. Is there anything I can do?"

"No," he said brokenly. "No. It doesn't matter. I'd hoped to see Mrs. Sothill. When will she be back?"

"You can never tell," said Basil. "Most irresponsible in some ways. Goes off for months at a time. But this time she has me to watch out for her. Was it about your evacués you wanted to see her? She was *very* glad to hear they had been happily settled. It meant she could go away with a clear conscience. That particular family had been something of an anxiety, if you understand me."

Mr. Harkness sat down uninvited. He sat on a gilt chair in that bright little room like a figure of death. He seemed disposed neither to speak nor to move.

"Mrs. Harkness well?" said Basil affably.

"Prostrate."

"And your paying guest?"

"She left this morning — as soon as the road was cleared. Our two maids went with her."

"I hope Doris is making herself useful about the house."

At the mention of that name Mr. Harkness broke. He came clean. "Mr. Seal, I can't stand it. We neither of us can. We've come to the end. You must take those children away."

"You surely wouldn't suggest sending them back to Birmingham to be bombed?"

This was an argument which Barbara often employed with good effect. As soon as Basil spoke he realized it was a false step. Suffering had purged Mr. Harkness of all hypocrisy. For the first time something like a smile twisted his lips.

"There is nothing would delight me more," he said.

"Tut, tut. You do yourself an injustice. Anyway it is against the law. I should like to help you. What can you suggest?"

"I thought of giving them weed-killer," said Mr. Harkness wistfully.

"Yes," said Basil, "that would be one way. Do you think Marlene could keep it down?"

"Or hanging."

"Come, come, Mr. Harkness, this is mere wishful thinking. We must be more practical."

"Everything I've thought of has had death in it; ours or theirs."

"I'm sure there must be a way," said Basil, and then, delicately, watching Mr. Harkness while he spoke for any expression of distrust or resentment, he outlined a scheme which had come to him, vaguely, when he first saw the Connollies, and had grown more precise during the past week. "The difficulty about billeting on the poor," he said, "is that the allowance barely covers what the children eat. Of course where they are nice, affectionate children people are often glad enough to have them. But one wouldn't call the Connollies nice or affectionate —" Mr. Harkness groaned.

"They are destructive, too. Well I needn't tell you that. The fact is that it would be inflicting a very considerable hardship — a *financial* hardship — to put them in a cottage. Now if the meagre allowance paid by the Government were *supplemented* — do you follow me?"

"You mean I might *pay* someone to take them. Of course I will, anything — at least almost anything. How much shall I offer? How shall I set about it?"

"Leave it to me," said Basil, suddenly dropping his urbane manner. "What's it worth to you to have those children moved?"

Mr. Harkness hesitated; with the quickening of hope came a stir of self-possession. One does not work in the East without acquiring a nose for a deal. "I should think a pound a week would make all the difference to a poor family," he said.

"How about a lump sum? People — poor people that is — will often be dazzled by the offer of a lump sum who wouldn't consider an allowance."

"Twenty-five pounds."

"Come, Mr. Harkness, that's what you proposed paying over six months. The war is going to last longer than that."

"Thirty. I can't go higher than thirty."

He was not a rich man, Basil reflected; very likely thirty was all he could afford. "I daresay I could find someone to take them for that," he said. "Of course you realize that this is all highly irregular."

"Oh, I realize that." Did he? Basil wondered;
perhaps he did. "Will you fetch those children
to-day?"

"To-day?"

"Without fail." Mr. Harkness seemed to be dictat-
ing terms now. "The cheque will be waiting for you.
I will make it out to bearer."

"What a long time you've been," said Barbara.
"Have you pacified him?"

"I've got to find a new home for the Connollies."

"Basil, you've let him off!"

"He was so pathetic. I softened."

"Basil, how very unlike you."

"I must get to work with that address book again.
We shall have to have the Connollies here for the
night. I'll find them a new home in the morning."

He drove over to North Grappling in the twilight.
On either side of the lane the new-dug snow was
heaped high, leaving a narrow, passable track. The
three Connollies were standing outside the apple-
green door waiting for him.

"The man with the beard said to give you this,"
said Doris.

It was an envelope containing a cheque; nothing
more. Neither Harkness appeared to see them off.

"Mister, am I glad to see you again!" said Doris.

"Jump in," said Basil.

"May I come in front with you?"

"Yes, jump in."

"Really? No kidding?"

"Come on, it's cold." Doris got in beside Basil. "You're here on sufferance."

"What does that mean?"

"You can sit here as long as you behave yourself, and as long as Micky and Marlene do too. Understand?"

"Hear that, you brats?" said Doris with sudden authority. "Behave, or I'll tan yer arses for yer. They'll be all right, mister, if I tell 'em."

They were all right.

"Doris, I think it's a very good game of yours making the kids be a nuisance, but we're going to play it my way in future. When you come to the house where I live you're to behave, always. See? I may take you to other houses from time to time. There you can usually be as bad as you like, but not until I give the word. See?"

"O.K. partner. Give us a cig."

"I'm beginning to like you, Doris."

"*I love you*," said Doris with excruciating warmth, leaning back and blowing a cloud of smoke over the solemn children in the back. "I love you more than anyone I ever seen."

"Their week with the Harknesses seems to have had an extraordinary effect on the children," said Barbara after dinner that night. "I can't understand it."

"Mr. Harkness said there were *imponderabilia* at Mill House. Perhaps it's that."

"Basil, you're up to something. I wish I knew what it was."

Basil turned on her his innocent blue eyes, as blue as hers and as innocent; they held no hint of mischief. "Just war work, Babs," he said.

"Slimy snake."

"I'm not."

"Crawly spider." They were back in the schoolroom, in the world where once they had played pirates. "Artful monkey," said Barbara, very fondly.

5. COMPANIES paraded at quarter-past eight; immediately after inspection men were fallen out for the company commanders' orderly room; that gave time to sift out the genuine requests from the spurious, deal with minor offences, have the charge sheets made out properly and the names entered in the guard report of serious defaulters for the C.O.

"Private Tatton charged with losing by neglect one respirator, anti-gas, value 18/6."

Private Tatton fell into a rambling account of having left this respirator in the N.A.A.F.I. and, going back for it ten minutes later, having found it gone.

"Case remanded for the commanding officer." Captain Mayfield could not give a punishment involving loss of pay.

"Case remanded for the commanding officer. About turn. As you were. I didn't say anything about saluting. About turn. Quick march."

Captain Mayfield turned to the IN basket on his table.

"O.C.T.U. candidates," said the Company Sergeant-Major.

"Who have we got? The Adjutant doesn't take nil returns."

"Well, sir, there's Brodie."

Brodie was a weedy solicitor who had appeared with the last draft.

"Really, Sergeant-Major, I can't see Brodie making much of an officer."

"He's not much good in the company, sir, and he's a man of very superior education."

"Well put him down for one. What about Sergeant Harris?"

"Not suitable, sir."

"He's a man of excellent character, fine disciplinarian, knows his stuff backwards, the men will follow him anywhere."

"Yessir."

"Well what have you got against him?"

"Nothing against him, sir. But we can't get on without Sergeant Harris in the company football."

"No. Well, who do you suggest?"

"There's our baronet, sir." The Sergeant-Major said this with a smile. Alastair's position in the ranks was a slight embarrassment to Captain Mayfield but it was a good joke to the Sergeant-Major.

"Trumpington? All right, I'll see him and Brodie right away."

The orderly brought them. The Sergeant-Major marched them in singly. "Quick march. Halt. Salute. Brodie, sir."

"Brodie. They want the names of two men from this company as O.C.T.U. candidates. I'm putting your name in. Of course the C.O. makes the decision. I don't say you *will* go to an O.C.T.U. I take it you would have no objection if the C.O. approves."

"None, sir, if you really think I should make a good officer."

"I don't suppose you'll make a *good* officer. They're very rare. But I daresay you'll make an officer of some kind."

"Thank you, sir."

"And as long as you're in my company you won't come into my office with a fountain pen sticking out of your pocket."

"Sorry, sir."

"Not so much talk," said the Sergeant-Major.

"All right, that's all, Sergeant-Major."

"About turn. Quick march. As you were. Swing the right arm forward as you step out."

"I believe we'll have to give him a couple of stripes before we can get rid of him. I'll see the Adjutant about that."

Alastair was marched in. He had changed little since he joined the Army. Perhaps there was a slight shifting of bulk from waistline to chest, but it was barely perceptible under the loose battle-dress.

Captain Mayfield addressed him in precisely the same words as those he had used to Brodie.

"Yes, sir."

"You don't want to take a commission?"

"No, sir."

"That's very unusual, Trumpington. Any particular reason?"

"I believe a lot of people felt like that in the last war."

"So I've heard. And a very wasteful business it was. Well if you won't, I can't make you. Afraid of responsibility, eh?"

Alastair made no answer. Captain Mayfield nodded and the Sergeant-Major marched him out.

"What d'you make of that?" asked Captain Mayfield.

"I've known men who think it's *safer* to stay in the ranks."

"Shouldn't think that's the case with Trumpington. He's a volunteer, over-age to have been called up."

"Very rum, sir."

"Very rum, Sergeant-Major."

Alastair took his time about returning to his platoon. At this time of the morning they were doing P.T. It was the one part of the routine he really hated. He lurked behind the cookhouse until his watch told him that they would have finished. When he reported back the platoon were putting on their jackets, panting and sticky. He fell in and marched with them to the dining-hut, where it was stuffy and fairly warm, to hear a lecture on hygiene from the medical officer. It dealt with the danger of flies; the medical officer described with appalling detail the journey of the fly from the latrine to the sugar basin; how its hairy feet carried the germs of dysentery; how it softened its food with contaminated saliva before it ate; how it excreted while it fed. This lecture always went down well. "Of course," he added rather lamely, "this may not seem very important at the moment" — snow lay heavy on every side of them — "but if we go to the East . . ."

When the lecture was finished the company fell out for twenty minutes; they smoked and ate chocolate and exchanged gossip, qualifying every noun, verb or adjective with the single, unvarying obscenity which punctuated all their speech like a hiccup; they stamped their feet and chafed their hands.

"What did the —— company commander want?"

"He wanted to send me to a —— O.C.T.U.," said Alastair.

"Well some —— are —— lucky. When are you off?"

"I'm staying here."

"Don't you want to be a —— officer?"

"Not —— likely," said Alastair.

When people asked Alastair, as they quite often did, why he did not put in for a commission, he sometimes said, "Snobbery. I don't want to meet the officers on social terms"; sometimes he said, "Laziness. They work too hard in war-time"; sometimes he said, "The whole thing's so crazy one might as well go the whole hog." To Sonia he said, "We've had a pretty easy life up to now. It's probably quite good for one to have a change sometimes." That was the nearest he ever came to expressing the nebulous satisfaction which lay at the back of his mind. Sonia understood it, but left it undefined. Once, much later, she said to Basil, "I believe I know what Alastair felt all that first winter of the war. It sounds awfully unlike him, but he was a much odder character than anyone knew. You remember that man who used to dress as an Arab and then went into the Air Force as a private because he thought the British Government had let the Arabs down? I forget his name but there were lots of books about him. . . . Well, I believe Alastair felt like that. You see he'd never done anything for the country and though we were always broke we had lots of money really and lots of fun. I believe he thought that perhaps if we hadn't had so much fun perhaps there wouldn't have been any war. Though how he could blame him-

self for Hitler I never quite saw. . . . At least I do
now in a way," she added. "He went into the ranks as
a kind of penance or whatever it's called, that religious
people are always supposed to do."

It was a penance whose austerities, such as they
were, admitted of relaxation.

After the stand-easy they fell in for platoon training. Alastair's platoon commander was away that
morning. He was sitting on a Court of Enquiry. For
three hours he and two other officers heard evidence,
and recorded it at length, on the loss of a swill tub from
H.Q. lines. At length it was clear either that there was
a conspiracy of perjury on the part of all the witnesses,
or that the tub had disappeared by some supernatural
means independent of human agency; the Court there-
fore entered a verdict that no negligence was attrib-
utable to anyone in the matter and recommended that
the loss be made good out of public funds. The Presi-
dent said, "I don't expect the C.O. will approve that
verdict. He'll send the papers back for fresh evidence
to be taken."

Meanwhile the platoon, left in charge of the Sergeant, split up into sections and practised immediate
action on the Bren gun.

"Gun fires two rounds and stops again. What do
you look at now, Trumpington?"

"Gas regulator." . . . Off with the magazine. Press,
pull back, press . . . "Number Two gun clear."

"What's he forgotten?"

A chorus, "Butt strap."

One man said, "Barrel-locking nut." He had said it once, one splendid day, when asked a question, and he had been right when everyone else was stumped, and he had been commended. So now he always said it, like a gambler obstinately backing the same colour against a long run of bad luck; it was bound to turn up again one day.

The Corporal ignored him. "Quite right, he's forgotten the butt strap. Down again, Trumpington."

It was Saturday. Work ended at twelve o'clock; as the platoon commander was away, they knocked off ten minutes earlier and got all the gear stowed so that as soon as the call was sounded off on the bugle they could run straight for their quarters. Alastair had his leave pass for reveille on Monday. He had no need to fetch luggage. He kept everything he needed at home. Sonia was waiting in the car outside the guardroom; they did not go away for week-ends but spent them, mostly in bed, in the furnished house which they had taken near by.

"I was pretty good with the Bren this morning," said Alastair. "Only one mistake."

"Darling, you are clever."

"And I managed to shirk P.T."

They had packed up ten minutes early too; altogether it had been a very satisfactory morning. And now he could look forward to a day and a half of privacy and leisure.

"I've been shopping in Woking," said Sonia, "and I've got all kinds of delicious food and all the weekly papers. There's a film there we might go and see."

"We might," said Alastair doubtfully. "It will probably be full of a lot of —— soldiers."

"Darling, I've never before heard words like that spoken. I thought they only came in print, in novels."

Alastair had a bath and changed into tweeds. (It was chiefly in order that he might wear civilian clothes that he stayed indoors during week-ends; for that and the cold outside and the ubiquitous military.) Then he took a whiskey-and-soda and watched Sonia cooking; they had fried eggs, sausages, bacon, and cold plum pudding; after luncheon he lit a large cigar; it was snowing again, piling up round the steel-framed windows, shutting out the view of the golf course; there was a huge fire and at tea-time they toasted crumpets.

"There's all this evening, and all to-morrow," said Sonia. "Isn't it lovely? You know, Alastair, you and I always seem to manage to have fun, don't we, wherever we are?"

This was February 1940, in that strangely cosy interlude between peace and war, when there was leave every week-end and plenty to eat and drink and plenty to smoke, when France stood firm on the Maginot Line and the Finns stood firm in Finland, and everyone said what a cruel winter they must be having in

Germany. During one of these week-ends Sonia conceived a child.

6. AS MR. BENTLEY had foretold, it was not long before Ambrose found himself enrolled on the staff of the Ministry of Information. He was in fact one of the reforms introduced at the first of the many purges. Questions had been asked about the Ministry in the House of Commons; the Press, hampered in so much else, was free to exploit its own grievances. Redress was promised and after a week of intrigue the new appointments were made. Sir Philip Hesketh-Smithers went to the Folk-dancing Department; Mr. Pauling went to Woodcuts and Weaving; Mr. Digby-Smith was given the Arctic Circle; Mr. Bentley himself, after a dizzy period in which, for a day, he directed a film about postmen, for another day filed press-cuttings from Istanbul, and for the rest of the week supervised the staff catering, found himself at length back beside his busts in charge of the men of letters. Thirty or forty officials retired thankfully into competitive commercial life, and forty or fifty new men and women appeared to take their places; among them, he never quite knew how, Ambrose. The Press, though sceptical of good results, congratulated the public upon maintaining a system of government in which the will

of the people was given such speedy effect. *The lesson of the muddle at the Ministry of Information — for muddle there undoubtedly was — is not that such things occur under a democracy, but that they are susceptible to remedy,* they wrote; *the wind of democratic criticism has blown, clear and fresh, through the departments of the Ministry; charges have been frankly made and frankly answered. Our enemies may ponder this portent.*

Ambrose's post as sole representative of Atheism in the Religious Department was not, at this stage of the war, one of great importance. He was in no position, had he wished it, to introduce statuary into his quarters. He had for his use a single table and a single chair. He shared a room and a secretary with a fanatical young Roman Catholic layman who never tired of exposing discrepancies between *Mein Kampf* and the encyclical *Quadragesimo anno*, a bland nonconformist minister, and a Church of England clergyman who had been brought in to succeed the importer of the mahogany prie-dieu. "We must reorientate ourselves to Geneva," this cleric said; "the first false step was taken when the Lytton report was shelved." He argued long and gently, the Roman Catholic argued long and fiercely, while the nonconformist sat as a bemused umpire between them. Ambrose's task consisted in representing to British and colonial atheists that Nazism was at heart agnostic with a strong tinge of religious superstition; he envied the lot of his colleagues who

had at their finger-tips long authentic summaries of
suppressed Sunday Schools, persecuted monks, and
pagan Nordic rites. His was uphill work; he served a
small and critical public; but whenever he discovered
in the pile of foreign newspapers which passed from
desk to desk any reference to German church-going, he
circulated it to the two or three magazines devoted to
his cause. He counted up the number of times the
word "God" appeared in Hitler's speeches and found
the sum impressive; he wrote a pointed little article to
show that Jew-baiting was religious in origin. He did
his best, but time lay heavy on his hands and, more
and more, as the winter wore on, he found himself
slipping away from his rancorous colleagues, to the
more human companionship of Mr. Bentley.

The great press of talent in search of occupation
which had thronged the Ministry during its first weeks
had now dropped to a mere handful; the doorkeeper
was schooled to detect and deter the job seekers. No
one wanted another reorganization for some time to
come. Mr. Bentley's office became an enclave of culture in a barbaric world. It was here that the *Ivory
Tower* was first discussed.

"Art for Art's sake, Geoffrey. Back to the lily and
the lotus, away from these dusty young *immortelles,*
these dandelions sprouting on the vacant lot."

"A kind of new *Yellow Book,*" suggested Mr. Bentley sympathetically.

Ambrose turned sharply from his contemplation of Mrs. Siddons. "*Geoffrey.* How *can* you be so unkind?"

"My dear Ambrose . . ."

"That's just what they'll call it."

"Who will?"

"Parsnip," said Ambrose with venom, "Pimpernell, Poppet and Tom. They'll say we're deserting the workers' cause."

"I'm not aware that I ever joined it," said Mr. Bentley. "I claim to be one of the very few living Liberals."

"We've allowed ourselves to be dominated by economists."

"I haven't."

"For years now we've allowed ourselves to think of nothing but concrete mixers and tractors."

"*I* haven't," said Mr. Bentley crossly. "I've thought a great deal about Nolleykins."

"Well," said Ambrose, "I've had enough. *Il faut en finir*" — and added: "*Nous gagnerons parce que nous sommes les plus forts.*"

Later he said, "I was never a Party member."

"Party?"

"Communist Party. I was what they call, in their horrible jargon, a fellow traveller."

"Ah."

"Geoffrey, they do the most brutal things, don't they, to Communists who try to leave the Party?"

"So I've heard."

"Geoffrey, you don't think they'd do that to fellow travellers, do you?"

"I don't expect so."

"But they *might?*"

"Oh yes, they *might.*"

"Oh dear."

Later he said, "You know, Geoffrey, even in fascist countries they have underground organizations. Do you think the underground organizations would get hold of us?"

"Who?"

"The fellow travellers."

"Really it's too ridiculous to talk like this of fellow travellers and the underground. It sounds like straphangers on the Bakerloo railway."

"It's all very well for you to laugh. You were never one of them."

"But my dear Ambrose, why should these political friends of your mind so very much, if you produce a purely artistic paper?"

"I heard of a 'cellist in America. He'd been a member of the Party and he accepted an invitation to play at an anniversary breakfast of the Revolutionary Dames. It was during the Scottsboro trials when feeling was running high. They tied him to a lamppost and covered him with tar and set him on fire."

"The Revolutionary Dames did?"

"No, no, the Communists."

After a long pause he said: —

"But Russia's doing very badly in Finland."

"Yes."

"If only we knew what was going to happen."

He returned pensively to the Religious Department.

"This is more in your line than mine," sa d the Catholic representative, handing him a cutting from a Swiss paper.

It said that Storm Troopers had attended a Requiem Mass in Salzburg. Ambrose clipped it to a piece of paper and wrote "Copies to *Free Thought*, the *Atheist Advertiser*, and to *Godless Sunday at Home*"; then he placed it in his basket marked OUT. Two yards distant the nonconformist minister was checking statistics about the popularity of beer-gardens among Nazi officials. The Church of England clergyman was making the most of some rather scrappy Dutch information about cruelty to animals in Bremen. There was no foundation here for an ivory tower, thought Ambrose, no cloud to garland its summit, and his thoughts began to soar larklike into a tempera, fourteenth-century sky; into a heaven of flat, blank blue with white clouds, cross-hatched with gold leaf on their sunward edges; a vast altitude painted with shaving soap on a panel of lapis lazuli; he stood on a high, sugary pinnacle, on a new Tower of Babel; like a muezzin calling his message to a world of domes and clouds; beneath him, between him and the absurd little figures bobbing and bending on their striped praying mats, lay fathoms of clear air where doves sported with the butterflies.

7. MOST OF Mrs. Sothill's Garden Party Only list were people of late middle age who, on retirement from work in the cities or abroad, had bought the smaller manor houses and the larger rectories; houses that once had been supported on the rent of a thousand acres and a dozen cottages now went with a paddock and a walled garden, and their life subsisted on unsupported pensions and savings. To these modest landholders the rural character of the neighbourhood was a matter of particular jealousy. Magnates like Freddy would eagerly sell off outlying farms for development. It was the G.P.O. list who suffered and protested. A narrow corner could not be widened or a tree lopped to clear the telegraph wires without it being noted and regretted in those sunny morning-rooms. These were benevolent, companionable people; their carefully limited families were "out in the world" and came to them only for occasional visits. Their daughters had flats and jobs and lives of their own in London; their sons were self-supporting in the services and in business. The tribute of Empire flowed gently into the agricultural countryside, tithe barns were converted into village halls, the boy scouts had a new bell tent and the district nurse a motor-car;

the old box pews were taken out of the churches, the galleries demolished, the Royal Arms and the Ten Commandments moved from behind the altar and replaced with screens of blue damask supported at the four corners with gilt Sarum angels; the lawns were close-mown, fertilized and weeded, and from their splendid surface rose clumps of pampas grass and yucca; year in, year out, gloved hands grubbed in the rockeries, gloved hands snipped in the herbaceous borders; baskets of bass stood beside trays of visiting-cards on the hall tables. Now in the dead depths of winter when ice stood thick on the lily ponds, and the kitchen gardens at night were a litter of sacking, these good people fed the birds daily with the crumbs from the dining-room table and saw to it that no old person in the village went short of coal.

It was this unfamiliar world that Basil contemplated in the leather-bound pages of Mrs. Sothill's address book. He contemplated it as a marauder might look down from the hills into the fat pastures below; as Hannibal's infantry had looked down from the snow-line as the first elephants tried the etched footholds which led to the Lombardy plains below them and went lurching and trumpeting over the edge.

After the successful engagement at North Grappling, Basil took Doris into the nearest town and fed her liberally on fried fish and chipped potatoes; afterwards he took her to the cinema, allowed her to hold his hand in a fierce and sticky grasp throughout the length of two deeply sentimental films, and brought her back to Malfrey in a state of entranced docility.

"You don't like blondes, do you?" she asked anxiously in the car.

"Yes, very much."

"More than brunettes?"

"I'm not particular."

"They say like goes to like. *She's* dark."

"Who?"

"Her you call your sister."

"Doris, you must get this idea out of your head. Mrs. Sothill *is* my sister."

"You aren't sweet on her?"

"Certainly not."

"Then you *do* like blondes," said Doris sadly.

Next day she disappeared alone into the village, returned mysteriously with a small parcel, and remained hidden all the morning in the bachelors' wing. Just before luncheon she appeared in the orangery with her head in a towel.

"I wanted you to see," she said, and uncovered a damp mop of hair which was in part pale yellow, in part its original black, and in part mottled in every intervening shade.

"Good heavens, child," said Barbara. "What have you done?"

Doris looked only at Basil. "D'you like it? I'll give it another go this afternoon."

"I wouldn't," said Basil. "I'd leave it just as it is."

"You like it?"

"I think it's fine."

"Not too streaky?"

"Not a bit too streaky."

If anything had been needed to complete the horror of Doris' appearance, that morning's work had done it.

Basil studied the address book with care. "Finding a new home for the Connollies," he said.

"Basil, we must do something to that poor child's head before we pass her on."

"Not a bit of it. It suits her. What d'you know of the Graces, of the Old Rectory, Adderford?"

"It's a pretty little house. He's a painter."

"Bohemian?"

"Not the least. Very refined. Portraits of children in water-colour and pastel."

"Pastel? He sounds suitable."

"She's rather delicate I believe."

"Perfect."

The Connollies stayed two days at the Old Rectory and earned twenty pounds.

8. LONDON was full again. Those who had left in a hurry returned; those who had made arrangements to go after the first air raid re-

mained. Margot Metroland shut her home and moved
to the Ritz; opened her home and moved back; decided
that after all she really preferred the Ritz and shut her
home, this time, though she did not know it, for ever.
No servant ever folded back the shutters from the long
windows; they remained barred until, later in the year,
they were blown into Curzon Street; the furniture was
still under dust sheets when it was splintered and
burned.

Sir Joseph Mainwaring was appointed to a position
of trust and dignity. He was often to be seen with generals now, and sometimes with an admiral. "Our first
war aim," he said, "is to keep Italy out of the war until
she is strong enough to come in on our side." He
summed up the situation at home by saying, "One
takes one's gas-mask to one's office but *not* to one's
club."

Lady Seal had not troubled him again about Basil.
"He's at Malfrey, helping Barbara with her evacués,"
she said. "The Army is very full just at present. Things
will be much easier when we have had some casualties."

Sir Joseph nodded but at heart he was sceptical.
There were not going to be many casualties. Why, he
had been talking to a very interesting fellow at the Beefsteak who knew a German Professor of History; this
Professor was now in England; they thought a great
deal of him at the Foreign Office; he said there were
fifty million Germans "ready to declare peace to-

morrow on our own terms." It was just a question of
outing those fellows in the Government. Sir Joseph
had seen many Governments outed. It was quite easy
in war-time — they had outed Asquith quite easily and
he was a far better fellow than Lloyd George, who
succeeded him. Then they outed Lloyd George and
then they outed Macdonald. Christopher Seal knew
how to do it. He'd soon out Hitler if he were alive and
a German.

Poppet Green was in London with her friends.
"Ambrose has turned fascist," she said.
"Not really?"
"He's working for the Government in the Ministry
of Information and they've bribed him to start a new
paper."
"Is it a fascist paper?"
"You bet it is."
"I heard it was to be called the *Ivory Tower*."
"That's fascist if you like."
"Escapist."
"Trotskyist."
"Ambrose never had the proletarian outlook. I can't
think why we put up with him as we did. Parsnip al-
ways said . . ."

Peter Pastmaster came into Bratt's wearing battle-
dress and, on his shoulder, the name of a regiment to
which he had not formerly belonged.

"Hullo. Why on earth are you dressed like that?"

Peter smirked as only a soldier can when he knows a secret. "Oh, no particular reason."

"Have they thrown you out of the regiment?"

"I'm seconded, temporarily, for special duty."

"You're the sixth chap I've seen in disguise this morning."

"That's the idea — security, you know."

"What's it all about?"

"You'll hear in time, I expect," said Peter with boundless smugness.

They went to the bar.

"Good morning, my lord," said Macdougal, the barman. "I see you're off to Finland too. Quite a number of our gentlemen are going to-night."

Angela Lyne was back in London; the affairs of the hospital were in order, her son was at his private school, transported at the outbreak of war from the East coast to the middle of Dartmoor. She sat at the place she called "home" listening to wireless news from Germany.

This place was a service flat and as smart and non-committal as herself, a set of five large rooms high up in the mansard floor of a brand-new block in Grosvenor Square. The decorators had been at work there while she was in France; the style was what passes for Empire in the fashionable world. Next year, had there been no

war, she would have had it done over again during
August.

That morning she had spent an hour with her brokers
giving precise, prudent directions for the disposition of
her fortune; she had lunched alone, listening to the
radio from Europe; after luncheon she had gone alone
to the cinema in Curzon Street. It was darkening when
she left the cinema and quite dark now outside, beyond the heavy crimson draperies which hung in a
dozen opulent loops and folds, girded with gold cord,
fringed with gold at the hem, over the new black shutters. Soon she would go out to dine with Margot at the
Ritz. Peter was off somewhere and Margot was trying
to get a party together for him.

She mixed herself a large cocktail; the principal ingredients were vodka and Calvados; the decorators had
left an electric shaker on the Pompeian side-table. It
was their habit to litter the house where they worked
with expensive trifles of this sort; parsimonious clients
sent them back; the vaguer sort believed them to be
presents for which they had forgotten to thank anyone,
used them, broke them and paid for them a year later
when the bills came in. Angela liked gadgets. She
switched on the electric shaker and, when her drink was
mixed, took the glass with her to the bathroom and
drank it slowly in her bath.

Angela never drank cocktails except in private; there
was something about them which bore, so faintly as

to be discernible to no one but herself, a suggestion of good fellowship and good cheer; an infinitely small invitation to familiarity — derived perhaps from the days of Prohibition, when gin had ceased to be Hogarthian and had become chic; an aura of naughtiness, of felony compounded; a memory of her father's friends who sometimes had raised their glasses to her, of a man in a ship who had said "À *tes beaux yeux.*" And so Angela, who hated human contact on any but her own terms, never drank cocktails except in solitude. Lately all her days seemed to be spent alone.

Steam from the bath formed in a mist, and later in great beads of water, on the side of the glass. She finished her cocktail and felt the fumes rise inside her. She lay for a long time in the water, scarcely thinking, scarcely feeling anything except the warm water round her and the spirit within her. She called for her maid, from next door, to bring her a cigarette; smoked it slowly to the end; called for an ash tray and then for a towel. Presently she was ready to face the darkness, and the intense cold, and Margot Metroland's dinner party.

She noticed in the last intense scrutiny before her mirrors that her mouth was beginning to droop a little at the corners. It was not the disappointed pout that she knew in so many of her friends; it was as the droop you sometimes saw in death masks, when the jaw had been set and the face had stiffened in lines which told those waiting round the bed that the will to live was gone.

At dinner she drank Vichy water and talked like a man. She said that France was no good any more and Peter used a phrase that was just coming into vogue, accusing her of being "fifth column." They went on to dance at the Suivi. She danced and drank her Vichy water and talked sharply and well like a very clever man. She was wearing a new pair of ear-rings — an arrow set with a ruby point, the shaft a thin bar of emerald that seemed to transfix the lobe; she had designed them for herself and had called for them that morning on her way home from seeing her man of business. The girls in the party noticed Angela's ear-rings; they noticed everything about her clothes; she was the best-dressed woman there, as she usually was, wherever she went.

She stayed to the end of the party and then returned to Grosvenor Square alone. Since the war there was no lift-man on duty after midnight. She shut herself in, pressed the button for the mansard floor and rose to the empty, uncommunicative flat. There were no ashes to stir in the grate; illuminated glass coals glowed eternally in an elegant steel basket; the temperature of the rooms never varied, winter or summer, day or night. She mixed herself a large whiskey and water and turned on the radio.

Tirelessly, all over the world, voices were speaking in their own and in foreign tongues. She listened and fidgeted with the knob; sometimes she got a burst of music, once a prayer. Presently she fetched another whiskey and water.

Her maid lived out and had been told not to wait up.
When she came in the morning she found Mrs. Lyne
in bed but awake; the clothes she had worn the evening
before had been carefully hung up, not broadcast about
the carpet as they used sometimes to be. "I shan't be
getting up this morning, Grainger," she said. "Bring
the radio here and the newspapers."

Later she had her bath, returned to bed, took two
tablets of Dial and slept, gently, until it was time to fit
the black plywood screens into the window frames and
hide them behind the velvet draperies.

9. "WHAT ABOUT Mr. and
Mrs. Prettyman-Partridge of the Malt House, Grantley
Green?"

Basil was choosing his objectives from the extreme
quarters of the Malfrey billeting area. He had struck
east and north. Grantley Green lay south where the
land of spur and valley fell away and flattened out into
a plain of cider orchards and market gardens.

"They're very old, I think," said Barbara. "I hardly
know them. Come to think of it, I heard something
about Mr. Prettyman-Partridge the other day. I can't
remember what."

"Pretty house? Nice things in it?"

"As far as I remember."

"People of regular habits? Fond of quiet?"

"Yes, I suppose so."

"They'll do."

Basil bent over the map tracing the road to Grantley Green which he would take next day.

He found the Malt House without difficulty. It had been a brew house in the seventeenth century and later was converted to a private house. It had a large, regular front of dressed stone, facing the village green. The curtains and the china in the window proclaimed that it was in "good hands." Basil noted the china with approval — large, black Wedgwood urns — valuable and vulnerable and no doubt well-loved. When the door opened it disclosed a view straight through the house to a white lawn and a cedar tree laden with snow.

The door was opened by a large and lovely girl. She had fair curly hair and a fair skin, huge, pale blue eyes, a large, shy mouth. She was dressed in a tweed suit and woollen jumper as though for country exercise, but the soft, fur-lined boots showed that she was spending the morning at home. Everything about this girl was large and soft and round and ample. A dress shop might not have chosen her as a mannequin but she was not a fat girl; a more civilized age would have found her admirably proportioned; Boucher would have painted her half-clothed in a flutter of blue and pink draperies, a butterfly hovering over a breast of white and rose.

"Miss Prettyman-Partridge?"

"No. Please don't say you've come to sell something. It's terribly cold standing here and if I ask you in I shall have to buy it."

"I want to see Mr. and Mrs. Prettyman-Partridge."

"They're dead. At least one is; the other sold us the house last summer. Is that all, please? I don't want to be rude but I must shut the door or freeze."

So that was what Barbara had heard about the Malt House. "May I come in?"

"Oh dear," said this splendid girl, leading him into the room with the Wedgwood urns. "Is it something to buy or forms to fill in or just a subscription? If it's the first two I can't help because my husband's away with the yeomanry; if it's a subscription I've got some money upstairs. I've been told to give the same as Mrs. Andrews, the doctor's wife. If you haven't been to her yet, come back when you find what she's good for."

Everything in the room was new; that is to say the paint was new and the carpets and the curtains, and the furniture had been newly put in position. There was a very large settee in front of the fireplace whose cushions, upholstered in toile-de-Jouy, still bore the impress of that fine young woman; she had been lying there when Basil rang the bell. He knew that if he put his hand in the round concavity where her hip had rested, it would still be warm; and that further cushion had been tucked under her arm. The book she had been reading was on the lambskin hearth-rug. Basil could reconstruct the position, exactly, where she had been sprawling with the languor of extreme youth.

The girl seemed to sense an impertinence in Basil's scrutiny. "Anyway," she said. "Why aren't you in khaki?"

"Work of national importance," said Basil. "I am the district billeting officer. I'm looking for a suitable home for three evacuated children."

"Well, I hope you don't call this suitable. I ask you. I can't even look after Bill's sheepdog. I can't even look after myself very well. What should I do with three children?"

"These are rather exceptional children."

"They'd have to be. Anyway I'm not having any thank you. There was a funny little woman called Harkness came to call here yesterday. I do think people might let up on calling in war-time, don't you? She told me the most gruesome things about some children that were sent to her. They had to bribe the man, literally bribe him with money, to get the brutes moved."

"These are the same children."

"Well for God's sake, why pick on me?"

Her great eyes held him dazzled, like a rabbit before the headlights of a car. It was a delicious sensation.

"Well, actually, I picked on the Prettyman-Partridges . . . I don't even know your name."

"I don't know yours."

"Basil Seal."

"Basil Seal?" There was a sudden interest in her voice. "How very funny."

"Why funny?"

"Only that I used to hear a lot about you once. Weren't you a friend of a girl called Mary Nichols?"

"Was I?" Was he? Mary Nichols? Mary Nichols?

"Well, she used to talk a lot about you. She was much older than me. I used to think her wonderful when I was sixteen. You met her in a ship coming from Copenhagen."

"I daresay. I've been to Copenhagen."

The girl was looking at him now with a keen and not wholly flattering attention. "So you're Basil Seal," she said. "Well I never . . ."

Four years ago in South Kensington, at Mary Nichols' home, there was a little back sitting-room on the first floor which was Mary's room. Here Mary entertained her girl friends to tea. Here she had come, day after day, to sit before the gas fire and eat Fullers' walnut cake and hear the details of Mary's Experience. "But aren't you going to see him again?" she asked. "No, it was something so beautiful, so complete in itself — " Mary had steeped herself in romantic literature since her Experience. "I don't want to spoil it." "I don't think he sounds half good enough for you, darling." "He's absolutely *different*. You mustn't think of him as one of the young men one meets at dances . . ." The girl did not go to dances yet, and Mary knew it.

Mary's tales of the young men she met at dances had
been very moving, but not as moving as this tale of
Basil Seal. The name had become graven on her mind.

And Basil, still standing, searched his memory. Mary
Nichols? Copenhagen? No, it registered nothing. It was
very consoling, he thought, the way in which an act of
kindness, in the fullness of time, returns to bless the
benefactor. One gives a jolly-up to a girl in a ship. She
goes her way, he goes his. He forgets; he has so many
benefactions of the kind to his credit. But she remem-
bers and then one day, when it is least expected, Fate
drops into his lap the ripe fruit of his reward, this
luscious creature waiting for him, all unaware, in the
Malt House, Grantley Green.

"Aren't you going to offer me a drink — on the
strength of Mary Nichols?"

"I don't think there's anything in the house. Bill's
away you see. He's got some wine downstairs in the
cellar, but the door's locked."

"I expect we could open it."

"Oh! I wouldn't do that. Bill would be furious."

"Well, I don't suppose he'll be best pleased to come
home on leave and find the Connolly family hacking
up his home. By the way, you haven't seen them yet;
they're outside in the car; I'll bring them in."

"*Please* don't!" There was genuine distress and appeal in those blue cow-eyes.

"Well, take a look at them through the window."

She went and looked. "Good God," said the girl.

"Mrs. Harkness wasn't far wrong. I thought she was laying it on thick."

"It cost her thirty pounds to get rid of them."

"Oh, but I haven't got anything like that" — again the distress and appeal in her wide blue eyes. "Bill makes me an allowance out of his pay. It comes in monthly. It's practically all I've got."

"I'll take payment in kind," said Basil.

"You mean the sherry?"

"I'd like a glass of sherry very much," said Basil.

When they got to work with the crowbar on the cellar door, it was clear that this high-spirited girl thoroughly enjoyed herself. It was a pathetic little cellar: a poor man's treasury. Half a dozen bottles of hock, a bin of port, a dozen or two of claret. "Mostly wedding presents," explained the girl. Basil found some sherry and they took it up to the light.

"I've no maid now," she explained. "A woman comes in once a week."

They found glasses in the pantry and a corkscrew in the dining-room.

"Is it any good?" she asked anxiously, while Basil tasted the wine.

"Delicious."

"I'm so glad. Bill knows about wine. I don't."

So they began to talk about Bill, who was married in July to this lovely creature, who had a good job in an architect's office in the near-by town, had settled at

Grantley Green in August, and in September had gone to join the yeomanry as a trooper . . .

Two hours later Basil left the Malt House and returned to his car. It was evidence of the compelling property of love that the Connolly children were still in their seats.

"Gawd, mister, you haven't half been a time," said Doris. "We're fair froze. Do we get out here?"

"No."

"We aren't going to muck up this house?"

"No, Doris, not this time. You're coming back with me."

Doris sighed blissfully. "I don't care how froze we are if we can come back with you," she said.

When they returned to Malfrey, and Barbara once more found the children back in the bachelors' wing, her face fell. "Oh, Basil," she said. "You've failed me."

"Well not exactly. The Prettyman-Partridges are dead."

"I knew there was something about them. But you've been a long time."

"I met a friend. At least the friend of a friend. A very nice girl. I think you ought to do something about her."

"What's her name?"

"D'you know, I never discovered. But her husband's called Bill. He joined Freddy's regiment as a trooper."

"Who's she a friend of?"

"Mary Nichols."

"I've never heard of her."

"Old friend of mine. Honestly, Babs, you'll like this girl."

"Well, ask her to dinner." Barbara was not enthusiastic; she had known too many of Basil's girls.

"I have. The trouble is she hasn't got a car. D'you mind if I go and fetch her?"

"Darling, we simply haven't the petrol."

"We can use the special allowance."

"Darling, I *can't*. This has nothing to do with billeting."

"Believe it or not Babs, it has."

10. THE FROST broke; the snow melted away; Colony Bog, Bagshot Heath, Chobham Common and all the little polygons of gorse and bush which lay between the high roads of Surrey — patches of rank land marked on the signposts W.D., marked on the maps as numbered training areas — reappeared from their brief period of comeliness.

"We can get on with the tactical training," said the C.O.

For three weeks there were platoon schemes and
company schemes. Captain Mayfield consumed his leisure devising ways of transforming into battlefields the
few acres of close, soggy territory at his disposal. For
the troops these schemes only varied according to the
distance of the training area from camp, and the distance that had to be traversed before the Cease Fire.
Then for three days in succession the C.O. was seen
to go out with the Adjutant in the Humber snipe, each
carrying a map case. "We're putting on a battalion
exercise," said Captain Mayfield. It was all one to his
troops. "It's our first battalion exercise. It's absolutely
essential that every man in the company shall be in
the picture all the time."

Alastair was gradually learning the new languages.
There was the simple tongue, the unchanging reitera-
tion of obscenity, spoken by his fellow soldiers. That
took little learning. There was also the language spoken
by his officers, which from time to time was addressed
to him. The first time that Captain Mayfield had asked
him, "Are you in the picture, Trumpington?" he supposed him to mean, was he personally conspicuous?
He crouched at the time, waterlogged to the knees, in
a ditch; he had, at the suggestion of Mr. Smallwood —
the platoon commander — ornamented his steel helmet
with bracken. "No, sir," he had said, stoutly.

Captain Mayfield had seemed rather gratified than
not by the confession. "Put these men in the picture,
Smallwood," he said, and there had followed a tedious

and barely credible narrative about the unprovoked aggression of Southland against Northland (who was not party to the Geneva gas protocol), about How support batteries, A.F.V.'s and F.D.L.'s.

Alastair learned, too, that all schemes ended in a "shambles," which did not mean, as he had feared, a slaughter, but a brief restoration of individual freedom of movement, when everyone wandered where he would, while Mr. Smallwood blew his whistle and Captain Mayfield shouted, "Mr. Smallwood, will you kindly get your platoon to hell out of here and fall them in on the road."

On the day of the battalion scheme they marched out of camp as a battalion. Alastair had been made mortar-man in Mr. Smallwood's platoon. It was a gamble, the chances of which were hotly debated. At the moment there were no mortars and he was given instead a light and easily manageable counterfeit of wood which was slung on the back of his haversack, relieving him of a rifle. At present it was money for old rope, but a day would come, spoken of as "When we get over 1098"; in that dire event he would be worse off than the riflemen. Two other men in the platoon had rashly put in to be anti-tank men; contrary to all expectations anti-tank rifles had suddenly arrived. One of these men had prudently gone sick on the eve of the exercise; the other went sick after it.

Water bottles were filled, haversack rations were packed in mess-tins, and, on account of Northland's frank obduracy at Geneva, gas respirators frustrated the aim of the designers of the equipment to leave the man's chest unencumbered. Thus they marched out and after ten minutes, at the command to march at ease, they began singing "Roll Out the Barrel," "We'll Hang Out the Washing on the Siegfried Line," and "The Quartermaster's Store." Presently the order came back to march tactically. They knew all about that; it meant stumbling along in the ditch; singing stopped; the man with the anti-tank rifle swore monotonously. Then the order came back, "Gas"; they put on their respirators and the man with the anti-tank rifle suffered in silence.

"Gas Clear. *Don't* put the respirators back in the haversacks. Leave them out a minute to dry."

They marched eight miles or so and then turned off the main road into a lane and eventually halted. It was now eleven o'clock.

"This is the battalion assembly position," announced Captain Mayfield. "The C.O. has just gone forward with his recce group to make his recce."

It was as though he were announcing to a crowd of pilgrims, "This is the Vatican. The Pope has just gone into the Sistine Chapel."

"It makes things much more interesting," said Mr. Smallwood rather apologetically, "if you try and understand what is going on. Yes, carry on smoking."

The company settled itself on the side of the road and began eating its haversack rations.

"I say, you know," said Mr. Smallwood. "There'll be a halt for dinner."

They ate, mostly in silence.

"Soon the C.O. will send for his O group," announced Captain Mayfield.

Presently a runner appeared, not running but walking rather slowly, and led Captain Mayfield away.

"The C.O. *has* sent for his O group," said Mr. Smallwood. "Captain Brown is now in command."

Captain Brown announced: "The C.O. has given out his orders. He is now establishing advanced Battalion H.Q. The company commanders are now making their recces. Soon *they* will send for *their* O groups."

"Can't think what they want *us* here for at all," said the man with the anti-tank rifle.

Three-quarters of an hour passed and then an orderly arrived with a written message for Captain Brown. He said to the three platoon commanders: "You're to meet the company commander at the third E in 'Bee Garden.' I'm bringing the company on to the B in Bee."

Mr. Smallwood and his orderly and his batman left platoon headquarters and drifted off uncertainly into the scrub.

"Get the company fallen in, Sergeant-Major."

Captain Brown was not quite happy about his position; they tacked along behind him across the common; several times they halted while Captain Brown worried over the map. At last he said, "This is the company assembly position. The company commander is now giving out orders to his O group."

At this moment, just as the men were beginning to settle down, Captain Mayfield appeared. "Where the hell are those platoon commanders?" he asked. "And what is the company doing here? I said the B in Bee, this is the E in Garden."

A discussion followed, inaudible to Alastair except for an occasional phrase, "ring contour," "track junction" and again and again "Well, the map's wrong." Captain Brown seemed to get the better of the argument; at any rate Captain Mayfield went away in search of his O group and left the company in possession.

Half an hour passed. Captain Brown felt impelled to explain the delay.

"The platoon commanders are making their recces," he said.

Presently the C.O. arrived. "Is this C Company?" he asked.

"Yes, sir."

"Well, what's happening? You ought to be on the start line by now." Then since it was clearly no use attacking Captain Brown about that, he said in a way Captain Brown had learned to dread: "I must have missed your sentries coming along. Just put me in the picture, will you, of your local defence?"

"Well, sir, we've just halted here . . ."

The C.O. led Captain Brown away.

"He's getting a rocket," said the anti-tank man. It

was the first moment of satisfaction he had known that day.

Captain Brown came back looking shaken and began posting air look-outs and gas sentries with feverish activity. While he was in the middle of it the platoon orderlies came back to lead the platoons to assembly positions. Alastair advanced with the platoon another half mile. Then they halted. Mr. Smallwood appeared and collected the section-commanders round him. The C.O. was there too, listening to Mr. Smallwood's orders. When they were finished he said, "I don't think you mentioned the R.A.P., did you, Smallwood?"

"R.A.P. sir? No, sir, I'm afraid I don't know where it is."

The C.O. led Mr. Smallwood out of hearing of his platoon.

"Now *he's* getting a rocket," said the anti-tank man with glee.

The section-commanders came back to their men. Mr. Smallwood's orders had been full of detail; start line, zero hour, boundaries inclusive and exclusive, objectives, supporting fire. "It's like this," said Corporal Deacon. "They're over there and we're here. So then we go for un."

Another half-hour passed. Captain Mayfield appeared. "For Christ's sake, Smallwood, you ought to be halfway up the ridge by this time."

"Oh," said Mr. Smallwood. "Sorry. Come on. Forward."

The platoon collected its equipment and toiled into action up the opposing slope. Major Bush, the second-in-command, appeared before them. They fired their blanks at him with enthusiasm. "Got him," said the man next to Alastair.

"You're coming under heavy fire," said the Major. "Most of you are casualties."

"He's a casualty himself."

"Well, what are you going to do, Smallwood?"

"Get down, sir."

"Well *get* down."

"Get down," ordered Mr. Smallwood.

"What are you going to do now?"

Mr. Smallwood looked round desperately for inspiration. "Put down smoke, sir."

"Well, *put* down smoke."

"Put down smoke," said Mr. Smallwood to Alastair.

The Major went on his way to confuse the platoon on their flank.

"Come on," said Mr. Smallwood. "We've got to get up this infernal hill sometime. We might as well do it now."

It was shorter than it looked; they were up in twenty minutes and at the summit there was a prolonged shambles. Bit by bit the whole battalion appeared from different quarters. C Company was collected and fallen in; then they were fallen out to eat their dinners. No one had any dinner left, so they lay on their backs and smoked.

Marching home the C.O. said, "Not so bad for a first attempt."

"Not so bad, Colonel," said Major Bush.

"Bit slow off the mark."

"A bit sticky."

"Smallwood didn't do too well."

"He was very slow off the mark."

"Well, I think we learned some lessons. The men were interested. You could see that."

It was dark by the time the battalion reached camp. They marched to attention passing the guardroom, split into companies, and halted on the company parade grounds.

"All rifles to be pulled through before supper," said Captain Mayfield. "Platoon sergeants collect empties. Foot inspection by platoons." Then he dismissed the company.

Alastair had time to slip away to the telephone box and summon Sonia before Mr. Mayfield came round the hut examining the feet with an electric torch. He pulled on a clean pair of socks, pushed his boots under his palliasse and put on a pair of shoes; then he was ready. Sonia was outside the guardroom, waiting for him in the car. "Darling, you smell very sweaty," she said. "What have you been doing?"

"I put down smoke," said Alastair proudly. "The whole advance was held up until I put down smoke."

"Darling, you *are* clever. I've got a tinned beefsteak and kidney pudding for dinner."

After dinner Alastair settled in a chair. "Don't let me go to sleep," he said. "I must be in by midnight."

"I'll wake you."

"I wonder if a real battle is much like that," said Alastair just before he dropped off.

Peter Pastmaster's expedition never sailed. He resumed his former uniform and his former habits. His regiment was in barracks in London; his mother was still at the Ritz; most of his friends were still to be found round the bar at Bratt's. With time on his hands and the prospect of action, for a few days imminent, now postponed, but always present as the basis of any future plans, Peter began to suffer from pangs of dynastic conscience. He was thirty-three years old. He might pop off any day. "Mama," he said, "d'you think I ought to marry?"

"Who?"

"Anyone."

"I don't see that you can say anyone *ought* to marry *anyone.*"

"Darling, don't confuse me. What I mean is supposing I get killed."

"I don't see a great deal in it for the poor girl," said Margot.

"I mean I should like to have a son."

"Well then you had better marry, darling. D'you know any girls?"

"I don't think I do."

"I don't think I do either, come to think of it. I believe Emma Granchester's second girl is very pretty — try her. There are probably lots of others. I'll make enquiries."

So Peter, little accustomed to their society, began, awkwardly at first, taking out a series of very young and very eligible girls; he quickly gained confidence; it was easy as falling off a log. Soon there were a dozen mothers who were old-fashioned enough to be pleasurably excited at the prospect of finding in their son-in-law all the Victorian excellencies of an old title, a new fortune, and a shapely leg in blue overalls.

"Peter," Margot said to him one day. "D'you ever give yourself time from debutantes to see old friends? What's become of Angela? I never see her now."

"I suppose she's gone back to the country."

"Not with Basil?"

"No, not with Basil."

But she was living still above the block of flats in Grosvenor Square. Below, layer upon layer of rich men and women came and went about their business, layer below layer down to street level; below that again, underground, the management were adapting the basement to serve as an air raid shelter. Angela seldom went beyond her door, except once or twice a week to visit the cinema; she always went alone. She had taken to wearing spectacles of smoked glass; she wore them indoors, as well as out; she wore them in the subdued, concealed lighting of her drawing-room, as she sat hour

after hour with the radio standing by the decanter and
glass at her elbow; she wore them when she looked at
herself in the mirror. Only Grainger, her maid, knew
what was the matter with Mrs. Lyne, and she only
knew the shell of it. Grainger knew the number of bottles, empty and full, in the little pantry; she saw Mrs.
Lyne's face when the blackout was taken down in the
morning. (She never had to wake Mrs. Lyne nowadays; her eyes were always open when the maid came
to call her; sometimes Mrs. Lyne was up and sitting in
her chair; sometimes she lay in bed, staring ahead, waiting to be called.) She knew the trays of food that came
up from the restaurant and went back, as often as not,
untasted. All this Grainger knew and, being a dull
sensible girl, she kept her own counsel; but, being a
dull and sensible girl, she was spared the knowledge of
what went on in Mrs. Lyne's mind.

So the snows vanished and the weeks of winter
melted away with them; presently, oblivious of the
hazards of war, the swallows returned to their ancestral
building grounds.

CHAPTER III

Spring

1. *T*WO EVENTS decided Basil to return to London. First, the yeomanry moved back to the country under canvas. Freddy telephoned to Barbara: —

"Good news," he said; "we're coming home."

"Freddy, how splendid," said Barbara, her spirits falling a little. "When?"

"I arrive to-morrow. I'm bringing Jack Cathcart; he's our second-in-command now. We're going to lay out a camp. We'll stay at Malfrey while we're doing it."

"Lovely," said Barbara.

"We'll be bringing servants, so we'll be self-supporting as far as that goes. There'll be a couple of sergeants. Benson can look after them. And I say, Barbara, what do you say to having the camp in the park?"

"Oh no, Freddy, for God's sake."

"We could open up the saloon and have the mess there. I could live in. You'd have to have old Colonel Sproggin and probably Cathcart, too, but you wouldn't mind that, would you?"

"Please, Freddy, don't decide anything in a hurry."

"Well I have practically decided. See you to-morrow. I say, is Basil still with you?"

"Yes."

"I can't see him getting on terribly well with Cathcart. Couldn't you give him a gentle hint?"

Barbara hung up sadly and went to make arrangements for Freddy's and Major Cathcart's reception.

Basil was at Grantley Green. He returned to Malfrey after dinner, to find Barbara still up.

"Darling, you've got to go away."

"Yes, how did you know?"

"Freddy's coming home."

"Oh damn Freddy; who cares for him? *Bill's* coming home."

"What does she say?"

"Believe it or not, she's as pleased as Punch."

"Ungrateful beast," said Barbara; and, after a pause, "You never wrote that book either."

"No, but we've had a lovely time, haven't we, Babs? Quite like the old days."

"I suppose you'll want some money."

"I could always do with some more, but as it happens I'm quite rich at the moment."

"Basil, how?"

"One thing and another. I tell you what I will do before I go. I'll get the Connollies off your hands again. I'm afraid I've been neglecting them rather in the last few weeks."

That led to the second deciding event.

On his way to and from Grantley Green, Basil had noticed a pretty stucco house standing in paddock and orchard, which seemed exactly suited to harbour the Connollies. He had asked Barbara about it, but she could tell him nothing. Basil was getting lax and confident now in his methods, and no longer bothered himself with much research before choosing his victims. The stucco house was marked down and next day he packed the Connollies into the car and drove over to do his business.

It was ten in the morning but he found the proprietor at breakfast. He did not appear to be quite the type that Basil was used to deal with. He was younger than the G.P.O. list. A game leg, stuck awkwardly askew, explained why he was not in uniform. He had got this injury in a motor race, he explained later to Basil. He had ginger hair and a ginger moustache and malevolent pinkish eyes. His name was Mr. Todhunter.

He was eating kidneys and eggs and sausages and bacon and an overcooked chop; his tea-pot stood on the hob. He looked like a drawing by Leech for a book by Surtees.

"Well," he said, cautious but affable. "I know about you. You're Mrs. Sothill's brother at Malfrey. I don't know Mrs. Sothill but I know all about her. I don't know Captain Sothill but I know about him. What can I do for you?"

"I'm the billeting officer for this district," said Basil.

"*Indeed.* I'm interested to meet you. Go on. You don't mind my eating, I'm sure."

Feeling a little less confident than usual, Basil went through his now stereotyped preface: . . . Getting harder to find billets, particularly since the anti-aircraft battery had come to South Grappling and put their men in the cottages there . . . important to stop the backwash to the towns . . . bad impression if the bigger houses seemed not to be doing their share . . . natural reluctance to employ compulsory powers but these powers *were* there, if necessary . . . three children who had caused some difficulty elsewhere . . .

Mr. Todhunter finished his breakfast, stood with his back to the fire and began to fill his pipe. "And what if I don't want these hard cases of yours?" he said. "What if I'd sooner pay the fine?"

Basil embarked on the second part of his recitation: . . . Official allowance barely covered cost of food . . . serious hardship to poor families . . . poor people valued their household gods even more than the rich . . . possible to find a cottage where a few pounds would make all the difference between dead loss and a small and welcome profit . . .

Mr. Todhunter heard him in silence. At last he said, "So *that's* how you do it. Thank you. That was most instructive, very instructive indeed. I liked the bit about household gods."

Basil began to realize that he was dealing with a fellow of broad and rather dangerous sympathies; someone like himself. "In more cultured circles I say *Lares et Penates.*"

"Household gods is good enough. Household gods is very good indeed. What d'you generally count on raising?"

"Five pounds is the worst, thirty-five the best I've had so far."

"So far? Do you hope to carry on long with this trade?"

"I don't see why not."

"Don't you? Well, I'll tell you something. D'you know who's billeting officer in this district? I am. Mrs. Sothill's district ends at the main road. You're muscling in on my territory when you come past the crossing. Now what have you got to say for yourself?"

"D'you mean to say that Grantley Green is yours?"

"Certainly."

"How damned funny."

"Why funny?"

"I can't tell you," said Basil. "But it *is* — exquisitely funny."

"So I'll ask you to keep to your own side of the road in future. Not that I'm ungrateful for your visit. It's given me some interesting ideas. I always felt there was money in this racket somehow, but I could never quite see my way to get it. Now I know. I'll remember about the household gods."

"Wait a minute," said Basil. "It isn't quite as easy as all that, you know. It isn't just a matter of having the

idea; you have to have the Connollies too. You don't
understand it, and I don't understand it, but the fact
remains that quite a number of otherwise sane human
beings are perfectly ready to take children in; they like
them; it makes them feel virtuous; they like the little
pattering feet about the house — I know it sounds
screwy but it's the truth. I've seen it again and again."

"So have I," said Mr. Todhunter. "There's no sense
in it, but it's a fact — they make household gods of
them."

"Now the Connollies are something quite special;
no one could make a household god of them. Come
and have a look."

He and Mr. Todhunter went out into the circle of
gravel in front of the porch, where Basil had left the car.

"Doris," he said. "Come out and meet Mr. Todhunter. Bring Micky and Marlene too."

The three frightful children stood in a line to be inspected.

"Take that scarf off your head, Doris. Show him your
hair."

In spite of himself Mr. Todhunter could not disguise
the fact that he was profoundly moved. "Yes," he said.
"I give you that. They *are* special. If it's not a rude
question, what did you pay for them?"

"I got them free. But I've put a lot of money into
them since — fried fish and cinemas."

"How did you get the girl's hair that way?"

"She did it herself," said Basil, "for love."

"They certainly are special," repeated Mr. Todhunter with awe.

"You haven't seen anything yet. You should see them in action."

"I can imagine it," said Mr. Todhunter. "Well, what d'you want for them?"

"Five pounds a leg and that's cheap, because I'm thinking of closing down the business anyhow."

Mr. Todhunter was not a man to haggle when he was on a good thing. "Done," he said.

Basil addressed the Connollies. "Well, children, this is your new headquarters."

"Are we to muck 'em about?" asked Doris.

"That's up to Mr. Todhunter. I'm handing you over to him now. You'll be working for him in future."

"Ain't we never going to be with you again?" asked Doris.

"Never again, Doris. But you'll find you like Mr. Todhunter just as much. He's very handsome, isn't he?"

"Not as handsome as you."

"No, perhaps not, but he's got a fine little red moustache, hasn't he?"

"Yes, it's a lovely moustache," Doris conceded; she looked from her old to her new master, critically. "But he's shorter than you."

"Dammit, girl," said Basil impatiently. "Don't you realize there's a war on? We've all got to make sacrifices. There's many a little girl would be very grateful for Mr. Todhunter. Look at his fine red nob."

"Yes, it *is* red."

Mr. Todhunter tired of the comparison and stumped indoors to fetch his cheque-book.

"Can't we muck his house up, just a bit?" said Micky wistfully.

"Yes, I don't see why not, just a bit."

"Mister," said Doris, near tears. "Kiss me once before you go."

"No. Mr. Todhunter wouldn't like it. He's terribly jealous."

"Is he?" she said lightening. "I love jealous men."

When Basil left her, her fervent, volatile affections were already plainly engaged with her new host. Marlene remained passive throughout the interview; she had few gifts, poor child, and those she was allowed to employ only on rare occasions. "Mayn't I be sick here, Doris? Just once?"

"Not here, ducky. Wait till the gentleman billets you."

"Will that be long?"

"No," said Mr. Todhunter decisively, "not long."

So the scourge of the Malfrey area moved south into the apple-growing country and the market gardens; and all over the park at Malfrey, dispersed irregularly under the great elms, tents sprang up; and the yeomanry officers set up their mess in the Grinling Gibbons saloon; and Barbara had Colonel Sproggin and Major Cathcart to live in the house; and Freddy made an agreeable sum of money out of the arrangement; and Bill spent many blissful uxorious hours in the Malt House, Grantley Green (he was quite satisfied with the explanation he was given about the cellar door). And Basil returned to London.

2. HE DECIDED to pay one of his rare, and usually rather brief, visits to his mother. He found her busy and optimistic, serving on half a dozen benevolent committees connected with comforts for the troops, seeing her friends regularly. The defeat of Finland had shocked her, but she found it a compensation that Russia was at last disclosed in the true light. She welcomed Basil to the house, heard his news of Barbara and gave him news of Tony. "I want to have a little talk with you sometime," she said, after half an hour's gossip.

Basil, had he not been inured to his mother's euphemisms, might have supposed that a little talk was precisely what she had just had; but he knew what a little talk meant; it meant a discussion of his "future."

"Have you arranged anything for to-night?"

"No, Mother, not yet."

"Then we will dine in. Just the two of us."

And that night after dinner she said, "Basil, I never

thought I should have to say this to you. I've been pleased, of course, that you were able to be of help to Barbara with her evacués, but now that you have returned to London, I must tell you that I do not think it is *man's* work. At a time like this you ought to be *fighting*."

"But Mother, as far as I know, no one's fighting much at the moment."

"Don't quibble, dear, you know what I mean."

"Well, I went to see that colonel when you asked me to."

"Yes. Sir Joseph explained that to me. They only want very young officers in the Guards. But he says that there are a number of other excellent regiments that offer a far better career. General Gordon was a Sapper, and I believe quite a number of the generals in this war were originally only Gunners. I don't want you just lounging about London in uniform like your friend Peter Pastmaster. He seems to spend his whole time with girls. That goose Emma Granchester is seriously thinking of him for Molly. So is Etty Flintshire and so is poor Mrs. Van Atrobus for *their* daughters. I don't know what they're thinking of. I knew his poor father. Margot led him a terrible dance. That was long before she married Metroland of course — before he was called Metroland, in fact. No," said Lady Seal, abruptly checking herself in the flow of reminiscence. "I want to see you doing something *important*. Now Sir Joseph has got me one of the forms you fill in to become an officer. It is called the Supplementary Reserve. Before you go to bed I want you to sign it. Then we'll see about getting it sent to the proper quarter. I'm sure that everything will be much easier now that that disgraceful Mr. Belisha has been outed."

"But you know, Mother, I don't really fancy myself much as a subaltern."

"No, dear," said Lady Seal decisively, "and if you had gone into the Army when you left Oxford you would be a major by now. Promotion is very quick in war-time because so many people get killed. I'm sure once you're in, they'll find great use for you. But you must begin somewhere. I remember Lord Kitchener told me that even he was once a subaltern."

Thus it was that Basil found himself again in danger of being started on a career. "Don't worry," said Peter. "No one ever gets taken off the Supplementary Reserve." But Basil did worry. He had a rooted distrust of official forms. He felt that at any moment a telegram might summon him to present himself at some remote barracks, where he would spend the war, like Alastair's Mr. Smallwood, teaching fieldcraft to thirty militiamen. It was not thus that he had welcomed the war as the ne'er-do-well's opportunity. He fretted about it for three days and then decided to pay a visit to the War Office.

He went there without any particular object in view, impelled by the belief that somewhere in that large organization was a goose who would lay eggs for

him. In the first days of the war, when he was seeking
to interest the authorities in the annexation of Liberia,
he had more than once sought an entrance. Perhaps,
he felt now, he had pitched a little too high. The Chief
of the Imperial General Staff was a busy man. This
time he would advance humbly.

The maelstrom which in early September had eddied
round the vestibule of the building seemed to have
subsided very little. There was a similar — perhaps,
he reflected sadly, an identical — crowd of officers of
all ranks attempting to gain admission. Among them
he saw a single civilian figure, whom he recognized
from his visit to the Ministry of Information.

"Hullo," he said. "Still hawking bombs?"

The little lunatic with the suitcase greeted him
with great friendliness. "They won't pay any attention. It's a most unsatisfactory office," he said. "They
won't let me in. I was sent on here from the Admi-
ralty."

"Have you tried the Air Ministry?"

"Why, bless you, it was them sent me to the Ministry of Information. I've tried them all. I will say for
the Ministry of Information they were uncommon
civil. Not at all like they are here. At the M. of I. they
were never too busy to see one. The only thing was,
I felt I wasn't getting anywhere."

"Come along," said Basil. "We'll get in."

Veterans of the Ashanti and the Zulu campaigns
guarded the entrance. Basil watched them stop a full

general. "If you'll fill in a form, sir, please, one of the boys will take you up to the Department." They were a match for anyone in uniform but Basil and the bag-man were a more uncertain quantity; a full general was just a full general, but a civilian might be anyone.

"Your passes, gentlemen, please."

"That's all right, Sergeant," said Basil. "I'll vouch for this man."

"Yes sir, but who are you, sir?"

"You ought to know by this time. M.I.9. We don't carry passes or give our names in my department."

"Very good, sir; beg pardon, sir. D'you know the way or shall I send a boy up with you?"

"Of course I know my way," said Basil sharply, "and you might take a look at this man. He won't give his name or show a pass, but I expect you'll see him here often."

"Very good, sir."

The two civilians passed through the seething military into the calm of the corridors beyond.

"I'm sure I'm very obliged," said the man with the suitcase; "where shall I go now?"

"The whole place lies open to you," said Basil. "Take your time. Go where you like. I think if I were you I should start with the Chaplain General."

"Where's he?"

"Up there," said Basil vaguely. "Up there and straight on."

The little man thanked him gravely, trotted off

down the corridor with the irregular, ill–co-ordinated
steps of the insane, and was lost to view up the bend
in the staircase. Not wishing to compromise himself
further by his act of charity, Basil took the opposing
turning. A fine vista lay before him of twenty or more
closed doors, any one of which might open upon pros-
perity and adventure. He strolled down the passage in
a leisurely but purposeful manner; thus, he thought,
an important agent might go to keep an appointment;
thus, in fact, Soapy Sponge might have walked in the
gallery of Jawleyford Court.

It was a vista full of potentiality; but lacking, at
the moment, in ornament — a vista of linoleum and
sombre dado; the light came solely from the far end,
so that a figure approaching appeared in silhouette,
and in somewhat indistinct silhouette; a figure now
approached and it was not until she was within a few
yards of Basil that he realized that here was the en-
richment which the austere architectural scheme demanded: a girl dressed in uniform with a lance-corporal's stripe on her arm — with a face of transparent,
ethereal silliness which struck deep into Basil's heart.
The classical image might have been sober fact, so
swift and silent and piercing was the dart of pleasure.
He turned in his tracks and followed the lance-corporal
down the lane of linoleum, which seemed, momentarily, as buoyant as the carpet of a cinema or theatre.

The lance-corporal led him a long way; she stopped
from time to time to exchange greetings with pass-

ers-by, showing to all ranks from full general to second-class scout the same cheerful affection; she was clearly a popular girl in these parts. At length she turned into a door marked ADDIS; Basil followed her in. There was another lance-corporal — male — in the room.

This lance-corporal sat behind a typewriter; he had a white, pimply face, large spectacles, and a cigarette in the corner of his mouth. He did not look up. The female lance-corporal smiled and said, "So now you know where I live. Drop in any time you're passing."

"What is ADDIS?" asked Basil.

"It's Colonel Plum."

"What's Colonel Plum?"

"He's a perfect lamb. Go and take a peek at him if you like. He's in there." She nodded towards a glass door marked KEEP OUT.

"Assistant Deputy Director Internal Security," said the male lance-corporal without looking up from his typing.

"I think I'd like to come and work in this office," said Basil.

"Yes, everyone says that. It was the same when I was in Pensions."

"I might take *his* job."

"You're welcome," said the male lance-corporal sourly. "Suspects, suspects, suspects, all day long — all with foreign names, none of them ever shot."

A loud voice from beyond the glass door broke into the conversation. "Susie, you slut, come here."

"That's him, the angel. Just take a peek while the door's open. He's got the sweetest little moustache."

Basil peered round the corner and caught a glimpse of a lean, military face and, as Susie had said, the sweetest little moustache. The Colonel caught a glimpse of Basil.

"Who the devil's that?"

"I don't know," said Susie lightly. "He just followed me in."

"Come here you," said the Colonel. "Who are you and what d'you want in my office?"

"Well," said Basil, "what the lance-corporal says is strictly true. I just followed her in. But since I'm here I can give you some valuable information."

"If you can you're unique in this outfit. What is it?"

Until now the word "Colonel" for Basil had connoted an elderly rock-gardener on Barbara's G.P.O. list. This formidable man of his own age was another kettle of fish. Here was a second Todhunter. What could he possibly tell him which would pass for valuable information?

"Can I speak freely before the lance-corporal?" he asked, playing for time.

"Yes, of course. She doesn't understand a word of any language."

Inspiration came. "There's a lunatic loose in the War Office," Basil said.

"Of course there is. There are some hundreds of them. Is that all you came to tell me?"

"He's got a suitcase full of bombs."

"Well, I hope he finds his way to the Intelligence Branch. I don't suppose you know his name? No; well, make out a card for him, Susie, with a serial number, and index him under SUSPECTS. If his bombs go off we shall know where he is; if they don't it doesn't matter. These fellows usually do more harm to themselves than to anyone else. Run along, Susie, and shut the door. I want to talk to Mr. Seal."

Basil was shaken. When the door shut he said, "Have we met before?"

"You bet we have. Djibouti 1936, St. Jean de Luz 1937, Prague 1938. You wouldn't remember me. I wasn't dressed up like this then."

"Were you a journalist?"

Vaguely at the back of Basil's mind was the recollection of an unobtrusive, discreet face among a hundred unobtrusive, discreet faces that had passed in and out of his ken from time to time. During the past ten years he had usually managed to find himself, on one pretext or another, on the outer fringe of contemporary history — in that half-world there were numerous slightly sinister figures whose orbits crossed and recrossed, ubiquitous men and women camp-followers of diplomacy and the press; among those shades he dimly remembered seeing Colonel Plum.

"Sometimes. We got drunk together once at the Basquebar, the night you fought the United Press correspondent."

"As far as I remember he won."

"You bet he did. I took you back to your hotel. What are you doing now besides making passes at Susie?"

"I thought of doing counter-espionage."

"Yes," said Colonel Plum. "Most people who come here seem to have thought of that. Hallo — " he added as a dull detonation shook the room slightly — "that sounds as if your man has had a success with his bombs. That was a straight tip, anyway. I daresay you'd be no worse in the job than anyone else."

Here it was at last, the scene that Basil had so often rehearsed; the scene, very slightly adapted by a later hand, in order to bring it up to date, from the adventure stories of his youth. Here was the lean, masterful man, who had followed Basil's career saying, "One day his country will have a use for him . . ."

"What are your contacts?"

What were his contacts? Alastair Digby-Vane-Trumpington, Angela Lyne, Margot Metroland, Peter Pastmaster, Barbara, the bride of Grantley Green, Mr. Todhunter, Poppet Green — *Poppet Green*; there was his chicken.

"I know some very dangerous Communists," said Basil.

"I wonder if they're on our files. We'll look in a minute. We aren't doing much about Communists at the moment. The politicians are shy of them for some reason. But we keep an eye on them, on the side, of course. I can't pay you much for Communists."

"As it happens," said Basil with dignity, "I came here to serve my country. I don't particularly want money."

"The devil you don't? Well, what *do* you want, then? You can't have Susie. I had the hell of a fight to get her away from the old brute in charge of Pensions."

"We can fight that out later. What I really want most at the moment is a uniform."

"Good God! Why?"

"My mother is threatening to make me a platoon commander."

Colonel Plum accepted this somewhat surprising statement with apparent understanding. "Yes," he said. "There's a lot to be said for a uniform. For one thing you'll have to call me 'sir' and if there's any funny stuff with the female staff I can take disciplinary action. For another thing it's the best possible disguise for a man of intelligence. No one ever suspects a soldier of taking a serious interest in the war. I think I can fix that."

"What'll my rank be?"

"Second Lieutenant, Crosse and Blackwell's regiment."

"Crosse and Blackwell?"

"General Service List."

"I say, can't you do anything better than that?"

"Not for watching Communists. Catch a fascist for me and I'll think about making you a Captain of Marines." At this moment the telephone bell rang. "Yes, ADDIS speaking . . . oh, yes, the bomb . . . yes, we know all about that . . . the Chaplain General? I say, that's bad . . . oh, only the Deputy Assistant Chaplain General and you think he'll recover. Well what's all the fuss about? . . . Yes, we know all about the man in this branch. We've had him indexed a long time. He's nuts — yes, N for nuts, U for uncle, nuts, you've got it. No I don't want to see him. Lock him up. There must be plenty of padded cells in this building, I should imagine."

News of the attempt to assassinate the Chaplain General reached the Religious Department of the Ministry of Information late in the afternoon, just when they were preparing to pack up for the day. It threw them into a fever of activity.

"Really," said Ambrose pettishly. "You fellows get all the fun. I shall be *most* embarrassed when I have to explain this to the editor of the *Godless Sunday at Home*."

Lady Seal was greatly shocked.

"Poor man," she said, "I understand that his eyebrows have completely gone. It must have been Russians."

3. FOR THE third time since his return to London, Basil tried to put a call through to Angela Lyne. He listened to the repeated buzz, five, six, seven times, then hung up the receiver. Still away, he thought; I should have liked to show her my uniform.

Angela counted the rings: five, six, seven; then there was silence in the flat; silence except for the radio which said ". . . dastardly attempt which has shocked the conscience of the civilized world. Messages of sympathy continue to pour into the Chaplain General's office from the religious leaders of four continents . . ."

She switched over to Germany, where a rasping, contemptuous voice spoke of "Churchill's attempt to make a second *Athenia* by bombing the military bishop."

She switched on to France where a man of letters gave his impressions of a visit to the Maginot Line. Angela filled her glass from the bottle at her elbow. Her distrust of France was becoming an obsession with her now. It kept her awake at night and haunted her dreams by day — long, tedious dreams born of barbituric; dreams which had no element of fantasy or surprise; utterly real, drab dreams which, like waking

life, held no promise of delight. She often spoke aloud
to herself nowadays — living, as she did, so much
alone; it was thus that lonely old women spoke, passing in the street with bags of rubbish in their hands,
squatting, telling their rubbish. Angela was like an old
woman squatting in a doorway picking over her day's
gleaning of rubbish, talking to herself while she sorted
the scraps of garbage. She had seen and heard old
women like that, often, at the end of the day, in the
side streets near the theatres.

Now she said to herself as loudly as though to someone sitting opposite on the white Empire day-bed:
"Maginot Line — Angela Lyne — both lines of least
resistance," and laughed at her joke until the tears
came and suddenly she found herself weeping in earnest.

Then she took a pull at herself. This wouldn't do
at all. She had better go out to the cinema.

Peter Pastmaster was taking a girl out that evening.
He looked very elegant and old-fashioned in his blue
patrol jacket and tight overall trousers. He and the
girl dined at a new restaurant in Jermyn Street.

She was Lady Mary Meadowes, Lord Granchester's
second daughter. In his quest for a wife Peter had nar-
rowed the field to three — Molly Meadowes; Sarah,
Lord Flintshire's daughter; and Betty, daughter of the
Duchess of Stayle. Since he was marrying for old-
fashioned, dynastic reasons, he proposed to make an

old-fashioned, dynastic choice from among the survivors of Whig oligarchy. He really could see very little difference between the three girls; in fact he sometimes caused offence by addressing them absent-mindedly by the wrong names. None of them carried a pound of superfluous flesh; they all had an enthusiasm for the works of Mr. Ernest Hemingway; all had pet dogs of rather similar peculiarities. They had all found that the way to keep Peter amused was to get him to brag about his past iniquities.

During dinner he told Molly about the time when Basil Seal had stood for Parliament and he and Sonia and Alastair had done him dirt in his constituency. She laughed dutifully at the incident of Sonia throwing a potato at the mayor.

"Some of the papers got it wrong and said it was a bun," he explained.

"What a lovely time you all seem to have had," said Lady Mary wistfully.

"All past and done with," said Peter primly.

"Is it? I *do* hope not."

Peter looked at her with a new interest. Sarah and Betty had taken this tale as though it were one of highwaymen — something infinitely old-fashioned and picturesque.

Afterwards they walked to the cinema next door.

The vestibule was in darkness except for a faint blue light in the box office. Out of the darkness the voice of the commissionaire announced: "No three and sixes. Plenty of room in the five and nines. Five and nines this way. Don't block up the gangway, please."

There was some kind of disturbance going on at the *guichet*. A woman was peering stupidly at the blue light and saying "I don't want five and nines. I want one three and sixpenny."

"No three and sixes. Only five and nines."

"But you don't understand. It isn't the price. The five and nines are too far away. I want to be *near*, in the three and sixpennies."

"No three and sixes. Five and nines," said the girl in the blue light.

"Come on, lady, make up your mind," said a soldier, waiting.

"She's got a look of Mrs. Cedric Lyne," said Molly.

"Why," said Peter, "it *is* Angela. What on earth's the matter with her?"

She had now bought her ticket and moved away from the window, trying to read what was on it in the half light and saying peevishly, "I *told* them it was too far away. I can't see if I'm far away. I *said* three and sixpence."

She held the ticket close up to her eyes, trying to read it; she did not notice the step, stumbled and sat down. Peter hurried forward.

"Angela, are you all right? Have you hurt yourself?"

"Perfectly all right," said Angela, sitting quietly in the twilight. "Not hurt at all thank you."

"Well, for God's sake get up."

Angela squinnied up at him from the step.

"*Peter*," she said, "I didn't recognize you. Too far away to recognize anyone in the five and ninepennies. *How* are you?"

"Angela, do get up."

He held out his hand to help her up. She shook it cordially. "How's Margot?" she said affably. "Haven't seen her lately. I've been so busy. Well that's not quite true. As a matter of fact I've not been altogether well."

A crowd was beginning to assemble in the twilight. From the darkness beyond came the voice of the commissionaire, policemanlike, saying, "What's going on here?"

"Pick her up, you coot," said Molly Meadowes.

Peter got behind Angela, put his arms round her and picked her up. She was not heavy.

"Ups-a-daisy," said Angela, making to sit down again.

Peter held her firm; he was glad of the darkness; this was no position for an officer of the Household Cavalry in uniform.

"A lady has fainted," said Molly in a clear, authoritative voice. "Please don't crowd round her," and to the commissionaire, "Call a cab."

Angela was silent in the taxi.

"I say," said Peter, "I can't apologize enough for letting you in for this."

"My dear man," said Molly, "don't be ridiculous. I'm thoroughly enjoying it."

"I can't think what's the matter with her," he said. "Can't you?"

When they reached Grosvenor Square, Angela got out of the taxi and looked about her, puzzled. "I thought we were going to the cinema," she said. "Wasn't it good?"

"It was full."

"I remember," said Angela, nodding vigorously. "Five and nines." Then she sat down again on the pavement.

"Look here," said Peter to Lady Mary Meadowes. "You take the taxi back to the cinema. Leave my ticket at the box-office. I'll join you in half an hour. I think I'd better see Angela home and get hold of a doctor."

"Bumbles," said Molly. "I'm coming up too."

Outside her door Angela suddenly rallied, found her key, opened the flat and walked steadily in. Grainger was still up.

"You need not have stayed in," said Angela. "I told you I shouldn't want you."

"I was worried. You shouldn't have gone out like that," and then seeing Peter, "Oh, good evening, my lord."

Angela turned and saw Peter, as though for the first time. "Hullo, Peter," she said. "Come in." She fixed Molly with eyes that seemed to focus with difficulty.

"You know," she said, "I'm sure I know you quite well, but I can't remember your name."

"Molly Meadowes," said Peter. "We just came to see you home. We must be going along now. Grainger, Mrs. Lyne isn't at all well. I think you ought to get her doctor."

"Molly Meadowes. My dear, I used to stay at Granchester when you were in the nursery. How old that sounds. You're very pretty, Molly, and you're wearing a lovely dress. Come in, both of you."

Peter frowned at Molly, but she went into the flat.

"Help yourself to something to drink, Peter," said Angela. She sat down in her armchair by the radio. "My dear," she said to Molly. "I don't think you've seen my flat. I had it done up by David Lennox just before the war. David Lennox. People say unkind things about David Lennox . . . Well, you can't blame them . . ." Her mind was becoming confused again. She made a resolute attempt to regain control of herself. "That's a portrait of me by John. Ten years ago; nearly done when I was married. Those are my books . . . my dear, I'm afraid I'm rather *distraite* this evening. You must forgive me," and, so saying, she fell into a heavy sleep.

Peter looked about him helplessly. Molly said to Grainger, "Had we better get her to bed?"

"When she wakes up. I shall be here. I can manage."

"Sure?"

"Quite sure."

"Well then, Peter, we'd better get back to our film."

"Yes," said Peter. "I'm awfully sorry for bringing you here."

"I wouldn't have missed it for anything," said Molly.

Peter was still puzzled by the whole business.

"Grainger," he said. "Had Mrs. Lyne been out this evening? To a party or anything?"

"Oh, no, my lord. She's been in all day."

"Alone?"

"Quite alone, my lord."

"Extraordinary thing. Well come on, Molly. Good night, Grainger. Take care of Mrs. Lyne. I think she ought to see a doctor."

"I'll take care of her," said Grainger.

They went down in the lift together, in silence, each full of thought. When they reached the hall Peter said, "Well, that was rum."

"Very rum."

"You know," said Peter, "if it had been anyone else but Angela, I should have thought she was tight."

"Darling, she was plastered."

"Are you sure?"

"My dear, stinko paralytico."

"Well, I don't know what to think. It certainly looked like it. But *Angela* . . . besides her maid said she hadn't been out all the evening. I mean to say people don't get tight alone."

Suddenly Molly put her arms round Peter's neck

and kissed him warmly. "Bless you," she said. "Now we'll go to that cinema."

It was the first time anyone had ever kissed Peter like that. He was so surprised that in the taxi he made no attempt to follow it up; so surprised that he thought about nothing else all through the film. "God Save the King" brought him back to reality with a jolt. He was still pensive while he led Molly to supper. It was hysteria, he decided; the girl was naturally upset at the scene they had been through. She's probably frightfully embarrassed about it now; best not to refer to it.

But Molly was not prepared to let the matter drop.

"Oysters," she said. "Only a dozen. Nothing else," and then, though the waiter was still beside her, "Were you surprised when I kissed you just now?"

"No," said Peter hastily, "certainly not. Not at all."

"Not at all? You mean to say you *expected* me to?"

"No, no. Of course not. You know what I mean."

"I certainly don't. I think it's very conceited of you not to be surprised. Do you always have this effect on girls, or is it just the uniform?"

"Molly, don't be a beast. If you must know, I *was* surprised."

"And shocked?"

"No, just surprised."

"Yes," said Molly, seeing it was not kind to tease him any more. "I was surprised, too. I've been wondering about it in the cinema."

"So have I," said Peter.

"*That's* how I like you," said Molly, as though she were a photographer catching a happy expression. She saw the likeness herself and added, "Hold it."

"Really, Molly, I don't understand you a bit to-night."

"Oh but you must, really you must, Peter. I'm sure you were a fascinating little boy."

"Come to think of it, I believe I was."

"You mustn't ever try playing the old rip again, Peter. Not with me, at any rate. Now don't pretend you don't understand that. I like you puzzled, Peter, but not *absolutely cretinous*. You know, I nearly despaired of you to-night. You would go on bucking about what a gay dog you'd been. I thought I could never go through with it."

"Through with what?"

"Marrying you. Mother's terribly keen I should, though I can't think why. I should have thought from her point of view you were about the end. But no, nothing else would do but that I must marry you. So I've tried to be good and I've let you bound away about the good old days till I thought I should have to pour something on your head. Thought I couldn't bear it any more and I'd decided to tell Mother it was off. Then we met Mrs. Lyne and everything was all right."

"It seemed awfully awkward to me."

"Of course it did. You looked like a little boy at

his private school when his father has come to the
sports in the wrong kind of hat. An adorable little
boy."

"Well," said Peter, "I suppose as long as you're
satisfied . . ."

"Yes, I think 'satisfied' is the word. You'll do. And
Sarah and Betty'll be as sick as cats."

"How did you decide?" asked Margot, when Peter
told her of his engagement.

"Well, as a matter of fact, I don't think I did. Molly
decided."

"Yes, that's usually the way. Now I suppose I shall
have to do something friendly about that ass Emma
Granchester."

"I really know Lady Metroland very little," said
Lady Granchester. "But I suppose now I must invite
her to luncheon. I'm afraid she's far too smart for us."
And by "smart" Lady Granchester meant nothing at
all complimentary.

But the mothers met and decided on an immediate
marriage.

4. THE NEWS of Peter's
engagement was not unexpected and, even had it
come as a surprise, would have been eclipsed in interest by the story of Angela Lyne's uncharacteristic

behaviour at the cinema. Peter and Molly, before
parting that night, had resolved to tell no one of the
incident; a renunciation from which each made certain implicit reservations. Peter told Margot because
he thought she ought to do something about it, Basil
because he was still dubious about the true explanation of the mystery and thought that Basil, if anyone
could, would throw light on it, and three members of
Bratt's because he happened to run into them at the
bar next morning when his mind was still full of the
matter. Molly told her two sisters and Lady Sarah
from long habit, because whenever she promised secrecy in any matter she meant, even at the time, to
tell these three. These initiates in their turn told their
cronies until it was widely known that the temperate,
cynical, aloof, impeccably dressed, sharply dignified
Mrs. Lyne — Mrs. Lyne who never "went out" in a
general sense but lived in a rarefied and enviable coterie — Mrs. Lyne whose conversation was that of a
highly intelligent man, who always cleverly kept out
of the gossip columns and picture papers, who for
fifteen years had set a high and wholly individual
standard of all that Americans meant by "poise"; this
almost proverbial lady had been picked up by Peter
in the gutter where she had been thrown struggling by
two bouncers from the cinema where she had created
a drunken disturbance.

It could scarcely have been more surprising had it
been Mrs. Stitch herself. It was indeed barely credible

and many refused to believe it. Drugs possibly, they conceded, but Drink was out of the question. What Parsnip and Pimpernell were to the intelligentsia, Mrs. Lyne and the bottle became to the fashionable world: topic number one.

They were still topic number one three weeks later at Peter's wedding. Basil persuaded Angela to come to the little party with which Lady Granchester honoured the occasion.

He had gone round to see her when Peter told him the news; not immediately, but within twenty-four hours of hearing it. He found her up and dressed, but indefinably raffish in appearance; her make-up was haphazard and rather garish, like a later Utrillo.

"Angela, you look awful."

"Yes, darling, I feel awful. You're in the Army!"

"No, the War Office."

She began talking intensely and rather wildly about the French. Presently she said, "I must leave you for a minute," and went into her bedroom. She came back half a minute later with an abstracted little smile; the inwardly happy smile of a tired old nun — almost. There was a difference.

"Angela," said Basil, "if you want a drink you might drink fair with a chap."

"I don't know what you mean," she said.

Basil was shocked. There had never been any humbug about Angela before, none where he was concerned anyway.

"Oh, come off it," he said.

Angela came off it. She began to weep.

"Oh, for Christ's sake," said Basil.

He went into her bedroom and helped himself to whiskey from the bottle by the bed.

"Peter was here the other evening with some girl. I suppose they've told everyone."

"He told *me*. Why don't you switch to rum? It's much better for you."

"Is it? I don't think I've ever tasted it. Should I like it?"

"I'll send you some round. When did you start on this bat?"

There was no humbug about Angela now. "Oh, weeks ago."

"It's not a bit like you."

"Isn't it, Basil? Isn't it?"

"You were always bloody to me when I had a bat."

"Yes, I suppose I was. I'm sorry. But then you see I was in love with you."

"Was?"

"Oh, I don't know. Fill up the glasses, Basil."

"That's the girl."

" 'Was' is wrong. I do love you, Basil."

"Of course you do. Is that how you take it?" he asked, respectfully.

"That's how I take it."

"Good and strong."

"Good and strong."

"But I think we'd be better suited to rum."

"Doesn't it smell rather?"

"I don't see it matters."

"Don't want to smell."

"Whiskey smells."

"Well, I suppose it doesn't matter. It's nice drinking with you, Basil."

"Of course it's nice. I think it's pretty mean of you to drink without me as you've been doing."

"I'm not mean."

"You usen't to be. But you have been lately, haven't you? Drinking by yourself."

"Yes, that was mean."

"Now listen, next time you want to go on a bat, let me know. Just ring me up and I'll come round. Then we can drink together."

"But I want to so often, Basil."

"Well, I'll come round often. Promise me."

"I promise."

"That's the girl."

The rum was a failure, but in general the new arrangement worked well. Angela drank a good deal less and Basil a good deal more than they had done for the last few weeks and both were happier as a result.

Margot tackled Basil on the matter. "What's the matter with her?" she asked.

"She doesn't like the war."

"Well, no one does."

"Don't they? I can't think why not. Anyway why shouldn't the girl have a drink?"

"You don't think we ought to get her into a home?"

"Good God no."

"But she sees nobody."

"She sees me."

"Yes, but . . ."

"Honestly, Margot, Angela's fine. A little break like this is what she's been needing all these years. I'll make her come to the wedding if you like and you can see for yourself."

So Angela came to the wedding. She and Basil did not make the church but they came to the little party at Lady Granchester's house afterwards, and stole the scene. Molly had had her moment of prominence; she had had her double line of troopers and her arch of cavalry sabres; she had had her veil of old lace. In spite of the war it was a pretty wedding. But at her mother's house all eyes were on Mrs. Lyne. Even Lady Anchorage and the Duchess of Stayle could not dissemble their interest.

"My dear, *there she is*."

There she was, incomparably dressed, standing by Basil, talking gravely to Sonia; she wore dark glasses; otherwise there was nothing unusual about her. A footman brought a tray of champagne. "Is there such a thing as a cup of tea?" she said. "Without cream or sugar."

Molly and Peter stood at one end of the long drawing-room, Angela at the other. As the guests filed past the bride and bridegroom and came into the straight, you could see them come to the alert at the sight of Angela and draw one another's attention to her. Her own coterie formed round her and she talked like a highly intelligent man. When the last of the guests had shaken hands with them — they were comparatively few — Molly and Peter joined the group at the far end.

"Molly, you are the prettiest girl I've ever seen," said Angela. "I'm afraid I was a bore the other night."

A silly girl would have been embarrassed and said, "No, not at all." Molly said, "Not a *bore*. You were rather odd."

"Yes," said Angela. " 'Odd' is the word. I'm not always like that, you know."

"May Peter and I come and see you again? He's only got a week, you know, and then we shall be in London."

"That's an unusually good girl Peter's picked for himself," said Angela to Basil when they were alone after the party at her flat. "You ought to marry someone like that."

"I could never marry anyone, except, I suppose, you."

"No, I don't believe you could, Basil."

When their glasses were filled she said, "I seem to be getting to the age when I enjoy weddings. I liked that girl this afternoon. D'you know who was here this morning? Cedric."

"How very odd."

"It was rather touching really. He came to say good-bye. He's off to-morrow. He couldn't say where, but I guess it's Norway. I never thought of him as a soldier, somehow, but he used to be one till he married me — a very bad one I believe. Poor Cedric, he's had a raw deal."

"He's not done so badly. He's enjoyed himself messing about with grottoes. And he's had Nigel."

"He brought Nigel this morning. They gave him a day away from school to say good-bye. You never knew Cedric when I married him. He was most romantic — genuinely. I'd never met anyone like him. Father's friends were all hard-boiled and rich — men like Metroland and Copper. They were the only people I ever saw. And then I met Cedric who was poor and very, very soft-boiled and tall and willowy and very unhappy in a boring smart regiment because he only cared about Russian ballet and baroque architecture. He had the most charming manner and he was always laughing up his sleeve about people like my father and his officers in the regiment. Poor Cedric, it used to be such fun finding things to give him. I bought him an octopus once and we had a case made for its tank, carved with dolphins and covered with silver leaf."

"It wouldn't have lasted, even if I hadn't come along."

"No, it wouldn't have lasted. I'm afraid the visit this morning was rather a disappointment to him. He'd planned it all in an attitude of high tragedy, and, my dear, I had such a hangover I had to keep my eyes shut nearly all the time he was here. He's worried about what will happen to the house if he gets killed."

"Why should he get killed?"

"Why, indeed? Except that he was always such a bad soldier. You know, when the war started I quite made up my mind you were for it."

"So did my mother. But I'm taking care of that. Which reminds me I ought to go and see Colonel Plum again. He'll be getting restive. I'll go along now."

"Will he be there?"

"He never leaves. A very conscientious officer."

Susie was there, too, waiting till the Colonel was free to take her out to dinner. At the sight of the office, some of Basil's elation began to fade away. Basil's job at the War Office looked as if it were going the way of all the others; once secured, it had few attractions for him. Susie was proving a disappointment; in spite of continued remonstrance, she still seemed to prefer Colonel Plum.

"Good evening, handsome," she said. "Plummy has been asking for you."

Basil went through the door marked KEEP OUT.

"Good evening, Colonel."

"You can call me 'sir.'"

"None of the best regiments call their commanding officers 'sir.' "

"You're not in one of the best regiments. You're General Service. What have you been doing all day?"

"You don't think it will improve the tone of the Department if I called you 'Colonel,' sir?"

"I do not. Where have you been and what have you been doing?"

"You think I've been drinking, don't you?"

"I bloody well know you have."

"But you don't know the reason. You wouldn't understand if I told you. I've been drinking out of chivalry. That doesn't make any sense to you, does it?"

"No."

"I thought it wouldn't. Coarse-grained, sir. If they put on my grave, 'He drank out of chivalry' it would simply be the sober truth. But you wouldn't understand. What's more you think I've been idle, don't you?"

"I do."

"Well, sir, that's where you're wrong. I have been following up a very interesting trail. I hope to have some valuable information very soon."

"What have you got up to date?"

"You wouldn't sooner wait until I can give you the whole case cut-and-dried?"

"No."

"Well, I'm on to a very dangerous woman who calls herself Green. Among her intimates she's known as

'Poppet.' She pretends to be a painter, but you have only to look at her work to realize it is a cloak for other activities. Her studio is the meeting place for a Communist cell. She has an agent in the United States named Parsnip; he has the alias of Pimpernell; he puts it about that he is a poet, two poets in fact, but there again, the work betrays him. Would you like me to quote some Parsnip to you?"

"No."

"I have reason to believe that Green is the head of an underground organization by which young men of military age are smuggled out of the country. Those are the lines I have been working on. What d'you think of them?"

"Rotten."

"I was afraid you might say that. It's your own fault. Give me time and I would have had a better story."

"Now you can do some work. Here's a list of thirty-three addresses of suspected fascists. Check them up."

"Now?"

"Now."

"Shan't I keep track of the woman Green?"

"Not in office hours."

"I can't think what you see in your Plum," said Basil when he regained the outer office. "It must simply be snobbery."

"It's not: it's love. The officer in the Pensions office was a full Colonel, so there."

"I expect you'll be reduced to subalterns, yet. And

by the way, Lance-Corporal, you can call me 'sir.'"

Susie giggled. "I believe you're drunk," she said.

"Drunk with chivalry," said Basil.

That evening Cedric Lyne left to rejoin his regiment. The forty-eight hours of embarkation leave were
over and although he had chosen to start an hour
earlier rather than travel by the special train, it was
only with difficulty that he found a carriage free from
brother officers who had made the same choice. They
were going to the North to embark at dawn next day
and sail straight into action.

The first-class carriage was quite full, four a side, and
the racks piled high with baggage. Black funnel-shaped
shields cast the light onto the passengers' laps; their
faces in the surrounding darkness were indistinguishable; a naval paymaster-commander slept peacefully
in one corner; two civilians strained their eyes over the
evening papers; the other four were soldiers. Cedric
sat between two soldiers, stared at the shadowy luggage
above the civilians' heads, and ruminated, chewing the
last, bitter essence from the events of the last two days.

Because he was thirty-five years of age, and spoke
French and was built rather for grace than smartness,
they had made Cedric battalion Intelligence officer.
He kept the war diary and on wet days was often borrowed by the company commanders to lecture on map
reading, security, and the order of battle of a German
infantry division. These were Cedric's three lectures

When they were exhausted he was sent on a gas course and after that on a course on interpretation of air photographs. On exercise he stuck pins in a map and kept a file of field messages.

"There really isn't very much you can do until we get into action," said his commanding officer. "You might ring up the photographers in Aldershot about taking that regimental group."

They put him in charge of the Officers' Mess and made his visits there hideous with complaints.

"We're out of *Kümmel* again, Cedric."

"Surely there's some perfectly simple way of keeping the soup hot, Lyne."

"If officers *will* take the papers to their quarters, the only answer is to order more papers."

"The Stilton has been allowed to go dry again."

That had been his life; but Nigel did not know this. For Nigel, at eight years of age, his father was a man at arms and a hero. When they were given embarkation leave, Cedric telephoned to Nigel's head-master and the child met him at their station in the country. Pride in his father and pleasure at an unforeseen holiday made their night at home an enthralling experience for Nigel. The home was given over to empty wards and an idle hospital staff. Cedric and his son stayed in the farm where, before she left, Angela had fitted up a few rooms with furniture from the house. Nigel was full of questions; why Cedric's buttons were differently arranged from the fathers' and brothers'

buttons of most of the fellows; what was the difference between a Bren and a Vickers; how much faster
were our fighters than the Germans'; whether Hitler
had fits, as one fellow said, and, if so, did he froth at
the mouth and roll his eyes as the girl at the lodge had
once done?

That evening, Cedric took a long farewell of his water garden. It was for the water principally that he and
Angela had chosen the place, ten years ago, when they
were first engaged. It rose in a clear and copious spring
in the hillside above the house and fell in a series of
natural cascades to join the considerable stream which
flowed more solemnly through the park. He and Angela had eaten a picnic lunch by this spring and looked
down on the symmetrical, rectangular building below.

"It'll do," said Angela. "I'll offer them fifteen thousand."

It never embarrassed Cedric to be married to a rich
woman. He had not married for money in any gross
sense, but he loved the rare and beautiful things which
money could buy, and Angela's great fortune made
her trebly rare and beautiful in his eyes.

It was surprising that they should have met at all.
Cedric had been for years in his regiment, kept there
by his father, who gave him an allowance, which he
could ill spare, on that condition alone. It was that or
an office for Cedric, and despite the tedious company,
there was just enough pageantry about peace-time
soldiering to keep his imagination engaged. Cedric

was accomplished; he was a beautiful horseman but hated the rigours of fox-hunting; he was a very fine shot and because that formed a single tenuous bond with his brother officers and because it was agreeable to do anything pre-eminently well, he accepted invitations to pheasant-shooting in houses where, when they were not at the coverts, he felt lost and lonely. Angela's father had a celebrated shoot in Norfolk; he had also, Cedric was told, a collection of French impressionists. Thither that autumn ten years ago Cedric had gone and had found the pictures too obvious and the birds too tame and the party tedious beyond description, except for Angela, past her debutante days, aloof now and living in a cool and mysterious solitude of her own creation. She had resisted at first every attempt on the defences she had built up against a noisy world and then, quite suddenly, she had accepted Cedric as being like herself a stranger in these parts, as being, unlike herself, full of understanding of another, more splendid, attainable world outside. Angela's father thought Cedric a poor fellow, settled vast sums on them, and let them go their own way.

And this was the way they had gone. Cedric stood by the spring, enshrined, now, in a little temple. The architrave was covered with stalactites, the dome was set with real shells and the clear water bubbled out from the feet of a Triton. Cedric and Angela had bought this temple on their honeymoon at a deserted villa in the hills behind Naples.

Below in the hillside lay the cave which Cedric had
bought the summer that Angela had refused to come
with him to Salzburg; the summer when she met Basil.
The lonely and humiliating years after that summer
each had its monument.

"Daddy, what are you waiting for?"

"I'm just looking at the grottoes."

"But you've seen them thousands of times. They're
always the same."

Always the same; joys for ever; not like men and
women with their loves and hates.

"Daddy, there's an aeroplane. Is it a Hurricane?"

"No, Nigel, a Spitfire."

"How d'you tell the difference?"

Then, on an impulse, he had said, "Nigel, shall we
go to London and see Mummy?"

"We might see 'The Lion Has Wings' too. The fellows say it's awfully decent."

"All right, Nigel, we'll see both."

So the two of them went to London by the early
morning train. "Let's surprise her," said Nigel, but
Cedric telephoned first, wryly remembering the story
of the pedantic adulterer — "My dear, it is *I* who am
surprised; you are *astounded*."

"I am coming round to see Mrs. Lyne."

"She isn't very well this morning."

"I'm sorry to hear that. Is she able to see people?"

"Yes, I think so, sir. I'll ask . . . yes, madam will be
very pleased to see you and Master Nigel."

They had not met for three years, since they had discussed the question of divorce. Cedric understood exactly what Angela had felt about that; it was curious, he reflected, how some people were shy of divorce because of their love of society; they did not want there to be any occasion when their presence might be an embarrassment, they wanted to keep their tickets for the Ascot enclosure. With Angela reluctance came from precisely the opposite motives; she could not brook any intrusion of her privacy; she did not want to answer questions in court or allow the daily paper a single item of information about herself. "It's not as though you wanted to marry anyone else, Cedric."

"You don't think the present arrangement makes me look rather foolish?"

"Cedric, what's come over you? You used not to talk like that."

So he had given way and that year had spanned the stream with a bridge in the Chinese Taste, taken direct from Batty Langley.

In the five minutes of waiting before Grainger took him into Angela's bedroom, he studied David Lennox's grisailles with distaste.

"Are they old, Daddy?"

"No, Nigel, they're not old."

"They're awfully feeble."

"They are." (Regency . . . This was the age of Waterloo and highwaymen and duelling and slavery

and revivalist preaching and Nelson having his arm off
with no anesthetic but rum, and Botany Bay — and
this is what they make of it.)

"Well, I prefer the pictures at home, even if they
are old. Is that Mummy?"

"Yes."

"Is that old?"

"Older than you, Nigel."

Cedric turned from the portrait of Angela. What a
nuisance John had been about the sittings! It was her
father who had insisted on their going to him.

"Is it finished?"

"Yes. It was very hard to make the man finish it,
though."

"It hardly looks finished now, does it, Daddy? It's all
sploshy."

Then Grainger opened the door. "Come in, Cedric,"
Angela called from her bed.

Angela was wearing dark glasses. Her make-up things
lay on the quilt before her, with which she had been
hastily doing her face. Nigel might have asked if it was
finished; it was sploshy, like the John portrait.

"I had no idea you were ill," said Cedric stiffly.

"I'm not really. Nigel, haven't you got a kiss for
Mummy?"

"Why are you wearing those glasses?"

"My eyes are tired, darling."

"Tired of what?"

"Cedric," said Angela petulantly, "for God's sake don't let him be a bore. Go with Miss Grainger into the next room, darling."

"Oh, all right," said Nigel. "Don't be long, Daddy."

"You and he seem to be buddies these days."

"Yes, it's the uniform."

"Funny your being in the Army again."

"I'm off to-night, abroad."

"France?"

"I don't think so. I mustn't tell about it. That's why I came to see you."

"About not talking about not going to France?" said Angela in something of her old teasing way.

Cedric began to talk about the house; he hoped Angela would keep on to it, even if anything happened to him; he thought he saw some glimmerings of taste in the boy; he might grow to appreciate it later. Angela was inattentive and answered absently.

"I'm afraid I'm tiring you."

"Well, I'm not feeling terribly well to-day. Did you want to see me about anything special?"

"No I don't think so. Just to say good-bye."

"Daddy," came a voice from the next room. "Aren't you coming?"

"Oh dear, I wish I could do something about it. I feel there's something I ought to do. It's quite an occasion really, isn't it? I'm not being beastly, Cedric, I really mean it. I think it's sweet of you to come. I only wish I felt up to doing something about it."

"Daddy, come on. We want to get to Bassett and Lowkes before lunch."

"Take care of yourself," said Angela.

"Why?"

"Oh, I don't know. Why will you all ask questions?"

And that had been the end of the visit. At Bassett and Lowkes, Nigel had chosen a model of a Blenheim bomber. "The fellows *will* be jealous," he said.

After luncheon they went to see "The Lion Has Wings," and then it was time to put Nigel into the train back to school. "It's been absolutely ripping, Daddy," he said.

"Has it really?"

"The rippingest two days I ever spent."

So after these ripping days Cedric sat in the half-dark, with the pool of light falling on the unread book on his knees, returning to duty.

Basil went to the Café Royal to keep his watch on "the woman Green." He found her sitting among her cronies and was greeted with tepid affection.

"So you're in the Army, now," she said.

"No, the great uniformed bureaucracy. How are all the Reds?"

"Very well thank you, watching your imperialists making a mess of your war."

"Been to many Communist meetings lately?"

"Why?"

"Just wondering."

"You sound like a police spy."

"That's the very last impression I want to make," and, changing the subject hastily, added, "Seen Ambrose lately?"

"He's over there now, the lousy fascist."

Basil looked where she indicated and saw Ambrose at a table by the rail of the opposing gallery, sitting with a little, middle-aged man of nondescript appearance.

"Did you say 'fascist'?"

"Didn't you know? He's gone to the Ministry of Information and he's bringing out a fascist paper next month."

"This is very interesting," said Basil. "Tell me some more."

Ambrose sat, upright and poised, with one hand on the stem of his glass and one resting stylishly on the balustrade. There was no particular feature of his clothes which could be mentioned as conspicuous; he wore a dark, smooth suit that fitted perhaps a little closely at waist and wrists, a shirt of plain, cream-coloured silk; a dark, white spotted bow tie; his sleek black hair was not unduly long (he went to the same barber as Alastair and Peter); his pale Semitic face gave no hint of special care, and yet it always embarrassed Mr. Bentley somewhat to be seen with him in public. Sitting there, gesticulating very slightly as he talked, wagging his head very slightly, raising his voice occasionally in a suddenly stressed uncommon epithet or in a fragment of slang absurdly embedded in his precise

and literary diction, giggling between words now and
then as something which he had intended to say
changed shape and became unexpectedly comic in the
telling — Ambrose, like this, caused time to slip back
to an earlier age than his own youth or Mr. Bentley's,
when amid a more splendid décor of red plush and gilt
caryatides *fin-de-siècle* young worshippers crowded to
the tables of Oscar and Aubrey.

Mr. Bentley smoothed his sparse grey hairs and
fidgeted with his tie and looked about anxiously for
fear he was observed.

The Café Royal, perhaps because of its distant as-
sociations with Oscar and Aubrey, was one of the places
where Ambrose preened himself, spread his feathers
and felt free to take wing. He had left his persecution
mania downstairs with his hat and umbrella. He defied
the universe.

"The decline of England, my dear Geoffrey," he said,
"dates from the day we abandoned coal fuel. No, I'm
not talking about distressed areas, but about distressed
souls, my dear. We used to live in a fog, the splendid,
luminous, tawny fogs of our early childhood. The
golden aura of the golden age. Think of it, Geoffrey,
there are children now coming to manhood who never
saw a London fog. We designed a city which was meant
to be seen in a fog. We had a foggy habit of life and a
rich, obscure, choking literature. The great catch in
the throat of English lyric poetry is just *fog*, my dear,
on the vocal cords. And out of the fog we could rule

the world; we were a Voice, like the Voice on Sinai smiling through the clouds. Primitive peoples always choose a God who speaks from a cloud. *Then* my dear Geoffrey," said Ambrose, wagging an accusing finger and fixing Mr. Bentley with a black accusing eye, as though the poor publisher were personally responsible for the whole thing, "*then,* some busybody invents electricity or oil fuel or whatever it is they use nowadays. The fog lifts, the world sees us as we are, and worse still we see ourselves as we are. It was a carnival ball, my dear, which when the guests unmasked at midnight was found to be composed entirely of impostors. Such a *rumpus*, my dear."

Ambrose drained his glass with a swagger, surveyed the café haughtily and saw Basil, who was making his way towards them.

"We are talking of Fogs," said Mr. Bentley.

"They're eaten hollow with Communism," said Basil, introducing himself in the part of *agent provocateur*. "You can't stop a rot that's been going on twenty years by imprisoning a handful of deputies. Half the thinking men in France have begun looking to Germany as their real ally."

"*Please* Basil, don't start politics. Anyway we were talking of Fogs, not Frogs."

"Oh, Fogs." Basil attempted to tell of a foggy adventure of his own, sailing a yawl round Bear Island, but Ambrose was elated to-night and in no mood for these loose leaves of Conrad drifting in the high wind of his talk. "We must return to the Present," he said prophetically.

"Oh dear," said Mr. Bentley. "Why?"

"Everyone is either looking back or forward. Those with reverence and good taste, like you, my dear Geoffrey, look back to an Augustan Age; those with generous hearts and healthy lives and the taste of the devil, like Poppet Green over there, look forward to a Marxian Jerusalem. We must accept the Present."

"You would say, wouldn't you," said Basil, persevering, "that Hitler was a figure of the Present?"

"I regard him as a page for *Punch*," said Ambrose. "To the Chinese scholar the military hero was the lowest of human types, the subject for ribaldry. We must return to Chinese scholarship."

"It's a terribly difficult language, I believe," said Mr. Bentley.

"I knew a Chink in Valparaiso . . ." began Basil; but Ambrose was now in full gallop.

"European scholarship has never lost its monastic character," he said. "Chinese scholarship deals with taste and wisdom, not with the memorizing of facts. In China the man whom we make a don sat for the Imperial examinations and became a bureaucrat. Their scholars were lonely men of few books and fewer pupils, content with a single concubine, a pine tree and the prospect of a stream. European culture has become conventual; we must make it coenobitic."

"I knew a hermit in the Ogaden Desert once . . ."

"Invasions swept over China; the Empire split up into warring kingdoms. The scholars lived their frugal and idyllic lives undisturbed, occasionally making exquisite private jokes which they wrote on leaves and floated downstream."

"I read a lot of Chinese poetry once," said Mr. Bentley, "in the translation, of course. I became fascinated by it. I would read of a sage who, as you say, lived frugally and idyllically. He had a cottage and a garden and a view. Each flower had its proper mood and phase of the climate; he would smell the jasmine after recovering from the toothache and the lotus when drinking tea with a monk. There was a little clearing where the full moon cast no shadow, where his concubine would sit and sing to him when he got drunk. Every aspect of this little garden corresponded to some personal mood of the most tender and refined sort. It was quite intoxicating to read."

"It is."

"This sage had no tame dog, but he had a cat and a mother. Every morning he greeted his mother on his knees and every evening, in winter, he put charcoal under her mattress and himself drew the bed-curtains. It sounded the most exquisite existence."

"It was."

"And then," said Mr. Bentley, "I found a copy of the *Daily Mirror* in a railway carriage and I read an article there by Godfrey Winn about his cottage and his flowers and his moods, and for the life of me, Ambrose, I couldn't see the difference between that young gentleman and Yuan Ts'e-tsung."

It was cruel of Mr. Bentley to say this, but it may be argued for him that he had listened to Ambrose for three hours and now that Basil had joined their table he wanted to go home to bed.

The interruption deflated Ambrose and allowed Basil to say, "These scholars of yours, Ambrose — they didn't care if their empire was invaded?"

"Not a hoot, my dear, not a *tinker's* hoot."

"And you're starting a paper to encourage this sort of scholarship."

Basil sat back and ordered a drink, as an advocate in a film will relax, saying in triumph, "Mr. District Attorney, *your* witness."

There were four hours of darkness to go when Cedric arrived at the port of embarkation. There was a glimmer of light in some of the offices along the quayside, but the quay itself and the ship were in complete darkness; the top-hamper was just discernible as a darker mass against the dark sky. An E.S.O. told Cedric to leave his gear on the quay. The advanced working party were handling that. He left his valise and carried his suitcase up the gangway; at the head an invisible figure directed him to the first-class quarters forward. He found his C.O. in the saloon.

"Hullo, Lyne. You're back already. Lucky. Billy Allgood broke his collar-bone on leave and isn't coming

with us. You'd better take charge of the embarkation.
There's a hell of a lot to do. Some blasted Highlanders
have come to the wrong ship and are all over our troop
decks. Had any dinner?"

"I got some oysters in London before starting."

"Very wise. I tried to get something kept hot. Told
them we should all be coming on board hungry, but
they're still working peace-time routine here. This is all
I could raise."

He pointed to a large, silvery tray where, disposed on
a napkin, lay a dozen lozenges of toast covered with
sardines, slivers of cheese and little glazed pieces of
tongue. This was the tray that was always brought to
the first-class saloon at ten o'clock at night.

"Come back when you've found your cabin."

Cedric found his cabin, perfectly in order, complete
with three towels of different sizes and the photograph
of a moustached man putting on his life jacket in the
correct manner. He left his suitcase and returned to
the C.O.

"Our men will be coming on board in an hour and
a half. I don't know what the devil these Highlanders
are doing. Find out and clear them off."

"Very good, Colonel."

Cedric plunged down again into the darkness and
found the E.S.O. They studied the embarkation orders
with the aid of a dimmed torch. There was no doubt
about it; the Highlanders were in the wrong ship. This
was the *Duchess of Cumberland*; they should be in the

Duchess of Clarence. "But the *Clarence* isn't here,"
said the E.S.O. "I daresay they were told to go to the
Cumberland by someone."

"By whom?"

"Not by me, old man," said the E.S.O.

Cedric went on board and looked for the C.O. of
the Highlanders and found him at length in his cabin
asleep in his battle-dress.

"These are my orders," said the Highland Colonel,
taking a sheaf of typewritten sheets from the pocket
on his thigh. They were already tattered and smeared
by constant reference. " '*Duchess of Cumberland.* Embark 2300 hrs. with full 1098 stores.' That's plain
enough."

"But our men come on board in an hour."

"Can't help you, I'm afraid. These are my orders."

He was not going to discuss the matter with a subaltern. Cedric fetched his C.O. Colonel to Colonel, they
talked the thing out and decided to clear the after
troop-decks. Cedric was sent to wake the Highland
duty officer. He found the duty Sergeant. Together
they went aft to the troop-decks.

There were dim lights along the ceiling — electric
bulbs recently daubed with blue paint, not yet scratched
clear by the troops. Equipment and kit-bags lay about
the deck in heaps; there were Bren gun boxes and ammunition and the huge coffin-shaped chests of the anti-
tank rifles.

"Oughtn't that to be stored in the armoury?" asked Cedric.

"Not unless you want to get it pinched."

Amid the heaps of stores half a battalion lay huddled in blankets. Very few of them, on this first night, had slung hammocks. These lay with the other gear, adding to the piles.

"We'll never get them moved to-night."

"We've got to try," said Cedric.

Very slowly the inert mass was got into movement. They began collecting their own gear and swearing monotonously. Working parties began man-handling the stores. They had to go up the ladders onto the main deck, forward through the darkness and down the forward hatches.

Presently a voice from the top of the ladder said, "Is Lyne down there?"

"Yes."

"I've been told to bring my company to this troop-deck."

"They'll have to wait."

"They're coming on board now."

"Well for God's sake stop them."

"But isn't this D deck?"

"Yes."

"Then this is where we are to come to. Who the hell are all these men?"

Cedric went up the ladder and to the head of the gangway. A stream of heavily laden men of his regiment were toiling up. "Go back," ordered Cedric.

"Who the hell's that?" asked a voice from the darkness.

"Lyne. Take your men back to the quay. They can't come on board yet."

"Oh but they've got to. D'you realize half of them've had nothing to eat since midday?"

"There's nothing to eat here till breakfast."

"Oh, but, I say, what rot. The R.T.O. at Euston said he'd telegraph through and have a hot meal ready on arrival. Where's the Colonel?"

The line of soldiers on the gangway turned about and began a slow descent. When the last of them was on the quay, invisible in the darkness, their officer came on board.

"You seem to have made a pretty good muck-up," he said.

The deck was full of the other regiment carrying stores.

"There's a man there smoking," shouted a ship's officer from above. "Put that cigarette out."

Matches began to spurt up on the quay. "Put those cigarettes out, down there."

"——y well travelling all the ——ing day. No ——ing supper. ——ed about on the ——ing quay. Now a —— won't let me have a ——ing smoke. I'm ——ing ——ed with being ——ed about by these ——ers."

A dark figure passed Cedric muttering desperately:

"Nominal rolls in triplicate. Nominal rolls in triplicate. Why the devil can't they tell us beforehand they want nominal rolls in triplicate?"

Another dark figure, whom Cedric recognized as the E.S.O. . . .

"I say, the men are supposed to strip down their equipment and pack it in green sea-bags before embarking."

"Oh," said Cedric.

"They don't seem to have done it."

"Oh."

"It upsets all the storage arrangements if they don't."

"Oh."

An orderly came up. "Mr. Lyne, sir, will you go and see the C.O.?"

Cedric went.

"Look here Lyne, aren't those infernal Scotsmen out of our troop-deck yet? I ordered that deck to be clear two hours ago. I thought you were looking after that."

"I'm sorry, Colonel. They're getting a move on now."

"I should bloody well hope so. And look here, half our men have had nothing to eat all day. Go up to the purser and see what you can rout out for them. And find out on the bridge exactly what the sailing orders are. When the troops come on board see that everyone knows where everything is. We don't want anything lost. We may be in action before the end of the week. I hear these Highlanders lost a lot of kit on the way up.

We don't want them making up deficiencies at our expense."

"Very good, sir."

As he went out on deck the ghostly figure brushed past him in the darkness muttering in tones that seemed to echo from another and even worse world, "Nominal rolls in triplicate. Nominal rolls in triplicate . . ."

At seven o'clock the Colonel said, "For God's sake someone take over from Lyne. He seems to have lain down on the job."

Cedric went to his cabin; he was unspeakably tired; all the events and emotions of the last forty-eight hours were lost in the single longing for sleep; he took off his belt and his shoes and lay on his bunk. Within a quarter of a minute he was unconscious; within five minutes he was awakened by a steward placing a tray by his side; it contained tea, an apple, a thin slice of brown bread and butter. That was how the day always began on this ship, whether she was cruising to the midnight sun or the West Indies. An hour later another steward passed by, striking a musical gong with a little hammer. That was the second stage of the day in this ship. He passed, tinkling prettily, through the first-class quarters, threading his path delicately between valises and kit-bags. Unshaven, ill-tempered officers, who had not been asleep all night, scowled at him as he passed. Nine months ago the ship had been in the Mediterranean and a hundred cultured spinsters had welcomed his music. It was all one to him.

After breakfast the Colonel saw all his officers in the smoking-room. "We've got to get everything out of the ship," he said. "It's got to be loaded tactically. We shan't be sailing until to-night anyway. I've just seen the Captain and he says he isn't fuelled yet. Also we're overloaded and he insists on our putting two hundred men ashore. Also, there's a field hospital coming on board this morning, that we've got to find room for. There is also Field Security Police, Field Force Institute, N.A.A.F.I., two Pay Corps officers, four chaplains, a veterinary surgeon, a press photographer, a naval beach party, some Marine anti-aircraft gunners, an air support liaison unit — whatever that is — and a detachment of Sappers to be accommodated. All ranks are confined to the ship. There will be no communication of any kind with the shore. Duty company will find sentries for the post and telephone boxes on the quay. That's all, gentlemen."

Everyone said, "Lyne made a nonsense of the embarkation."

5. WHEN MR. BENTLEY, in the first flush of patriotic zeal, left publishing and took service with the Ministry of Information, it was agreed between him and the senior partner that his room should be kept for his use and that he should

come in whenever he could to keep an eye on his interests. Mr. Rampole, the senior partner, would see to the routine of the office.

Rampole and Bentley was not a large or a very prosperous firm; it owed its continued existence largely to the fact that both partners had a reasonable income derived from other sources. Mr. Bentley was a publisher because ever since he was a boy, he had had a liking for books; he thought them a Good Thing; the more of them the merrier. Wider acquaintance had not increased his liking for authors, whom he found as a class avaricious, egotistical, jealous and ungrateful, but he had always the hope that one day one of these disagreeable people would turn out to be a messiah of genius. And he liked the books themselves; he liked to see in the window of the office the dozen bright covers which were that season's new titles; he liked the sense of vicarious authorship which this spectacle gave him. Not so old Rampole. Mr. Bentley often wondered why his senior partner had ever taken to publishing and why, once disillusioned, he persisted in it. Old Rampole deplored the propagation of books. "It won't do," he always said whenever Mr. Bentley produced a new author, "no one ever reads first novels."

Once or twice a year old Rampole himself introduced an author, always with well-justified forecasts of the book's failure. "Terrible thing," he would say. "Met old So-and-so at the club. Got button-holed. Fellow's just retired from Malay States. Written his reminiscences. We shall have to do them for him. No getting out of it now. One comfort, he won't ever write another book."

That was one superiority he had over Mr. Bentley which he was fond of airing. His authors never came back for more, like Mr. Bentley's young friends.

The idea of the *Ivory Tower* was naturally repugnant to old Rampole. "I've never known a literary review succeed yet," he said.

He had a certain grudging regard for Ambrose because he was one of the few writers on their list who were incontestably profitable. Other writers always involved an argument, Mr. Bentley having an ingenious way of explaining over-advances and overhead charges and stock in hand in such a way that he seemed to prove that obvious failures had indeed succeeded. But Ambrose's books sold fifteen thousand copies. He didn't like the fellow but he had to concede him a certain knack of writing. It shocked him that Ambrose should be so blind to his own interests as to propose such a scheme.

"Has the fellow got money?" he asked Mr. Bentley privately.

"Very little, I think."

"Then what is he thinking of? What's he *after*?"

To Ambrose he said, "But a literary review, now of all times!"

"Now *is* the time of all times," said Ambrose. "Don't you *see*?"

"No, I don't. Costs are up and going higher. Can't get paper. Who'll want to read this magazine anyway? It isn't a woman's paper. It isn't, as I see it, a man's. It isn't even topical. Who's going to advertise in it?"

"I wasn't thinking of having advertisements. I thought of making it something like the old *Yellow Book*."

"Well, that was a failure," said old Rampole triumphantly, "in the end."

But presently he gave his consent. He always gave his consent in the end to all Mr. Bentley's suggestions. That was the secret of their long partnership. He had registered his protest. No one could blame him. It was all Bentley's doing. Often he had opposed Mr. Bentley's projects out of habit, on the widest grounds that publication of any kind was undesirable. In the case of the *Ivory Tower* he stood on firm ground and knew it. It gave him positive satisfaction to detect his partner in such indefensible folly. So Mr. Bentley's room, which was the most ornamental in the fine old building which they used as their offices, became the editorial room of Ambrose's paper.

There was not, at this stage, much editorial work to be done.

"There's one criticism I foresee," said Mr. Bentley, studying the proof sheets: "the entire issue seems to be composed by yourself."

"No one's to guess that," said Ambrose. "If you like we'll put some pseudonyms in." Ambrose had always rather specialized in manifestoes. He had written one at school; he had written a dozen at the University; once, in the late twenties, he and his friends Hat and Malpractice had even issued the invitation to a party in the form of a manifesto. It was one of his many reasons for shunning Communism — that its manifesto had been written for it, once and for all, by somebody else. Surrounded, as he believed himself to be, by enemies of all kinds, Ambrose found it exhilarating from time to time to trumpet his defiance. The first number of the *Ivory Tower* somewhat belied the serenity and seclusion which it claimed, for Ambrose had a blow for every possible windmill.

"The Minstrel Boys, or *Ivory Tower* v. *Manhattan Skyscraper*" defined once and for all Ambrose's attitude in the great Parsnip-Pimpernell controversy. "Hermit or Choirmaster" was an expansion of Ambrose's theme at the Café Royal: "Culture must be coenobitic not conventual." He struck ferocious unprovoked blows at those who held that literature was of value to the community. Mr. J. B. Priestley came in for much personal abuse in these pages. There followed "The Bakelite Tower," an onslaught on David Lennox and the decorative school of fashionable artists. "Majors and Mandarins" followed, where was defined the proper degrees of contempt and abhorrence due to the military, and among the military Ambrose included by name all statesmen of an energetic and warlike disposition.

"It's all very controversial," said Mr. Bentley sadly. "When you first told me about it, I thought you meant it to be a purely artistic paper."

"We must show people where we stand," said Ambrose. "Art will follow — anyway, there's 'Monument to a Spartan.'"

"Yes," said Mr. Bentley. "There's that."

"It covers fifty pages, my dear. All Pure Art."

He said this with a facetious, shop assistant's intonation as though he were saying "All Pure Silk"; he said it as though it were a joke, but in his heart he believed — and he knew Mr. Bentley understood him in this sense — he was speaking the simple truth. It *was* all pure art.

He had written it two years ago on his return from Munich after his parting with Hans. It was the story of Hans. Now, after the passage of two years, he could not read it without tears. To publish it was a symbolic action of the laying down of an emotional burden he had carried too long.

"Monument to a Spartan" described Hans, as Ambrose had loved him, in every mood; Hans immature, the provincial petit-bourgeois youth floundering and groping in the gloom of Teutonic adolescence, unsuccessful in his examinations, world-weary, brooding about suicide among the conifers, uncritical of direct authority, unreconciled to the order of the universe; Hans affectionate, sentimental, roughly sensual, guilty; above all Hans guilty, haunted by the taboos of the forest; Hans credulous, giving his simple and generous acceptance to all the nonsense of Nazi leaders; Hans reverent to those absurd instructors who harangued the youth camps, resentful at the injustices of man to man, at the plots of the Jews and the encirclement of his country, at the blockade and disarmament; Hans loving his comrades, finding in a deep tribal emotion an escape from the guilt of personal love, Hans singing with his Hitler youth comrades, cutting trees with them, making roads, still loving his old friend, puzzled that he could not fit the old love into the scheme of the new; Hans growing a little older, joining the Brown Shirts, lapped in a kind of benighted chivalry, bemused in a twilight where the demagogues and party hacks loomed and glittered like Wagnerian heroes; Hans faithful to his old friend, like a woodcutter's boy in a fairy tale who sees the whole forest peopled with the great ones of another world and, rubbing his eyes, returns at evening to his hut and his fireside. The Wagnerians shone in Ambrose's story as they did in Hans's eyes. He austerely denied himself any hint of satire. The blustering, cranky, boneheaded party men were all heroes and philosophers. All this Ambrose had recorded with great delicacy and precision at a time when his heart was consumed by the final tragedy. Hans's Storm Troop comrades discover that his friend is a Jew; they have resented this friend before because in their gross minds they know him to represent something personal and private in a world where only the mob and the hunting pack have the right to live. So the mob and the hunting pack fall on Hans's friendship. With a mercy they are far from feeling they save Hans from facing the implications of his discovery. For him, alone, it would have been the great climacteric of his retarded adolescence; the discovery that his own, personal conviction conflicted with the factitious convictions drummed into him by the crooks and humbugs he took for his guides. But the hunting pack and the mob left Hans no time to devise his own, intense punishment; that at least was spared him in the swift and savage onslaught; that was left to Ambrose returning by train to England.

It was a story which a popular writer would have spun out to 150,000 words; Ambrose missed nothing; it was all there, delicately and precisely, in fifty pages of the *Ivory Tower*.

"Quite frankly, Geoffrey, I regard this as a major work of art."

"Yes, Ambrose, I know you do. So do I. I only wish we were publishing it without all the controversial stuff."

"Not controversial, Geoffrey. We invite acceptance, not argument. We are showing our credentials and *laissez-passer*. That's all."

"Old Rampole won't like it," said Mr. Bentley.

"We won't let old Rampole see it," said Ambrose.

"I'm on to a very good thing, Colonel."

"Will you kindly address me as 'sir' in this office?"

"You wouldn't prefer to be called 'chief'?"

"You'll call me 'sir' or get out of that uniform."

"It's funny," said Basil. "I should much sooner be called 'chief.' In fact that's what Susie does call me. However, sir, may I tell you about my discovery?"

When Basil had told him, Colonel Plum said: "That's all right as far as it goes. We can't take any action, of course. This fellow Silk is a well-known writer, working in the Ministry of Information."

"He's a most dangerous type. I know him well. He was living in Munich before the war — never out of the Brown House."

"That's as may be, but this isn't Spain. We can't go arresting people for what they say in a private conversation in a café. I've no doubt we shall come to that eventually, but at the present stage of our struggle for freedom, it just can't be done."

"But this paper he's starting."

"Yes, that's another matter. But Rampole and Bentley are a perfectly respectable little firm. I can't apply for a search warrant until I've got something to go on. We've got pretty wide powers, but we have to be careful how we use them. We'll keep an eye on this paper and if it seems dangerous we'll stop it. Meanwhile get to work. Here's an anonymous denunciation of a retired admiral in South Kensington. There won't be anything in it. See what the police know about him."

"Don't we ever investigate night clubs? I'm sure they're bursting with enemy agents."

Susie said, "I do. You don't."

A quiet day at the Ministry of Information . . . The more energetic neutral correspondents had mostly left the country by now, finding Axis sources a happier hunting-ground for front-page news. The Ministry could get on with its work undisturbed. That afternoon a film was showing in the Ministry theatre; it dealt with otter-hunting and was designed to impress neutral countries with the pastoral beauty of English life. The Religious Department were all keen film-goers. Basil found the room empty. On Ambrose's table lay two sets of galley-proofs of the new magazine. Basil pocketed one of them. There was also a passport; Basil took it up with interest. He had never seen an Irish one before. It was made out for a Father Flanagan, S.J., Professor of Dublin University. The photograph showed a cadaverous face of indeterminate age. Father Flanagan was in his leisure from higher education the correspondent of an Irish newspaper. He wanted to visit the Maginot Line during his vacation and after numerous disappointments had found his way to the Religious Department of the Ministry of Information, where the Roman Catholic director had promised to try and get him a visa. Basil took this too; an additional passport often came in useful. Then he sauntered away.

He took the proofs home and read until dinner, marking a passage here and there as material to his brief. The style throughout was homogeneous but the authors' names were multiform. Ambrose rather let himself go on names: "Hucklebury Squib," "Bartholomew Grass," "Tom Barebones-Abraham." Only "Monument to a Spartan" bore Ambrose's own name. Later that evening Basil sought Ambrose where he was sure to find him, at the Café Royal.

"I've been reading your magazine," he said.

"So it *was* you. I thought one of those nasty Jesuits had stolen it. They're always flapping in and out the Department like jackdaws. Geoffrey Bentley was in a great stew about it. He doesn't want old Rampole to see a copy until the thing's out."

"Why should the Jesuits want to show your magazine to old Rampole?"

"They're up to any mischief. What d'you think of it?"

"Well," said Basil, "I think you might have made it a bit stronger. You know what you want to do is to shock people a bit. That's the way to put a new magazine across. You can't shock people nowadays with sex, of course; I don't mean that. But suppose you had a little poem in praise of Himmler — something like that?"

"I don't believe that would be a good idea; besides as far as I know no one has written a poem like that."

"I daresay I could rake one up for you."

"No," said Ambrose. "What did you think of 'Monument to a Spartan'?"

"All the first part is first-rate. I suppose they made you put on that ending?"

"Who?"

"The Ministry of Information."

"They've had nothing to do with it."

"Haven't they? Well, of course, you know best. I can only say how it reads to an outsider. What I felt was: Here is a first-class work of art; something no one but you could have written. And then, suddenly, it degenerates into mere propaganda. Jolly good propaganda, of course; I wish half the stuff your Ministry turns out was as good — but propaganda. An atrocity story — the sort of stuff American journalists turn out by the ream. It glares a bit, you know, Ambrose. Still, of course, we all have to make sacrifices in war-time. Don't think I don't respect you for it. But artistically, Ambrose, it's shocking."

"Is it?" said Ambrose, dismayed. "Is that how it reads?"

"Leaps to the eye, old boy. Still it ought to give you a leg up in the Department."

"Basil," said Ambrose solemnly, "if I thought that was how people would take it, I'd scrap the whole thing."

"Oh, I shouldn't do that. The first forty-five pages

are grand. Why don't you leave it like that, with Hans still full of his illusions marching into Poland?"

"I might."

"And you could bring Himmler in, just at the end, in a kind of apotheosis of Nazism."

"No."

"Well, Himmler isn't necessary. Just leave Hans in the first exhilaration of victory."

"I'll think about it . . . D'you really mean that intelligent readers would think I was writing propaganda?"

"They couldn't think anything else, old boy, could they?"

A week later, by the simple process of going to Rampole and Bentley's office and asking for one, Basil obtained an advance copy of the new magazine. He turned eagerly to the last page and found that "Monument to a Spartan" now ended as he had suggested; he read it again with relish; to anyone ignorant of Ambrose's private history it bore one plain character — the triumphant paean of Hitler youth; Doctor Ley himself might have been the author. Basil took the magazine with him to the War Office; before approaching Colonel Plum he marked with a red chalk the "Monument to a Spartan" and passages in the preceding articles which cast particular ridicule upon the Army and the War Cabinet and which urged on the artist the duty of non-resistance to violence. Then he laid it on Colonel Plum's desk.

"I think, sir, you promised to make me a Captain of Marines if I caught a fascist."

"It was a figurative expression."

"Meaning what?"

"That you might have done something to excuse your presence in my office. What have you got there?"

"Documentary evidence. A fifth column nest."

"Well, put it down. I'll have a look at it when I've time."

It was not Colonel Plum's habit to show enthusiasm before subordinates, but as soon as Basil was gone he began reading the marked passages with close attention. Presently he called for Basil.

"I believe you're on to something here," he said. "I'm taking this round to Scotland Yard. Who are these men Squib, Grass and Barebones-Abraham?"

"Don't you think they sound like pseudonyms?"

"Nonsense. When a man chooses an alias he calls himself Smith or Brown."

"Have it your own way, sir. I shall be interested to see them in the dock."

"There won't be any dock. We shall get this bunch under a special warrant."

"Shall I come round to Scotland Yard with you?"

"No."

"Just for that I won't introduce him to Barebones·

Abraham," said Basil when the Colonel was gone.

"Have we really caught some fifth column at last?" asked Susie.

"I don't know about 'we'; *I* have."

"Will they be shot?"

"Not all of them I should think."

"Seems a shame really," said Susie. "I expect they're only a bit touched."

In the pleasure of setting his trap, Basil had not looked forward to its consequences. When Colonel Plum returned to his office two hours later, things seemed to have gone far beyond Basil's control. "They're pleased as Punch at Scotland Yard," he said. "Handing out some very handsome bouquets. The whole thing is buttoned-up. We've taken out a special warrant for authors, publishers and printers, but I don't think we need worry the printers much. To-morrow morning the man Silk will be arrested at the Ministry of Information; simultaneously Rampole and Bentley's will be surrounded and entered, all copies of the paper and all correspondence seized. All the office staff will be held pending investigation. What we need now is a description of the men Grass, Squibb and Barebones-Abraham. You might get on to that. I'm going round to see the Home Secretary now."

There was, at first hearing, a lot about this speech which displeased Basil, and more still when he began to turn the thing over in his mind. In the first place Colonel Plum seemed to be getting all the credit and all the fun. It was he himself, Basil felt, who should be going to see the Home Secretary; *he* should have been to Scotland Yard to make arrangements for the morrow's raid; *he* should have had the handsome bouquets of which Colonel Plum had spoken. It was not for this that he had planned the betrayal of an old friend. Colonel Plum was putting on altogether too much dog.

In the second place the sensation of being on the side of the law was novel to Basil and not the least agreeable. Police raids, for Basil, had in the past always meant escaping over the tiles or through the area; it made him ashamed to hear these things spoken of with tolerance and familiarity.

In the third place he was not absolutely happy in his mind about what Ambrose might say. Even though he was to be deprived of the right of public trial, there would presumably be some kind of investigation at which he would be allowed to give an account of himself. Basil's share in editing "Monument to a Spartan" was, he felt, better kept as a good story to tell in the right company at the right time — not to be made the subject of official and semi-legal enquiry.

And in the fourth place Basil had from long association an appreciable softness of disposition towards Ambrose. Other things being equal, he wished him well rather than ill.

These considerations, in that order of importance, worked in Basil's mind.

Ambrose's flat lay in the neighbourhood of the Ministry of Information; it was the top floor of a large Bloomsbury mansion; where the marble stairs changed to deal, Ambrose ascended into what had once been the servants' bedrooms; it was an attic and, so-called, satisfied the ascetic promptings which had affected Ambrose in the year of the great slump. There was, however, little else about the flat to suggest hardship. He had the flair of his race for comfort and for enviable possessions. There were expensive continental editions of works on architecture, there were deep armchairs, an object like an ostrich egg sculptured by Brancusi, a gramophone with a prodigious horn, and a library of records — these and countless other features made the living-room dear to him. It is true that the bath was served only by a gas-burning apparatus which at the best gave a niggardly trickle of warm water and, at the worst, exploded in a cloud of poisonous vapours, but apparatus of this kind is the hall-mark of the higher intellectuals all the world over. Ambrose's bedroom compensated for the dangers and discomforts of the bathroom. In this flat he was served by a motherly old Cockney who teased him at intervals for not marrying.

To this flat Basil came very late that night. He had delayed his arrival on purely artistic grounds. Colonel Plum might deny him the excitements of Scotland Yard and the Home Office, but there should be every circumstance of melodrama here. Basil knocked and rang for some time before he made himself heard. Then Ambrose came to the door in a dressing-gown.

"Oh God," he said. "I suppose you're drunk" — for no friend of Basil's who maintained a fixed abode in London could ever consider himself immune from his occasional nocturnal visits.

"Let me in. We haven't a moment to spare." Basil spoke in a whisper. "The police will be here at any moment."

Slightly dazed with sleep, Ambrose admitted him. There are those for whom the word "police" holds no terror. Ambrose was not of them. All his life he had been an outlaw and the days in Munich were still fresh in his memory, when friends disappeared suddenly in the night, leaving no address.

"I've brought you this," said Basil, "and this and this." He gave Ambrose a clerical collar, a black clerical vest ornamented with a double line of jet buttons, and an Irish passport. "You are Father Flanagan returning to Dublin University. Once in Ireland you'll be safe."

"But surely there's no train at this time."

"There's one at eight. You mustn't be found here. You can sit in the waiting-room at Euston till it comes in. Have you got a breviary?"

"Of course not."

"Then read a racing paper. I suppose you've got a dark suit."

It was significant both of Basil's fine urgency of manner, and of Ambrose's constitutionally guilty disposition, that he was already clothed as a clergyman before he said, "But what have I done? Why are they after me?"

"Your magazine. It's being suppressed. They're rounding up everyone connected with it."

Ambrose asked no more. He accepted the fact as a pauper accepts the condition of being perpetually "moved on." It was something inalienable from his state; the artist's birthright.

"How did you hear about it?"

"In the War Office."

"What am I to do about all this?" asked Ambrose helplessly. "The flat, and the furniture, and my books, and Mrs. Carver?"

"I tell you what. If you like I'll move in and take care of it for you until it's safe to come back."

"Would you really, Basil?" said Ambrose, touched. "You're being very kind."

For some time now Basil had felt himself unfairly handicapped in his pursuit of Susie by the fact of his living with his mother. He had not thought of this solution. It had come providentially, with rapid and exemplary justice all too rare in life; goodness was being rewarded quite beyond his expectations, if not beyond his deserts.

"I'm afraid the geyser is rather a bore," said Ambrose apologetically.

They were not far from Euston Station. Packing was the work of a quarter of an hour.

"But, Basil, I *must* have *some* clothes."

"You are an Irish priest. What d'you think the Customs are going to say when they open a trunk full of Charvet ties and crêpe-de-Chine pyjamas?"

Ambrose was allowed one suitcase.

"I'll look after all this for you," said Basil, surveying the oriental profusion of expensive underclothes which filled the many drawers and presses of the bedroom. "You'll have to walk to the station, you know."

"Why, for God's sake?"

"Taxi might be traced. Can't take any chances."

The suitcase had seemed small enough when Basil first selected it as the most priestly of the rather too smart receptacles in Ambrose's box-room; it seemed enormous as they trudged northward through the dark streets of Bloomsbury. At last they reached the classic columns of the railway terminus. It is not a cheerful place at the best of times, striking a chill in the heart of the gayest holiday-maker. Now in war-time, before dawn on a cold spring morning, it seemed the entrance to a sepulchre.

"I'll leave you here," said Basil. "Keep out of sight until the train is in. If anyone speaks to you, tell your beads."

"I haven't any beads."

"Then contemplate. Go into an ecstasy. But don't open your mouth or you're done."

"I'll write to you when I get to Ireland."

"Better not," said Basil, cheerfully.

He turned away and was immediately lost in the darkness. Ambrose entered the station. A few soldiers slept on benches, surrounded by their kit and equipment. Ambrose found a corner darker, even, than the general gloom. Here, on a packing-case that seemed by its smell to contain fish of a sort, he sat waiting for dawn; black hat perched over his eyes, black overcoat wrapped close about his knees, mournful, black eyes open, staring into the blackness. From the fishy freight below him water oozed slowly onto the pavement making a little pool, as though of tears.

Mr. Rampole was not, as many of his club acquaintances supposed, a bachelor, but a widower of long standing. He lived in a small but substantial house at Hampstead and there maintained in servitude a spinster daughter. On this fateful morning his daughter saw him off from the front gate as had been her habit years without number, at precisely 8:45. Mr. Rampole paused in the flagged path to comment on the buds which were breaking everywhere in the little garden.

Look well at those buds, old Rampole; you will not see the full leaf.

"I'll be back at six," he said.

Presumptuous Rampole, who shall tell what the day will bring forth? Not his daughter, who returned, unmoved by the separation, to eat a second slice of toast in the dining-room; not old Rampole, who strode at a good pace towards the Hampstead Underground.

He showed his season ticket to the man at the lift.

"I shall have to get it renewed the day after to-morrow," he said affably, and tied a knot in the corner of his large white handkerchief to remind him of the fact.

There is no need for that knot, old Rampole; you will never again travel in the Hampstead Underground.

He opened his morning paper as he had done, five days a week, years without number. He turned first to the Deaths, then to the correspondence, then, reluctantly, to the news of the day.

Never again, old Rampole, never again.

The police raid on the Ministry of Information, like so many similar enterprises, fell flat. First, the plain-clothes men had the utmost difficulty in getting past the gate-keeper.

"Is Mr. Silk expecting you?"

"We hope not."

"Then you can't see him."

When finally they were identified and allowed to pass, there was a confused episode in the Religious Department, where they found only the non-conformist minister, whom, too zealously, they proceeded to hand-cuff. It was explained that Ambrose was unaccountably absent from duty that morning. Two constables were left to await his arrival. All through the day they sat there, casting a gloom over the Religious Department. The plain-clothes men proceeded to Mr. Bentley's room, where they were received with great frankness and charm.

Mr. Bentley answered all their questions in a manner befitting an honest citizen. Yes, he knew Ambrose Silk both as a colleague at the Ministry and, formerly, as one of their authors at Rampole's. No, he had almost nothing to do with publishing these days; he was too busy with all this (an explanatory gesture which embraced the dripping sink, the Nollekens busts and the page of arabesques beside the telephone). Mr. Rampole was in entire charge of the publishing firm. Yes, he thought he had heard of some magazine which Silk was starting. The *Ivory Tower?* Was that the name? Very likely. No, he had no copy. Was it already out? Mr. Bentley had formed the impression that it was not yet ready for publication. The contributors? Hucklebury Squib, Bartholomew Grass, Tom Barebones-Abraham? Mr. Bentley thought he had heard the names; he might have met them in literary circles in the old days. He had the idea that Barebones-Abraham was rather below normal height, corpulent, bald — yes, Mr. Bentley was quite sure he was bald as an egg; he spoke with a stammer and dragged his left leg as he walked. Hucklebury Squib was a very tall young man — easily recognizable, for he had lost the lobe of his left ear in extraordinary circumstances when sailing before the mast; he had a front tooth missing and wore gold ear-rings.

The plain-clothes men recorded these details in shorthand. This was the sort of witness they liked, circumstantial, precise, unhesitating.

When it came to Bartholomew Grass, Mr. Bentley's invention flagged. He had never seen the man. He rather thought it might be the pseudonym for a woman.

"Thank you, Mr. Bentley," said the chief of the plain-clothes men. "I don't think we need trouble you any more. If we want you I suppose we can always find you here."

"Always," said Mr. Bentley sweetly. "I often, whimsically, refer to this little table as my grindstone. I keep my nose to it. We live in arduous times, Inspector."

A posse of police went to Ambrose's flat, where all they got was a piece of his housekeeper's mind.

"Our man's got away," they reported when they returned to their superiors.

Colonel Plum, the Inspector of Police and Basil were summoned late that afternoon to the office of the Director of Internal Security.

"I can't congratulate you," he said, "on the way this case has been handled. I'm not blaming you, Inspector, or you, Seal," and he fixed Colonel Plum with a look of detestation. "We were clearly onto a very dangerous set of men and you let four out of five slip through your fingers. I've no doubt that at this moment they are sitting in a German submarine, laughing at us."

"We've got Rampole, sir," said Colonel Plum. "I'm inclined to think he's the ringleader."

"I'm inclined to think he's an old booby."

"He has behaved in the most hostile and defiant manner throughout. He refuses to give any particulars about any of his accomplices."

"He threw a telephone directory at one of our men," said the Inspector, "and used the following expressions about them: 'nincompoops,' 'jacks-in-office . . .' "

"Yes, yes, I have the report. Rampole is obviously a violent and thoroughly unreasonable type. It won't do him any harm to cool his heels for the rest of the war. But he's not the ringleader. This fellow Bare-bones-Abraham is the man I want and you haven't been able to find a trace of him."

"We've got his description."

"A fat lot of good that is when he's halfway back to Germany. No, the whole thing has been grossly mismanaged. The Home Secretary takes a very poor view of it. *Somebody talked* and I mean to find out who."

When the interview, painfully protracted, came to an end, the Director told Basil to remain behind.

"Seal," he said, "I understand you were the first man to get onto this gang. Have you any idea how they were warned?"

"You put me in a very difficult position, sir."

"Come, come, my boy, this is no time for petty loyalties when your country's future is at stake."

"Well, sir, I've felt for some time that there's been too much feminine influence in our Department. Have you seen Colonel Plum's secretary?"

"Hokey-pokey, eh?"

"You could call it that, sir."

"Enemy agent, eh?"

"Oh no, sir. Have a look at her."

The Director sent for Susie. When she had gone he said, "No, not an enemy agent."

"Certainly not, sir, but a frivolous, talkative girl. Colonel Plum's intimacy . . ."

"Yes, I quite understand. You did perfectly right to tell me."

"What did he want, sending for me like that and just staring?" asked Susie.

"I think I've arranged a promotion for you."

"Ooh, you are sweet."

"I'm just moving into a new flat."

"Lucky you," said Susie.

"I wish you'd come and advise me about the decorations. I'm no good at that kind of thing."

"Oh no?" said Susie in a voice she had learned at the cinema. "And what would Colonel Plum say?"

"Colonel Plum won't have anything to say. You're rising far above ADDIS."

"Ooh."

Next morning Susie received an official intimation that she was to move to the Director's office.

"Lucky you," said Basil.

She had admired all Ambrose's decorations except the Brancusi sculpture. That had been put away, out of sight, in the box-room.

At Brixton Gaol Mr. Rampole enjoyed many privileges that were not accorded to common criminals. There was a table in his cell and a tolerably comfortable chair. He was allowed, at his own expense, some additions to prison fare. He might smoke. The *Times* was delivered to him every morning and for the first time in his life he accumulated a small library. Mr. Bentley from time to time brought him papers for which his signature was required. In every way his life was much easier than it would have been in similar circumstances in any other country.

But Mr. Rampole was not content. There was an obnoxious young man next to him who, when they met at exercise, said, "Heil Mosley," and at night attempted to tap out messages of encouragement in Morse. Moreover Mr. Rampole missed his club and his home at Hampstead. In spite of a multitude of indulgences he faced the summer without enthusiasm.

In a soft, green valley where a stream ran through close-cropped, spongy pasture and the grass grew down below the stream's edge, and merged there with the water-weed — where a road ran between grass verges

and tumbled walls, and the grass merged into moss
which spread upwards and over the tumbled stones of
the walls, outwards over the pocked metalling and deep
ruts of the road; where the ruins of a police barracks,
built to command the road through the valley, burnt
in the Troubles, had once been white, then black, and
now were one green with the grass and the moss and
the water-weed; where the smoke of burned turf drifted
down from the cabin chimneys and joined the mist
that rose from the damp, green earth; where the prints
of ass and pig, goose and calf and horse, mingled indif-
ferently with those of barefoot children; where the soft,
resentful voices rose and fell in the smoky cabins, merg-
ing with the music of the stream and the treading and
shifting and munching of the beasts at pasture; where
mist and smoke never lifted and the sun never fell direct, and evening came slowly in infinite gradations of
shadow; where the priest came seldom because of the
rough road and the long climb home to the head of
the valley, and no one except the priest ever came from
one month's end to another — there stood an inn
which was frequented in bygone days by fishermen.
Here in the summer nights when their sport was over,
they had sat long over their whiskey and their pipes
— professional gentlemen from Dublin and retired
military men from England. No one fished the stream
now and the few trout that remained were taken by
ingenious and illicit means without respect for season

or ownership. No one came to stay; sometimes a couple on a walking tour, once or twice a party of motorists, paused for supper, hesitated, discussed the matter and then regretfully pushed on to the next village. Here Ambrose came, perched on an outside-car, from the railway station over the hill six miles distant.

He had discarded his clerical disguise, but there was something about his melancholy air and his precision of speech which made the landlord, who had never had contact before with an intellectual Jew, put him down as a "spoilt priest." He had heard about this inn from a garrulous fellow in the packet-boat; it was kept by a distant connection of this man's wife's, and though he had not himself visited the place, he never lost an opportunity of putting in a good word for it.

Here Ambrose settled, in the only bedroom whose windows were unbroken. Here he intended to write a book, to take up again the broken fragments of his artistic life. He spread foolscap paper on the dining-room table; and the soft, moist air settled on it and permeated it so that when, on the third day, he sat down to make a start, the ink spread and the lines ran together, leaving what might have been a brush stroke of indigo paint where there should have been a sentence of prose. Ambrose laid down the pen, and because the floor sloped where the house had settled, it rolled down the table, and down the floor-boards and under the mahogany sideboard, and lay there among napkin rings and small coins and corks and the sweepings of half

a century. And Ambrose wandered out into the mist
and the twilight, stepping soundlessly on the soft,
green turf.

In London Basil set Susie to work. She wanted to
be taken out in the evenings too often and in too expensive a style. He set her to work with needle and
silk and embroidery scissors, picking off the AS from
the monograms on Ambrose's crêpe-de-Chine underclothes and substituting a B.

6. LIKE HORSES in a rid-
ing school, line ahead to the leading mark, changing
the rein, circling to the leading mark on the opposite
wall, changing rein again, line ahead again, orderly and
regular and graceful, the aeroplanes manoeuvred in
the sharp sunlight. The engines sang in the morning
sky, the little black bombs tumbled out, turning over
in the air, drifting behind the machines, breaking in
silent upheavals of rock and dust which were already
subsiding when the sound of the explosions shook the
hillside where Cedric Lyne sat with his binoculars,
trying to mark their fall.

There was no sign of spring in this country. Everywhere the land lay frozen and dead, deep snow in the

hills, thin ice in the valleys; the buds on the thorn were hard and small and black.

"I think they've found A Company, Colonel," said Cedric.

Battalion Headquarters were in a cave in the side of the hill — a shallow cave made by a single great rock which held up the accumulations of smaller stone which in years had slid down from above and settled round it. The Colonel and the Adjutant and Cedric had room to sit here; they had arrived by night and had watched dawn break over the hills. Immediately below them the road led farther inland, climbing the opposing heights in a series of bends and tunnels. At their feet, between them and the opposite escarpment, the land lay frozen and level. The reserve company was concealed there. The Headquarter troops formed a small protective perimeter round the cave. Twenty yards away under another rock two signallers lay with a portable wireless set.

"Ack, Beer, Charley, Don . . . Hullo Lulu, Koko calling; acknowledge my signal; Lulu to Koko — over."

They had marched forward all the preceding night. When they arrived at the cave Cedric had first been hot and sweaty, then, after they halted in the chill of dawn, cold and sweaty. Now with the sun streaming down on them he was warm and dry and a little sleepy.

The enemy were somewhere beyond the farther hills. They were expected to appear late that afternoon.

"That's what they'll do," said the Colonel. "Make their assault in the last hour of daylight so as to avoid a counterattack. Well, we can hold them for ever on this front. I wish I felt sure of our left flank."

"The Loamshires are falling back there. They ought to be in position now," said the Adjutant.

"I know. But where are they? They ought to have sent over."

"All this air activity in front means they'll come this way," said the Adjutant.

"I hope so."

The high school finished its exercise, took up formation in arrow shape and disappeared droning over the hills. Presently a reconnaissance plane appeared and flew backwards and forwards overhead, searching the ground like an old woman after a lost coin.

"Tell those bloody fools to keep their faces down," said the Colonel.

When the aeroplane had passed he lit his pipe and stood in the mouth of the cave looking anxiously to his left.

"Can you see anything that looks like the Loamshires?"

"Nothing, Colonel."

"The enemy may have cut in across them yesterday evening. That's what I'm afraid of. Can't you get brigade?" he said to the signalling Corporal.

"No answer from brigade, sir. We keep trying. Hullo Lulu, Koko calling, acknowledge my signal, acknowledge my signal; Koko to Lulu — over . . ."

"I've a good mind to push D Company over on that flank."

"It's outside our boundary."

"Damn the boundary."

"We'd be left without a reserve if they come straight down the road."

"I know, that's what's worrying me."

An orderly came up with a message. The Colonel read it and passed it to Cedric to file. "C Company's in position. That's all our forward companies reported. We'll go round and have a look at them."

Cedric and the Colonel went forward, leaving the Adjutant in the cave. They visited the company Headquarters and asked a few routine questions. It was a simple defensive scheme, three companies up, one in reserve in the rear. It was suitable ground for defence. Unless the enemy had infantry tanks — and all the reports said he had not — the road could be held as long as ammunition and rations lasted.

"Made a water recce?"

"Yes, Colonel, there's a good spring on the other side of those rocks. We're refilling bottles by relays now."

"That's right."

A Company had been bombed, but without casualties, except for a few cuts from splintered rock. They were unshaken by the experience, rapidly digging dummy trenches at a distance from their positions

to draw the fire when the aeroplanes returned. The
Colonel returned from his rounds in a cheerful mood;
the regiment was doing all right. If the flanks held they
were sitting pretty.

"We're through to Lulu, sir," said the signalling
Corporal.

The Colonel reported to brigade Headquarters that
he was in position; air activity; no casualties; no sign
of enemy troops. "I've no contact on the left flank . . .
Yes, I know it's beyond the brigade boundary . . . I
know the Loamshires ought to be there. But *are* they?
Our . . . Yes, but that flank's completely in the air,
if they don't turn up . . ."

It was now midday. Battalion Headquarters ate
some luncheon — biscuits and chocolate; the Adjutant had a flask of whiskey. No one was hungry, but
they drank their bottles empty and sent the orderlies
to refill them at the spring B Company had found.
When the men came back the Colonel said, "I'm not
happy about the left flank. Lyne, go across and see
where those bloody Loamshires are."

It was two miles along a side track to the mouth of
the next pass, where the Loamshires should be in defence. Cedric left his servant behind at battalion Headquarters. It was against the rules, but he was weary of
the weight of dependent soldiery which throughout
the operations encumbered him and depressed his
spirits. As he walked alone he was exhilarated with the
sense of being one man, one pair of legs, one pair of

eyes, one brain, sent on a single, intelligible task; one man alone could go freely anywhere on the earth's surface; multiply him, put him in a drove and by each addition of his fellows you subtract something that is of value, make him so much less a man; this was the crazy mathematics of war. A reconnaissance plane came overhead. Cedric moved off the path but did not take cover, did not lie on his face or gaze into the earth and wonder if there was a rear gunner, as he would have done if he had been with Headquarters. The great weapons of modern war did not count in single lives; it took a whole section to make a target worth a burst of machine-gun fire; a platoon or a motor lorry to be worth a bomb. No one had anything against the individual; as long as he was alone he was free and safe; there's danger in numbers; divided we stand, united we fall, thought Cedric, striding happily towards the enemy, shaking from his boots all the frustration of corporate life. He did not know it but he was thinking exactly what Ambrose had thought when he announced that culture must cease to be conventual and become coenobitic.

He came to the place where the Loamshires should have been. There was no sign of them. There was no sign of any life, only rock and ice and beyond, in the hills, snow. The valley ran clear into the hills, parallel with the main road he had left. They may be holding it, higher up, he thought, where it narrows, and he set off up the stony track towards the mountains.

And there he found them; twenty of them under the command of a subaltern. They had mounted their guns to cover the track at its narrowest point and were lying, waiting for what the evening would bring. It was a ragged and weary party.

"I'm sorry I didn't send across to you," said the subaltern. "We were all in. I didn't know where you were exactly and I hadn't a man to spare."

"What happened?"

"It was all rather a nonsense," said the subaltern, in the classic phraseology of his trade which comprehends all human tragedy. "They bombed us all day yesterday and we had to go to ground. We made a mile or two between raids but it was sticky going. Then at just before sunset they came clean through us in armoured cars. I managed to get this party away. There may be a few others wandering about, but I rather doubt it. Luckily the Jerries decided to call it a day and settled down for a night's rest. We marched all night and all to-day. We only arrived an hour ago."

"Can you stop them here?"

"What d'you think?"

"No."

"No, we can't stop them. We may hold them up half an hour. They may think we're the forward part of a battalion and decide to wait till to-morrow before they attack. It all depends what time they arrive. Is there any chance of your being able to relieve us?"

"Yes. I'll get back right away."

"We could do with a break," said the subaltern.

Cedric ran most of the way to the cave. The Colonel heard his story grimly.

"Armoured cars or tanks?"

"Armoured cars."

"Well there's a chance. Tell D Company to get on the move," he said to the Adjutant. Then he reported to brigade Headquarters on the wireless what he had heard and what he was doing. It was half an hour before D Company was on its way. From the cave they could see them marching along the track where Cedric had walked so exuberantly. As they watched they saw the column a mile away halt, break up and deploy.

"We're too late," said the Colonel. "Here come the armoured cars."

They had overrun the party of Loamshires and were spreading fanwise across the low plain. Cedric counted twenty of them; behind them an endless stream of lorries full of troops. At the first shot the lorries stopped and under cover of the armoured cars the infantry fell in on the ground, broke into open order and began their advance with parade-ground deliberation. With the cars came a squadron of bombers, flying low along the line of the track. Soon the whole battalion area was full of bursting bombs.

The Colonel was giving orders for the immediate withdrawal of the forward companies.

Cedric stood in the cave. It was curious, he thought,

that he should have devoted so much of his life to caves.

"Lyne," said the Colonel. "Go up to A Company and explain what's happening. If they come in now from the rear the cars may jink round and give the other companies a chance to get out."

Cedric set out across the little battlefield. All seemed quite unreal to him still.

The bombers were not aiming at any particular target; they were plastering the ground in front of their cars, between battalion Headquarters and the mouth of the valley where A Company were dug in. The noise was incessant and shattering. Still it did not seem real to Cedric. It was part of a crazy world where he was an interloper. It was nothing to do with him. A bomb came whistling down, it seemed from directly over his head. He fell on his face and it burst fifty yards away, bruising him with a shower of small stones.

"Thought they'd got him," said the Colonel. "He's up again."

"He's doing all right," said the Adjutant.

The armoured cars were shooting it out with D Company. The infantry spread out in a long line from hillside to hillside and were moving steadily up. They were not firing yet; just tramping along behind the armoured cars abreast, an arm's length apart. Behind them another wave was forming up. Cedric had to go across this front. The enemy were still out of effective rifle range from him, but spent bullets were singing round him among the rocks.

"He'll never make it," said the Colonel.

I suppose, thought Cedric, I'm being rather brave. How very peculiar. I'm not the least brave, really; it's simply that the whole thing is so damned silly.

A Company were on the move now. As soon as they heard the firing, without waiting for orders, they were doing what the Colonel intended, edging up the opposing hillside among the boulders, getting into position where they could outflank the outflanking party. It did not matter now whether Cedric reached them. He never did; a bullet got him, killing him instantly while he was a quarter of a mile away.

Summer

 Summer came and
with it the swift sequence of historic events which left
all the world dismayed and hardly credulous; all, that
is to say, except Sir Joseph Mainwaring, whose courtly
and ponderous form concealed a peppercorn lightness
of soul, a deep unimpressionable frivolity, which left
him bobbing serenely on the great waves of history
which splintered more solid natures to matchwood.
Under the new administration he found himself translated to a sphere of public life where he could do no
serious harm to anyone, and he accepted the change
as a well-earned promotion. In the dark hours of German victory he always had some light anecdote; he
believed and repeated everything he heard; he told
how — he had it on the highest authority — the German infantry was composed of youths in their teens,
who were intoxicated before the battle with dangerous
drugs; "those who are not mown down by machine
guns die within a week," he said. He told, as vividly
as if he had been there and seen it himself, of Dutch
skies black with descending nuns, of market women
who picked off British officers, sniping over their stalls
with sub-machine-guns, of waiters who were caught on

hotel roofs marking the rooms of generals with crosses as though on a holiday postcard. He believed, long after hope had been abandoned in more responsible quarters, that the French line was intact. "There is a little bulge," he explained. "All we have to do is to pinch it out," and he illustrated the action with his finger and thumb. He daily maintained that the enemy had outrun his supplies and was being lured on to destruction. Finally when it was plain, even to Sir Joseph, that in the space of a few days England had lost both the entire stores and equipment of her regular Army, and her only ally — that the enemy were less than twenty-five miles from her shores — that there were only a few battalions of fully armed, fully trained troops in the country — that she was committed to a war in the Mediterranean with a numerically superior enemy — that her cities lay open to air attack from fields closer to home than the extremities of her own islands; that her sea-routes were threatened from a dozen new bases — Sir Joseph said: "Seen in the proper perspective I regard this as a great and tangible success. Germany set out to destroy our Army and failed; we have demonstrated our invincibility to the world. Moreover, with the French off the stage, the last obstacle to our proper understanding with Italy is now removed. I never prophesy but I am confident that before the year is out they will have made a separate and permanent peace with us. The Germans have wasted their strength. They cannot possibly repair their losses. They have squandered the flower of their Army. They have enlarged their boundaries beyond all reason and given themselves an area larger than they can possibly hold down. The war has entered into a new and more glorious phase."

And in this last statement, perhaps for the first time in his long and loquacious life, Sir Joseph approximated to reality; he had said a mouthful.

A *new and more glorious phase:* Alastair's battalion found itself overnight converted from a unit in the early stages of training into first-line troops. Their 1098 stores arrived; a vast profusion of ironmongery which, to his pride, included Alastair's mortar. It was a source of pride not free from compensating disadvantages. Now, when the platoon marched, Alastair's pouches were filled with bombs and his back harnessed to the unnaturally heavy length of steel piping; the riflemen thought they had the laugh on him.

Parachute landings were looked for hourly. The duty company slept in their boots and stood-to at dawn and dusk. Men going out of camp carried charged rifles, steel helmets, anti-gas capes. Week-end leave ceased abruptly. Captain Mayfield began to take a censorious interest in the swill tubs; if there was any waste of food, he said, rations would be reduced. The C.O. said, "There is no such thing nowadays as working hours" and to show what he meant ordered a series of parades after tea. A training memorandum was issued which had the most formidable effect upon Mr. Smallwood; now, when the platoon returned exhausted from field exercises, Mr. Smallwood gave them twenty minutes arms drill before they dismissed; this was the "little bit extra" for which the memorandum called. The platoon referred to it as "——ing us about."

Then with great suddenness the battalion got orders to move to an unknown destination. Everyone believed this meant foreign service and a great breath of exhilaration inflated the camp. Alastair met Sonia outside the guardroom.

"Can't come out to-night. We're moving. I don't know where. I think we're going into action."

He gave her instructions about where she should go and what she should do while he was away. They now knew that she was to have a child.

There was a special order that no one was to come to the station to see the battalion off; no one in fact was supposed to know they were moving. To make secrecy absolute they entrained by night, disturbing the whole district with the tramp of feet and the roar of lorries going backwards and forwards between camp and station, moving their stores.

Troops in the train manage to achieve an aspect of peculiar raffishness; they leave camp in a state of ceremonial smartness; they parade on the platform as though on the barrack square; they are detailed to their coaches and there a process of transformation and decay sets in; coats are removed, horrible packages of food appear, dense clouds of smoke obscure the windows, in a few minutes the floor is deep in cigarette ends, lumps of bread and meat, waste paper; in repose the bodies assume attitudes of extreme abandon; some look like corpses that have been left too long unburied; others like the survivors of some Saturnalian debauch. Alastair stood in the corridor most of the night, feeling that for the first time he had cut away from the old life.

Before dawn it was well known, in that strange jungle process by which news travels in the ranks, that they were not going into action but to "Coastal ——ing Defence."

The train travelled, as troop trains do, in a series of impetuous rushes between long delays. At length in the middle of the forenoon they arrived at their destination and marched through a little seaside town of round fronted stucco Early Victorian boarding-houses, an Edwardian bandstand, and a modern, concrete bathing pool, three feet deep, blue at the bottom, designed to keep children from the adventure and romance of the beach. (Here there were no shells or star-fish, no jelly-fish to be melted, no smooth pebbles of glass to be found, no bottles that might contain messages from shipwrecked sailors, no wave which, bigger than the rest, suddenly knocked you off your feet. The nurses might sit round this pool in absolute peace of mind.) Two miles out, through a suburb of bungalows and converted railway carriages, there was a camp prepared for them in the park of what, in recent years, had been an unsuccessful holiday club.

That night Alastair summoned Sonia by telephone and she came next day, taking rooms in the hotel. It was a simple and snug hotel and Alastair came there in the evenings when he was off duty. They tried to recapture the atmosphere of the winter and spring, of the days in Surrey when Alastair's life as a soldier had been a novel and eccentric interruption of their domestic routine; but things were changed. The war had entered on a new and more glorious phase. The night in the train when he thought he was going to action stood between Alastair and the old days.

The battalion were charged with the defence of seven miles of inviting coastline, and they entered with relish into the work of destroying local amenities. They lined the sands with barbed wire and demolished the steps leading from esplanade to beach; they dug weapon pits in the corporation's gardens, sandbagged the bow-windows of private houses and with the co-operation of some neighbouring sappers blocked the roads with dragons'-teeth and pill-boxes; they stopped and searched all cars passing through this area and harassed the inhabitants with demands to examine their identity cards. Mr. Smallwood sat up on the golf course every night for a week, with a loaded revolver, to investigate a light which was said to have been seen flashing there. Captain Mayfield discovered that telegraph posts are numbered with brass-headed nails and believed it to be

the work of the fifth column; when mist came rolling
in from the sea one evening, the Corporal in command
of Alastair's section reported an enemy smoke screen,
and for miles round word of invasion was passed from
post to post.

"I don't believe you're enjoying the Army any more,"
said Sonia after three weeks of Coastal Defence.

"It isn't that. I feel I could be doing something more
useful."

"But, darling, you told me your mortar was one of
the key points of the defence."

"So it is," said Alastair loyally.

"So what?"

"So what?" Then Alastair said, "Sonia, would you
think it bloody of me if I volunteered for special
service?"

"Dangerous?"

"I don't suppose so really. But very exciting. They're
getting up special parties for raiding. They go across to
France and creep up behind Germans and cut their
throats in the dark." He was excited, turning a page in
his life, as, more than twenty years ago lying on his
stomach before the fire, with a bound volume of
Chums, he used to turn over to the next instalment of
the serial.

"It doesn't seem much of a time to leave a girl," said
Sonia, "but I can see you want to."

"They have special knives and Tommy-guns and
knuckle dusters; they wear rope-soled shoes."

"Bless you," said Sonia.

"I heard about it from Peter Pastmaster. A man in his regiment is raising one. Peter's got a troop in it. He says I can be one of his section commanders; they can fix me up with a commission apparently. They carry rope ladders round their waists and files sewn in the seams of their coats to escape with. D'you mind very much if I accept?"

"No, darling. I couldn't keep you from the rope ladder. Not from the rope ladder I couldn't. I see that."

Angela had never considered the possibility of Cedric's death. She received the news in an official telegram and for some days would speak to no one, not even to Basil, about the subject. When she mentioned it, she spoke from the middle rather than from the beginning or the end of her progression of thought.

"I knew we needed a death," she said. "I never thought it was his."

Basil said, "Do you want to marry me?"

"Yes, I think so. Neither of us could ever marry anyone else, you know."

"That's true."

"You'd like to be rich, wouldn't you?"

"Will anyone be rich after this war?"

"If anyone is, I shall be. If no one is, I don't suppose it matters so much being poor."

"I don't know that I want to be rich," said Basil, after a pause. "I'm not acquisitive, you know. I only enjoy the funnier side of *getting* money — not having it."

"Anyway it's not an important point. The thing is that we aren't separable any more."

"Let nothing unite us but death. You always thought I was going to die, didn't you?"

"Yes."

"The dog it was that died. . . . Anyway this is no time to be thinking of marrying. Look at Peter. He's not been married six weeks and there he is joining a gang of desperadoes. What's the sense of marrying with things as they are? I don't see what there is to marriage, if it isn't looking forward to a comfortable old age."

"The only thing in war-time is not to think ahead. It's like walking in the blackout with a shaded torch. You can just see as far as the step you're taking."

"I shall be a terrible husband."

"Yes, darling, don't I know it? But you see one can't expect anything to be perfect now. In the old days if there was one thing wrong it spoiled everything; from now on for all our lives, if there's one thing right the day is made."

"That sounds like poor Ambrose, in his Chinese mood."

Poor Ambrose had moved West. Only the wide, infested Atlantic lay between him and Parsnip. He had taken rooms in a little fishing town and the great waves pounded on the rocks below his windows. The days passed and he did absolutely nothing. The fall of France had no audible echo on that remote shore.

This is the country of Swift, Burke, Sheridan, Wellington, Wilde, T. E. Lawrence, he thought; this is the people who once lent fire to an imperial race, whose genius flashed through two stupendous centuries of culture and success, who are now quietly receding into their own mists, turning their backs on the world of effort and action. Fortunate islanders, thought Ambrose, happy, drab escapists, who have seen the gold lace and the candlelight and left the banquet before dawn revealed stained table linen and a tipsy buffoon!

But he knew it was not for him; the dark, nomadic strain in his blood, the long heritage of wandering and speculation, allowed him no rest. Instead of Atlantic breakers he saw the camels swaying their heads resentfully against the lightening sky, as the caravan woke to another day's stage in the pilgrimage.

Old Rampole sat in his comfortable cell and turned his book to catch the last, fading light of evening. He was absorbed and enchanted. At an age when most men are rather more concerned to preserve familiar joys than to seek for new, at, to be exact, the age of sixty-two, he had suddenly discovered the delights of light literature.

There was an author on the list of his firm of whom Mr. Bentley was slightly ashamed. She wrote under the name of Ruth Mountdragon, a pseudonym which hid the identity of a Mrs. Parker. Every year for seven-

teen years Mrs. Parker had written a novel dealing with
the domestic adventures of a different family; radically
different that is to say in name, exhibiting minor dif-
ferences of composition and circumstance, but spiritu-
ally as indistinguishable as larches; they all had the qual-
ity of "charm"; once it was a colonel's family of three
girls in reduced circumstances on a chicken farm, once
it was an affluent family on a cruise in the Adriatic,
once a newly-married doctor in Hampstead; all the
permutations and combinations of upper-middle-class
life had been methodically exploited for seventeen
years; but the charm was constant. Mrs. Parker's public
was not vast, but it was substantial; it lay, in literary
appreciation, midway between the people who liked
some books and disliked others, and the people who
merely liked reading, inclining rather to the latter
group. Mr. Rampole knew her name as one of the authors who were not positively deleterious to his pocket,
and consequently when his new manner of life and the
speculative tendencies which it fostered caused him to
take up novel reading, he began on her. He was transported into a strange world of wholly delightful, esti-
mable people whom he had rightly supposed not to
exist. With each page a deeper contentment settled
on the old publisher. He had already read ten books
and looked forward eagerly to rereading them when he
came to the end of the seventeenth. Mr. Bentley was
even engaged to bring Mrs. Parker to visit him at a
future, unspecified date. The prison chaplain was also

an admirer of Mrs. Parker's. Old Rampole gained great
face from disclosing her real name. He half-promised
to allow the chaplain to meet her. He was happier than
he could remember ever having been.

Peter Pastmaster and the absurdly youthful Colonel
of the new force were drawing up a list of suitable officers in Bratt's Club.

"Most of war seems to consist of hanging about," he
said. "Let's at least hang about with our own friends."

"I've a letter from a man who says he's a friend of
yours. Basil Seal."

"Does he want to join?"

"Yes. Is he all right?"

"Perfect," said Peter. "A tough nut."

"Right. I'll put him down with Alastair Trumpington as your other subaltern."

"No. For God's sake don't do that. But make him
liaison officer."

"You see, I know everything about you," said Angela.

"There's one thing you don't know," said Basil. "If
you really want to be a widow again, we'd better marry
quick. I don't think I told you. I'm joining a new
racket."

"Basil, what?"

"Very secret."

"But why?"

"Well you know things haven't been quite the same

at the War House lately. I don't know quite why it is, but Colonel Plum doesn't seem to love me as he did. I think he's a bit jealous about the way I pulled off the *Ivory Tower* business. We've never really been matey since. Besides, you know, that racket was all very well in the winter, when there wasn't any real war. It won't do now. There's only one serious occupation for a chap now, that's killing Germans. I have an idea I shall rather enjoy it."

"Basil's left the War Office," said Lady Seal.

"Yes," said Sir Joseph, with sinking heart. Here it was again: the old business. The news from all over the world might be highly encouraging — and, poor booby, he believed it was; we might have a great new secret weapon — and, poor booby, he thought we had; he might himself enjoy a position of great trust and dignity — poor booby, he was going, that afternoon, to address a drawing-room meeting on the subject of "Hobbies for the A.T.S." — but in spite of all this, Basil was always with him, a grim *memento mori* staring him out of countenance. "Yes," he said. "I suppose he has."

"He has joined a special *corps d'élite* that is being organized. They are going to do great things."

"He has actually joined?"

"Oh, yes."

"There's nothing I can do to help him?"

"Dear Jo, always so kind. No. Basil has arranged it

all himself. I expect that his excellent record at the War Office helped. It isn't every boy who would settle to a life of official drudgery when everyone else was going out for excitement — like Emma's silly girl in the fire brigade. No, he did his duty where he found it. And now he is getting his reward. I am not quite sure what they are going to do, but I know it is very dashing and may well have a decisive effect on the war."

The grey moment was passed; Sir Joseph, who had not ceased smiling, now smiled with sincere happiness.

"There's a new spirit abroad," he said. "I see it on every side."

And, poor booby, he was bang right.

THE END